DOROTHY L. SAYERS

THE UNPLEASANTNESS AT THE BELLONA CLUB

WITH A NEW INTRODUCTION
BY ELIZABETH GEORGE

NEW ENGLISH LIBRARY
Hodder & Stoughton

First p........................... Britain i........... Ernest Benn
First pub................................ 1968
....................................glish Library

In................ © Susan Elizabeth George 2003

The right of Dorothy L. Sayers to be identified as the Author
of the Work has been asserted in accordance with the
Copyright, Designs and Patents Act 1988.

11

A CIP catalogue record for this title
is available from the British Library

ISBN 978-0-450-01630-1

Typeset in Sabon by Hewer Text Ltd, Edinburgh
Printed and bound by
Clays Ltd, St Ives plc

Hodder and Stoughton
A division of Hodder Headline
338 Euston Road
London NW1 3BH

I came to the wonderful detective novels of Dorothy L.
Sayers in a way that would probably make that distinguished novelist spin in her grave. Years ago, actor Ian
Carmichael starred in the film productions of a good
chunk of them, which I eventually saw on my public
television station in Huntington Beach, California. I
recall the host of the show reciting the impressive, salient
details of Sayers' life and career – early female graduate
of Oxford, translator of Dante, among other things – and
I was much impressed. But I was even more impressed
with her delightful sleuth Lord Peter Wimsey, and I soon
sought out her novels.

Because I had never been – and still am not today – a great
reader of detective fiction, I had not heard of this marvellous
character. I quickly became swept up in everything about
him: from his foppish use of language to his family relations. In very short order, I found myself thoroughly
attached to Wimsey, to his calm and omnipresent manservant Bunter, to the Dowager Duchess of Denver (was
ever there a more deliciously alliterative title?), to the stuffy
Duke and the unbearable Duchess of Denver, to Viscount
St. George, to Charles Parker, to Lady Mary. . . . In
Dorothy L. Sayers' novels, I found the sort of main character I loved when I turned to fiction: someone with a 'real'
life, someone who wasn't just a hero who conveniently had
no relations to mess up the workings of the novelist's plot.

Dorothy L. Sayers, as I discovered, had much to teach

me both as a reader and as a future novelist. While many detective novelists from the Golden Age of mystery kept their plots pared down to the requisite crime, suspects, clues, and red herrings, Sayers did not limit herself to so limited a canvas in her work. She saw the crime and its ensuing investigation as merely the framework for a much larger story, the skeleton – if you will – upon which she could hang the muscles, organs, blood vessels and physical features of a much larger tale. She wrote what I like to call the tapestry novel, a book in which the setting is realised (from Oxford, to the dramatic coast of Devon, to the flat bleakness of the Fens), in which throughout both the plot and the subplots the characters serve functions surpassing that of mere actors on the stage of the criminal investigation, in which themes are explored, in which life and literary symbols are used, in which allusions to other literature abound. Sayers, in short, did what I call 'taking no prisoners' in her approach to the detective novel. She did not write down to her readers; rather, she assumed that her readers would rise to her expectations of them.

I found in her novels a richness that I had not previously seen in detective fiction. I became absorbed in the careful application of detail that characterized her plots: whether she was educating me about bell ringing in *The Nine Tailors*, about the unusual uses of arsenic in *Strong Poison*, about the beauties of architectural Oxford in *Gaudy Night*. She wrote about everything from cryptology to vinology, making unforgettable that madcap period between wars that marked the death of an overt class system and heralded the beginning of an insidious one.

What continues to be remarkable about Sayers' work, however, is her willingness to explore the human condition. The passions felt by characters created eighty years ago are as real today as they were then. The motives behind people's behavior are no more complex now than they were in 1923 when Lord Peter Wimsey took his first public bow. Times have changed, rendering Sayers' England in so many ways unrecognizable to today's reader. But one of the true pleasures inherent to picking up a Sayers novel now is to see how the times in which we live alter our perceptions of the world around us, while doing nothing at all to alter the core of our humanity.

When I first began my own career as a crime novelist, I told people that I would rest content if my name was ever mentioned positively in the same sentence as that of Dorothy L. Sayers. I'm pleased to say that that occurred with the publication of my first novel. If I ever come close to offering the reader the details and delights that Sayers offered in her Wimsey novels, I shall consider myself a success indeed.

The reissuing of a Sayers novel is an event, to be sure. As successive generations of readers welcome her into their lives, they embark upon an unforgettable journey with an even more unforgettable companion. In time of dire and immediate trouble, one might well call upon a Sherlock Holmes for a quick solution to one's trials. But for the balm that reassures one about surviving the vicissitudes of life, one could do no better than to anchor onto a Lord Peter Wimsey.

Elizabeth George
Huntington Beach, California
May 27, 2003

OLD MOSSY-FACE

'WHAT in the world, Wimsey, are you doing in this Morgue?' demanded Captain Fentiman, flinging aside the *Evening Banner* with the air of a man released from an irksome duty.

'Oh, I wouldn't call it that,' retorted Wimsey amiably. 'Funeral Parlour at the very least. Look at the marble. Look at the furnishings. Look at the palms and the chaste bronze nude in the corner.'

'Yes, and look at the corpses. Place always reminds me of that old thing in *Punch*, you know – "Waiter, take away Lord Whatsisname, he's been dead two days." Look at Old Ormsby there, snoring like a hippopotamus. Look at my revered grandpa – dodders in here at ten every morning, collects the *Morning Post* and the armchair by the fire, and becomes part of the furniture till the evening. Poor old devil! Suppose I'll be like that one of these days. I wish to God Jerry had put me out with the rest of 'em. What's the good of coming through for this sort of thing? What'll you have?'

'Dry Martini,' said Wimsey. 'And you? Two dry Martinis, Fred, please. Cheer up. All this remembrance-day business gets on your nerves, don't it? It's my belief most of us would only be too pleased to chuck these community hysterics if the beastly newspapers didn't run it for all it's worth. However, it don't do to say so. They'd hoof me out of the Club if I raised my voice beyond a whisper.'

1

'They'd do that anyway, whatever you were saying,' said Fentiman gloomily. 'What *are* you doing here?'

'Waitin' for Colonel Marchbanks,' said Wimsey. 'Bung-ho!'

'Dining with him?'

'Yes.'

Fentiman nodded quietly. He knew that young Marchbanks had been killed at Hill 60, and that the Colonel was wont to give a small, informal dinner on Armistice night to his son's intimate friends.

'I don't mind old Marchbanks,' he said, after a pause. 'He's a dear old boy.'

Wimsey assented.

'And how are things going with you?' he asked.

'Oh, rotten as usual. Tummy all wrong and no money. What's the damn good of it, Wimsey? A man goes and fights for his country, gets his inside gassed out, and loses his job, and all they give him is the privilege of marching past the Cenotaph once a year and paying four shillings in the pound income tax. Sheila's queer, too – overwork, poor girl. It's pretty damnable for a man to have to live on his wife's earnings, isn't it? I can't help it, Wimsey. I go sick and have to chuck jobs up. Money – I never thought of money before the War, but I swear nowadays I'd commit any damned crime to get hold of a decent income.'

Fentiman's voice had risen in nervous excitement. A shocked veteran, till then invisible in a neighbouring armchair, poked out a lean head like a tortoise and said 'Sh!' viperishly.

'Oh, I wouldn't do that,' said Wimsey lightly. 'Crime's a skilled occupation, y'know. Even a comparative imbecile like myself can play the giddy sleuth on the amateur Moriarty. If you're thinkin' of puttin' on a false moustache and lammin' a millionaire on the head, don't do it. That disgustin' habit you have of smoking cigarettes down to the last millimetre would betray you anywhere. I'd only have to come on with a magnifyin' glass and a pair of callipers to say "The criminal is my dear old friend George Fentiman. Arrest that man!" You might not think it, but I am ready to sacrifice my nearest and dearest in order to curry favour with the police and get a par. in the papers.'

Fentiman laughed, and ground out the offending cigarette stub on the nearest ashtray.

'I wonder anybody cares to know you,' he said. The strain and bitterness had left his voice and he sounded merely amused.

'They wouldn't,' said Wimsey, 'only they think I'm too well-off to have any brains. It's like hearing that the Earl of Somewhere is taking a leading part in a play. Everybody takes it for granted he must act rottenly. I'll tell you my secret. All my criminological investigations are done for me by a 'ghost' at three pounds a week, while I get the head-lines and frivol with well-known journalists at the Savoy.'

'I find you refreshing, Wimsey,' said Fentiman languidly. 'You're not in the least witty, but you have a kind of obvious facetiousness which reminds me of the less exacting class of music-hall.'

'It's the self-defence of the first-class mind against the superior person,' said Wimsey. 'But, look here, I'm sorry to hear about Sheila. I don't want to be offensive, old man, but why don't you let me—?'

'Damned good of you,' said Fentiman, 'but I don't care to. There's honestly not the faintest chance I could ever pay you, and I haven't quite got to the point yet—'

'Here's Colonel Marchbanks,' broke in Wimsey, 'we'll talk about it another time. Good evening, Colonel.'

'Evening, Peter, Evening, Fentiman. Beautiful day it's been. No – no cocktails, thanks, I'll stick to whisky. So sorry to keep you waiting like this, but I was having a yarn with poor old Grainger upstairs. He's in a baddish way, I'm afraid. Between you and me, Penberthy doesn't think he'll last out the winter. Very sound man, Penberthy – wonderful, really, that he's kept the old man going so long with his lungs in that frail state. Ah, well! it's what we must all come to. Dear me, there's your grandfather, Fentiman. He's another of Penberthy's miracles. He must be ninety, if he's a day. Will you excuse me for a moment? I must just go and speak to him.'

Wimsey's eyes followed the alert, elderly figure as it crossed the spacious smoking-room, pausing now and again to exchange greetings with a fellow-member of the Bellona Club. Drawn close to the huge fireplace stood a great chair with ears after the Victorian pattern. A pair of spindle shanks with neatly-buttoned shoes propped on a footstool was all that was visible of General Fentiman.

'Queer, isn't it,' muttered his grandson, 'to think that for Old Mossy-face the Crimea is still *the* War, and the Boer business found him too old to go out. He was given his commission at seventeen, you know – was wounded at Majuba—'

He broke off. Wimsey was not paying attention. He was still watching Colonel Marchbanks.

The Colonel came back to them, walking very quietly and precisely. Wimsey rose and went to meet him.

'I say, Peter,' said the Colonel, his kind face gravely troubled, 'just come over here a moment. I'm afraid something rather unpleasant has happened.'

Fentiman looked round, and something in their manner made him get up and follow them over to the fire.

Wimsey bent down over General Fentiman and drew the *Morning Post* gently away from the gnarled old hands, which lay clasped over the thin chest. He touched the shoulder – put his hand under the white head huddled against the side of the chair. The Colonel watched him anxiously. Then, with a quick jerk, Wimsey lifted the quiet figure. It came up all of a piece, stiff as a wooden doll.

Fentiman laughed. Peal after hysterical peal shook his throat. All round the room, scandalised Bellonians creaked to their gouty feet, shocked by the unmannerly noise.

'Take him away!' said Fentiman, 'take him away. He's been dead two days! So are you! So am I! We're all dead and we never noticed it!'

2

THE QUEEN IS OUT

IT is doubtful which occurrence was more disagreeable to the senior members of the Bellona Club – the grotesque death of General Fentiman in their midst or the indecent neurasthenia of his grandson. Only the younger men felt no sense of outrage; they knew too much. Dick Challoner – known to his intimates as Tin-Tummy Challoner, owing to the fact that he had been fitted with a spare part after the second battle of the Somme – took the gasping Fentiman away into the deserted library for a stiffener. The Club Secretary hurried in, in his dress-shirt and trousers, the half-dried lather still clinging to his jaws. After one glance he sent an agitated waiter to see if Dr Penberthy was still in the Club. Colonel Marchbanks laid a large silk handkerchief reverently over the rigid face in the armchair and remained quietly standing. A little circle formed about the edge of the hearth-rug, not quite certain what to do. From time to time it was swelled by fresh arrivals, whom the news had greeted in the hall as they wandered in. A little group appeared from the bar. 'What, old Fentiman?' they said. 'Good God, you don't say so. Poor old blighter. Heart gone at last, I suppose'; and they extinguished cigars and cigarettes, and stood by, not liking to go away again.

Dr Penberthy was just changing for dinner. He came down hurriedly, caught just as he was going out to an Armistice dinner, his silk hat tilted to the back of his head, his coat and muffler pushed loosely open. He was a thin, dark man with the abrupt manner which distinguishes the Army Surgeon from the West End practitioner. The group by the fire made way for him, except Wimsey, who hung rather foolishly upon the big elbow-chair, gazing in a helpless way at the body.

Penberthy ran practised hands quickly over neck, wrists and knee joints.

'Dead several hours,' he pronounced sharply. '*Rigor* well established – beginning to pass off.' He moved the dead man's left leg in illustration; it swung loose at the knee. 'I've been expecting this. Heart very weak. Might happen any moment. Anyone spoken to him today?'

He glanced round interrogatively.

'I saw him here after lunch,' volunteered somebody. 'I didn't speak.'

'I thought he was asleep,' said another.

Nobody remembered speaking to him. They were so used to old General Fentiman, slumbering by the fire.

'Ah, well,' said the doctor. 'What's the time? Seven?' He seemed to make a rapid calculation. 'Say five hours for *rigor* to set in – must have taken place very rapidly – he probably came in at his usual time, sat down and died straight away.'

'He always walked from Dover Street,' put in an elderly man. 'I told him it was too great an exertion at his age. You've heard me say so, Ormsby.'

'Yes, yes, quite,' said the purple-faced Ormsby. 'Dear me, just so.'

'Well, there's nothing to be done,' said the doctor. 'Died in his sleep. Is there an empty bedroom we can take him to, Culyer?'

'Yes, certainly,' said the Secretary. 'James, fetch the key of number sixteen from my office and tell them to put the bed in order. I suppose, eh, doctor? – when the *rigor* passes off we shall be able to – eh?'

'Oh, yes, you'll be able to do everything that's required. I'll send the proper people in to lay him out for you. Somebody had better let his people know – only they'd better not show up till we can get him more presentable.'

'Captain Fentiman knows already,' said Colonel Marchbanks. 'And Major Fentiman is staying in the Club – he'll probably be in before long. Then there's a sister, I think.'

'Yes, old Lady Dormer,' said Penberthy, 'she lives round in Portman Square. They haven't been on speaking terms for years. Still, she'll have to know.'

'I'll ring them up,' said the Colonel. 'We can't leave it to Captain Fentiman, he's in no fit state to be worried, poor fellow. You'll have to have a look at him, doctor, when you've finished here. An attack of the old trouble – nerves, you know.'

'All right. Ah! is the room ready, Culyer? Then we'll move him. Will somebody take his shoulders – no, not you, Culyer' (for the Secretary had only one sound arm), 'Lord Peter, yes, thank you – lift carefully.'

Wimsey put his long, strong hands under the stiff arms; the doctor gathered up the legs; they moved away. They looked like a dreadful little Guy Fawkes procession, with that humped and unreverend manikin bobbing and swaying between them.

The door closed after them, and a tension seemed removed. The circle broke up into groups. Somebody lit a cigarette. The planet's tyrant, dotard Death, had held his grey mirror before them for a moment and shown them the image of things to come. But now it was taken away again. The unpleasantness had passed.

Fortunate, indeed, that Penberthy was the old man's own doctor. He knew all about it. He could give a certificate. No inquest. Nothing undesirable. The members of the Bellona Club could go to dinner.

Colonel Marchbanks turned to go through the far door towards the library. In a narrow ante-room between the two rooms there was a convenient telephone-cabinet for the use of those members who did not wish to emerge into the semi-publicity of the entrance-hall.

'Hi, Colonel! not that one. That instrument's out of order,' said a man called Wetheridge, who saw him go. 'Disgraceful, I call it. I wanted to use the phone this morning, and – oh! hallo! the notice has gone. I suppose it's all right again. They ought to let one know.'

Colonel Marchbanks paid little attention to Wetheridge. He was the Club grumbler, distinguished even in that fellowship of the dyspeptic and peremptory – always threatening to complain to the committee, harassing the secretary and constituting a perennial thorn in the sides of his fellow-members. He retired, murmuring, to his chair and the evening paper, and the Colonel stepped into the telephone-cabinet to call up Lady Dormer's house in Portman Square.

Presently he came out through the library into the entrance-hall, and met Penberthy and Wimsey just descending the staircase.

'Have you broken the news to Lady Dormer?' asked Wimsey.

'Lady Dormer is dead,' said the Colonel. 'Her maid tells me she passed quietly away at half-past ten this morning.'

9

3

HEARTS COUNT MORE THAN DIAMONDS

ABOUT ten days after that notable Armistice Day, Lord Peter Wimsey was sitting in his library, reading a rare fourteenth-century manuscript of Justinian. It gave him particular pleasure, being embellished with a large number of drawings in sepia, extremely delicate in workmanship, and not always equally so in subject. Beside him on a convenient table stood a long-necked decanter of priceless old port. From time to time he stimulated his interest with a few sips, pursing his lips thoughtfully, and slowly savouring the balmy after-taste.

A ring at the front door of the flat caused him to exclaim 'Oh, hell!' and cock an attentive ear for the intruder's voice. Apparently the result was satisfactory, for he closed the Justinian and had assumed a welcoming smile when the door opened.

'Mr Murbles, my lord.'

The little elderly gentleman who entered was so perfectly the family solicitor as really to have no distinguishing personality at all, beyond a great kindness of heart and a weakness for soda-mint lozenges.

'I am not disturbing you, I trust, Lord Peter.'

Good lord, no, sir. Always delighted to see you. Bunter, a glass for Mr Murbles. Very glad you've turned up, sir. The Cockburn '86 always tastes a lot better in company – discernin' company, that is. Once knew a fellow who polluted it with a Trichinopoly. He was not asked again. Eight months later, he committed suicide. I

10

don't say it was on that account. But he was ear-marked for a bad end, what?'

'You horrify me,' said Mr Murbles gravely. 'I have seen many men sent to the gallows for crimes with which I could feel much more sympathy. Thank you, Bunter, thank you. You are quite well, I trust?'

'I am in excellent health, I am obliged to you, sir.'

'That's good. Been doing any photography lately?'

'A certain amount, sir. But merely of a pictorial description, if I may venture to call it so. Criminological material, sir, has been distressingly deficient of late.'

'Perhaps Mr Murbles has brought us something,' suggested Wimsey.

'No,' said Mr Murbles, holding the Cockburn '86 beneath his nostrils and gently agitating the glass to release the ethers, 'no, I can't say I have, precisely. I will not disguise that I have come in the hope of deriving benefit from your trained habits of observation and deduction, but I fear – that is, I trust – in fact, I am confident – that nothing of an undesirable nature is involved. The fact is,' he went on, as the door closed upon the retreating Bunter, 'a curious question has arisen with regard to the sad death of General Fentiman at the Bellona Club, to which, I understand, you were a witness.'

'If you understand that, Murbles,' said his lordship cryptically, 'you understand a damn' sight more than I do. I did not witness the death – I witnessed the discovery of the death – which is a very different thing, by a long chalk.'

'By how long a chalk?' asked Mr Murbles eagerly. 'That is just what I am trying to find out.'

'That's very inquisitive of you,' said Wimsey. 'I think perhaps it would be better' – he lifted his glass and tilted it thoughtfully, watching the wine coil down in thin flower petallings from rim to stem – 'if you were to tell me exactly what you want to know . . . and why. After all . . . I'm a member of the Club . . . family associations chiefly, I suppose . . . but there it is.'

Mr Murbles looked up sharply, but Wimsey's attention seemed focused upon the port.

'Quite so,' said the solicitor. 'Very well. The facts of the matter are these. General Fentiman had, as you know, a sister Felicity, twelve years younger than himself. She was very beautiful and very wilful as a girl, and ought to have made a very fine match, but for the fact that the Fentimans, though extremely well-descended, were anything but well-off. As usual, at that period, all the money there was went to educating the boy, buying him a commission in a crack regiment and supporting him there in the style which was considered indispensable for a Fentiman. Consequently there was nothing left to furnish a marriage-portion for Felicity, and that was rather disastrous for a young woman sixty years ago.

'Well, Felicity got tired of being dragged through the social round in her darned muslins and gloves that had been to the cleaners – and she had the spirit to resent her mother's perpetual strategies in the match-making line. There was a dreadful, decrepit old viscount, eaten up with diseases and dissipations, who would have been delighted to totter to the altar with a handsome young creature of eighteen, and I am sorry to say that the girl's father and mother did everything they could to force her into accepting this disgraceful proposal. In fact, the engagement was announced and the wedding day fixed, when, to the extreme horror of the family, Felicity calmly informed them one morning that she had gone out before breakfast and actually got married, in the most indecent secrecy and haste, to a middle-aged man called Dormer, very honest and abundantly wealthy, and – horrid to relate – a prosperous manufacturer. Buttons, in fact – made of papier mâché or something, with a patent indestructible shank – were the revolting antecedents to which this headstrong young Victorian had allied herself.

'Naturally there was a terrible scandal, and the parents did their best – seeing that Felicity was a minor – to get the marriage annulled. However, Felicity checkmated their plans pretty effectually by escaping from her bedroom – I fear, indeed, that she actually climbed down a tree in the back garden, crinoline and all – and running away with her husband. After which, seeing that the worst had happened – indeed, Dormer, a man of prompt action, lost no time in putting his bride in the family way – the old people put the best face they could on it in the grand Victorian manner. That is, they gave their consent to the marriage, forwarded their daughter's belongings to her new home in Manchester, and forbade her to darken their doors again.'

'Highly proper,' murmured Wimsey. 'I'm determined never to be a parent. Modern manners and the break-up of the fine old traditions have simply ruined the business. I shall devote my life and fortune to the endowment of research on the best method of producin' human beings decorously and unobtrusively from eggs. All parental responsibility to devolve upon the incubator.'

'I hope not,' said Mr Murbles, 'My own profession is largely supported by domestic entanglements. To proceed: Young Arthur Fentiman seems to have shared the family views. He was disgusted at having a brother-in-law in buttons, and the jests of his mess-mates did nothing to sweeten his feelings towards his sister. He became impenetrably military and professional, crusted over before his time, and refused to acknowledge the existence of anybody called Dormer. Mind you, the old boy was a fine soldier, and absolutely wrapped up in his army associations. In due course he married – not well, for he had not the means to entitle him to a noble wife, and he would not demean himself by marrying money, like the unspeakable Felicity. He married a suitable gentlewoman with a few thousand pounds. She died (largely, I believe, owing to the military regularity with which her husband ordained that she should perform her maternal functions), leaving a numerous but feeble family of children. Of these, the only one to attain maturity was the father of the two Fentimans you know – Major Robert and Captain George Fentiman.'

'I don't know Robert very well,' interjected Wimsey. 'I've met him. Frightfully hearty and all that – regular army type.'

'Yes, he's of the old Fentiman stock. Poor George inherited a weakly strain from his grandmother, I'm afraid.'

'Well, nervous, anyhow,' said Wimsey, who knew better than the old solicitor the kind of mental and physical strain George Fentiman had undergone. The War pressed hardly upon imaginative men in responsible positions. 'And then he was gassed and all that, you know,' he added apologetically.

'Just so,' said Mr Murbles. 'Robert, you know, is unmarried and still in the army. He's not particularly well-off, naturally, for none of the Fentimans ever had a bean, as I believe one says nowadays; but he does very well. George—'

'Poor old George! All right, sir, you needn't tell me about him. Usual story. Decentish job – imprudent

14

marriage – chucks everything to join up in 1914 – invalided out – job gone – no money – heroic wife keeping the home fires burning – general fedupness. Don't let's harrow our feelings. Take it as read.'

'Yes, I needn't go into that. Their father is dead, of course, and up till ten days ago there were just the two surviving Fentimans of the earlier generation. The old General lived on the small fixed income which came to him through his wife and his retired pension. He had a solitary little flat in Dover Street and an elderly man-servant, and he practically lived at the Bellona Club. And there was his sister, Felicity.'

'How did she come to be Lady Dormer?'

'Why, that's where we come to the interesting part of the story. Henry Dormer—'

'The button-maker?'

'The button-maker. He became an exceedingly rich man indeed – so rich, in fact, that he was able to offer financial assistance to certain exalted persons who need not be mentioned, and so, in time, and in consideration of valuable services to the nation not very clearly speci-fied in the Honours List, he became Sir Henry Dormer, Bart. His only child – a girl – had died, and there was no prospect of any further family, so there was, of course, no reason why he should not be made a baronet for his trouble.'

'Acid man, you are,' said Wimsey. 'No reverence, no simple faith or anything of that kind. Do lawyers ever go to heaven?'

'I have no information on that point,' said Mr Murbles dryly. 'Lady Dormer—'

'Did the marriage turn out well otherwise?' inquired Wimsey.

'I believe it was perfectly happy,' replied the lawyer;

15

'an unfortunate circumstance in one way, since it entirely precluded the possibility of any reconciliation with her relatives. Lady Dormer, who was a fine, generous-hearted woman, frequently made overtures of peace, but the General held sternly aloof. So did his son – partly out of respect for the old boy's wishes, but chiefly, I fancy, because he belonged to an Indian regiment and spent most of his time abroad. Robert Fentiman, how-ever, showed the old lady a certain amount of attention, paying occasional visits and so forth, and so did George at one time. Of course, they never let the General know a word about it, or he would have had a fit. After the War, George rather dropped his great-aunt – I don't know why.'

'I can guess,' said Wimsey. 'No job – no money, y'know. Didn't want to look pointed. That sort of thing, what?'

'Possibly. Or there may have been some kind of quarrel. I don't know. Anyway, those are the facts. I hope I am not boring you, by the way?'

'I am bearing up,' said Wimsey, 'waiting for the point where the money comes in. There's a steely legal glitter in your eye, sir, which suggests that the thrill is not far off.'

'Quite correct,' said Mr Murbles. 'I now come – thank you, well, yes – I will take just one more glass. I thank Providence I am not of a gouty constitution. Yes, Ah! – We now come to the melancholy event of November 11th last, and I must ask you to follow me with the closest attention.'

'By all means,' said Wimsey politely.

'Lady Dormer,' pursued Mr Murbles, leaning ear-nestly forward, and punctuating every sentence with sharp little jabs of his gold-mounted eye-glasses, held in his right finger and thumb, 'was an old woman, and had been ailing for a very long time. However, she was still the headstrong and vivacious personality that she had been as a girl, and on the fifth of November she was suddenly seized with a fancy to go out at night and see a display of fireworks at the Crystal Palace or some such place – it may have been Hampstead Heath or the White City – I forget, and it is of no consequence. The important thing is that it was a raw, cold evening. She insisted on undertaking her little expedition nevertheless, enjoyed the entertainment as heartily as the youngest child, imprudently exposed herself to the night air and caught a severe cold which, in two days' time, turned to pneumonia. On November 10th she was sinking fast, and scarcely expected to live out the night. Accordingly, the young lady who lived with her as her ward – a distant relative, Miss Ann Dorland – sent a message to General Fentiman that if he wished to see his sister alive he should come immediately. For the sake of our common human nature, I am happy to say that this news broke down the barrier of pride and obstinacy that had kept the old gentleman away so long. He came, found Lady Dormer just conscious, though very feeble, stayed with her about half an hour and departed, still stiff as a ramrod, but visibly softened. This was about four o'clock in the afternoon. Shortly afterwards Lady Dormer became unconscious, and, indeed, never moved or spoke again, passing peacefully away in her sleep at half-past ten the following morning.

'Presumably the shock and nervous strain of the interview with his long-estranged sister had been too much for the old General's feeble system, for, as you know, he died at the Bellona Club at some time – not yet clearly ascertained – on the same day, the eleventh of November.

'Now then, at last – and you have been very patient

with my tedious way of explaining all this – we come to the point at which we want your help.'

Mr Murbles refreshed himself with a sip of port, and, looking a little anxiously at Wimsey, who had closed his eyes and appeared to be nearly asleep, he resumed.

'I have not mentioned, I think, how I come to be involved in this matter myself. My father was the Fentimans' family solicitor, a position to which I naturally succeeded when I took over the business at his death. General Fentiman, though he had little enough to leave, was not the sort of disorderly person who dies without making a proper testamentary disposition. His retired pension, of course, died with him, but his small private estate was properly disposed by will. There was a small legacy – fifty pounds – to his manservant (a very attached and superior fellow); then one or two trifling bequests to old military friends and the servants at the Bellona Club (rings, medals, weapons and small sums of a few pounds each). Then came the bulk of his estate, about £2,000, invested in sound securities, and bringing in an income of slightly over £100 per annum. These securities, specifically named and enumerated, were left to Captain George Fentiman, the younger grandson, in a very proper clause, which stated that the testator intended no slight in thus passing over the older one, Major Robert, but that, as George stood in the greater need of monetary help, being disabled, married, and so forth, whereas his brother had his profession and was without ties, George's greater necessity gave him the better claim to such money as there was. Robert was finally named as executor and residuary legatee, thus succeeding to all such personal effects and moneys as were not specifically devised elsewhere. Is that clear?'

'Clear as a bell. Was Robert satisfied with that arrangement?'

'Oh, dear, yes; perfectly. He knew all about the will beforehand and had agreed that it was quite fair and right.'

'Nevertheless,' said Wimsey, 'it appears to be such a small matter on the face of it, that you must be concealing something perfectly devastating up your sleeve. Out with it, man, out with it! Whatever the shock may be, I am braced to bear it.'

'The shock,' said Mr Murbles, 'was inflicted on me, personally, last Friday by Lady Dormer's man of business – Mr Pritchard, of Lincoln's Inn. He wrote to me, asking if I could inform him of the exact hour and minute of General Fentiman's decease. I replied, of course, that, owing to the peculiar circumstances under which the event took place, I was unable to answer his question as precisely as I could have wished, but that I understood Dr Penberthy to have given it as his opinion that the General had died some time in the forenoon of November 11th. Mr Pritchard then asked if he might wait upon me without delay, as the matter he had to discuss was of the most urgent importance. Accordingly I appointed a time for the interview on Monday afternoon, and when Mr Pritchard arrived he informed me of the following particulars.

'A good many years before her death, Lady Dormer – who, as I said before, was an eminently generous-minded woman – made a will. Her husband and her daughter were then dead. Henry Dormer had few relations, and all of them were fairly wealthy people. By his own will he had sufficiently provided for these persons, and had left the remainder of his property, amounting to something like seven hundred thousand pounds, to his wife, with the express stipulation that she was to consider it as her own, to do what she liked with, without any restriction whatsoever. Accordingly, Lady Dormer's will divided this very handsome fortune – apart from certain charitable and personal bequests with which I need not trouble you – between the people who, for one reason and another, had the greatest claims on her affection. Twelve thousand pounds were to go to Miss Ann Dorland. The whole of the remainder was to pass to her brother, General Fentiman, if he was still living at her death. If, on the other hand, he should predecease her, the conditions were reversed. In that case the bulk of the money came to Miss Dorland, and fifteen thousand pounds were to be equally divided between Major Robert Fentiman and his brother George.'

Wimsey whistled softly.

'I quite agree with you,' said Mr Murbles. 'It is a most awkward situation. Lady Dormer died at precisely 10.37 a.m. on November 11th. General Fentiman died that same morning at some time, presumably after 10 o'clock, which was his usual hour for arriving at the Club, and certainly before 7 p.m., when his death was discovered. If he died immediately on his arrival, or at any time up to 10.36, then Miss Dorland is an important heiress, and my clients the Fentimans get only seven thousand pounds or so apiece. If, on the other hand, his death occurred even a few seconds after 10.37, Miss Dorland receives only twelve thousand pounds, George Fentiman is left with the small pittance bequeathed to him under his father's will – while Robert Fentiman, the residuary legatee, inherits a very considerable fortune of well over half a million.'

'And what,' said Wimsey, 'do you want me to do about it?'

'Why,' replied the lawyer, with a slight cough, 'it occurred to me that you, with your – if I may say so – remarkable powers of deduction and analysis, might be able to solve the extremely difficult and delicate problem of the precise moment of General Fentiman's decease. You were in the Club when the death was discovered, you saw the body, you know the places and the persons involved, and you are, by your standing and personal character, exceptionally well fitted to carry out the necessary investigations without creating any – ahem! – public agitation or – er – scandal, or, in fact notoriety, which would, I need hardly say, be extremely painful to all concerned.'

'It's awkward,' said Wimsey, 'uncommonly awkward.'

'It is indeed,' said the lawyer with some warmth, 'for, as we are now situated, it is impossible to execute either will or – or, in short, do anything at all. It is most unfortunate that the circumstances were not fully understood at the time, when the – um – the body of General Fentiman was available for inspection. Naturally, Mr Pritchard was quite unaware of the anomalous situation, and as I knew nothing about Lady Dormer's will, I had no idea that anything beyond Dr Penberthy's certificate was, or ever could become, necessary.'

'Couldn't you get the parties to come to some agreement?' suggested Wimsey.

'If we are unable to reach any satisfactory conclusion about the time of the death, that will probably be the only way out of the difficulty. But at the moment there are certain obstacles—'

'Somebody's being greedy, eh? You'd rather not say more definitely, I suppose? No. H'm, well! From a purely detached point of view it's a very pleasin' and pretty little problem, you know.'

'You will undertake to solve it for us, then, Lord Peter?'

Wimsey's fingers tapped out an intricate fugal passage on the arm of his chair.

'If I were you, Murbles, I'd try again to get a settlement.'

'Do you mean,' asked Mr Murbles, 'that you think my clients have a losing case?'

'No – I can't say that. By the way, Murbles, who is your client – Robert or George?'

'Well, the Fentiman family in general. I know, naturally, that Robert's gain is George's loss. But none of the parties wishes anything but that the actual facts of the case should be determined.'

'I see. You'll put up with anything I happen to dig out?'

'Of course.'

'However favourable or unfavourable it may be?'

'I should not lend myself to any other course,' said Mr Murbles, rather stiffly.

'I know that, sir. But – well! – I only mean that – Look here, sir! when you were a boy, did you ever go about pokin' sticks and things into peaceful, mysterious-lookin' ponds, just to see what was at the bottom?'

'Frequently,' replied Mr Murbles. 'I was extremely fond of natural history and had a quite remarkable collection (if I may say so at this distance of time) of pond fauna.'

'Did you ever happen to stir up a deuce of a stink in the course of your researches?'

'My dear Lord Peter – you are making me positively uneasy.'

'Oh, I don't know that you need be. I am only giving you a general warning, you know. Of course, if you wish it, I'll investigate this business like a shot.'

'It's very good of you,' said Mr Murbles.

'Not at all. *I* shall enjoy it all right. If anything odd comes of it, that's your funeral. You never know, you know.'

'If you decide that no satisfactory conclusion can be arrived at,' said Mr Murbles, 'we can always fall back on the settlement. I am sure all parties wish to avoid litigation.'

'In case the estate vanishes in costs? Very wise. I hope it may be feasible. Have you made any preliminary inquiries?'

'None to speak of. I would rather you undertook the whole investigation from the beginning.'

'Very well. I'll start tomorrow and let you know how it gets on.'

The lawyer thanked him and took his departure. Wimsey sat pondering for a short time, then rang the bell for his manservant.

'A new notebook, please, Bunter. Head it "Fentiman", and be ready to come round with me to the Bellona Club tomorrow, complete with camera and the rest of the outfit.'

'Very good, my lord. I take it your lordship has a new inquiry in hand?'

'Yes, Bunter – quite new.'

'May I venture to ask if it is a promising case, my lord?'

'It has its points. So has a porcupine. No matter. Begone, dull care! Be at great pains, Bunter, to cultivate a detached outlook on life. Take example by the bloodhound, who will follow up with equal and impartial zest the trail of a parricide or of a bottle of aniseed.'

'I will bear it in mind, my lord.'

Wimsey moved slowly across to the little black baby grand that stood in the corner of the library.

'Not Bach this evening,' he murmured to himself.

'Bach for tomorrow, when the grey matter begins to revolve.' A melody of Parry's formed itself crooningly under his fingers. 'For man walketh in a vain shadow . . . he heapeth up riches and cannot tell who shall gather them.' He laughed suddenly, and plunged into an odd, noisy, and painfully inharmonious study by a modern composer in the key of seven sharps.

4

LORD PETER LEADS A CLUB

'You are quite sure this suit is all right, Bunter?' said Lord Peter anxiously.

It was an easy lounge suit, tweedy in texture, and a trifle more pronounced in colour and pattern than Wimsey usually permitted himself. While not unsuitable for town wear, it yet diffused a faint suggestion of hills and the sea.

'I want to look approachable,' he went on, 'but on no account loud. I can't help wondering whether that stripe of invisible green wouldn't have looked better if it had been a remote purple.'

This suggestion seemed to disconcert Bunter. There was a pause while he visualised a remote purple stripe. At length, however, the palpitating balance of his mind seemed to settle definitely down.

'No, my lord,' he said firmly. 'I do not think purple would be an improvement. Interesting – yes; but, if I may so express myself, decidedly less affable.'

'Thank goodness,' said his lordship. 'I'm sure you're right. You always are. And it would have been a bore to get it changed now. You are sure you've removed all the newness, eh? Hate new clothes.'

'Positive, my lord. I assure your lordship that the garments have every appearance of being several months old.'

'Oh, all right. Well, give me the malacca with the foot-rule marked on it – and where's my lens?'

'Here, my lord.' Bunter produced an innocent-looking monocle, which was, in reality, a powerful magnifier. 'And the finger-print powder is in your lordship's right-hand coat pocket.'

'Thanks. Well, I think that's all. I'll go on now, and I want you to follow on with the doings in about an hour's time.'

The Bellona Club is situated in Piccadilly, not many hundred yards west of Wimsey's own flat, which overlooks the Green Park. The commissionaire greeted him with a pleased smile.

'Mornin', Rogers. How are you?'

'Very well, my lord. I thank you.'

'D'you know if Major Fentiman is in the Club, by the way?'

'No, my lord. Major Fentiman is not residing with us at present. I believe he is occupying the late General Fentiman's flat, my lord.'

'Ah, yes – very sad business, that.'

'Very melancholy, my lord. Not a pleasant thing to happen in the Club. Very shocking, my lord.'

'Yes – still, he was a very old man. I suppose it had to be some day. Queer to think of 'em all sittin' round him there and never noticin', eh, what?'

'Yes, my lord. It gave Mrs Rogers quite a turn when I told her about it.'

'Seems almost unbelievable, don't it? Sittin' round all those hours – must have been several hours, I gather, from what the doctor says. I suppose the old boy came in at his usual time, eh?'

'Ah! regular as clockwork, the General was. Always on the stroke of ten. "Good morning, Rogers," he'd say, a bit stiff-like, but very friendly. And then, "Fine morning," he'd say, as like as not. And sometimes ask after

Mrs Rogers and the family. A fine old gentleman, my lord. We shall all miss him.'

'Did you notice whether he seemed specially feeble or tired that morning at all?' inquired Wimsey casually, tapping a cigarette on the back of his hand.

'Why, no, my lord. I beg your pardon; I fancied you knew. I wasn't on duty that day, my lord. I was kindly given permission to attend the ceremony at the Cenotaph. Very grand sight it was, too, my lord. Mrs Rogers was greatly moved.'

'Oh, of course, Rogers – I was forgetting. Naturally, you would be there. So you didn't see the General to say good-bye, as it were. Still, it wouldn't have done to miss the Cenotaph. Matthews took over duty, I suppose?'

'No, my lord, Matthews is laid up with 'flue, I am sorry to say. It was Weston who was at the door all morning, my lord.'

'Weston? Who's he?'

'He's new, my lord, Took the place of Briggs. You recollect Briggs – his uncle died and left him a fish-shop.'

'Of course he did; just so. When does Weston come on parade? I must make his acquaintance.'

'He'll be here at one o'clock, when I go to my lunch, my lord.'

'Oh, right! I'll probably be about then. Hallo, Penberthy! You're just the man I want to see. Had your morning's inspiration? Or come in to look for it?'

'Just tracking it to its lair. Have it with me.'

'Right you are, old chap – half a mo' while I deposit my outer husk, I'll follow you.'

He glanced irresolutely at the hall-porter's desk, but seeing the man already engaged with two or three inquiries, plunged abruptly into the cloak-room, where the attendant, a bright Cockney with a Sam Weller face and an artificial leg, was ready enough to talk about General Fentiman.

'Well, now, my lord, that's funny you should ask me that,' he said, when Wimsey had dexterously worked in an inquiry as to the time of the General's arrival at Bellona. 'Dr Penberthy was askin' the same question. It's a fair puzzle that is. I could count on the fingers of one 'and the mornings I've missed seein' the General come in. Wonderful regular, the General was, and him being such a very old gentleman, I'd make a point of being 'andy, to 'elp him off with his overcoat and such. But there! He must 'a' come in a bit late that morning, for I never see him, and I thought at lunchtime, "The General must be ill," I thinks. And I goes round, and there I see his coat and 'at 'ung up on his usual peg, So I must 'a' missed him. There was a lot of gentlemen in and out that morning, my lord, bein' Armistice Day. A number of members come up from the country and wanting their 'ats and boots attended to, my lord, so that's how I came not to notice, I suppose.'

'Possibly. Well, he was in before lunch, at any rate.'

'Oh, yes, my lord. 'Alf-past twelve I goes off, and his hat and coat were on the peg then, because I seen 'em.'

'That gives us a *terminus ad quem*, at any rate,' said Wimsey, half to himself.

'I beg your lordship's pardon.'

'I was saying, that shows he came in before half-past twelve – and later than ten o'clock, you think?'

'Yes, my lord, I couldn't say to a fraction, but I'm sure if 'e'd arrived before a quarter-past ten I should have seen 'im. But after that, I recollect I was very busy, and he must 'a' slipped in without me noticing him.'

'Ah, yes – poor old boy! Still, no doubt he'd have liked

to pass out quietly like that. Not a bad way to go home, Williamson.'

'Very good way, my lord. We've seen worse than that. And what's it all come to, after all? They're all sayin' as it's an unpleasant thing for the Club, but *I* say, where's the odds? There ain't many 'ouses what somebody ain't died in, some time or another. We don't think any the worse of the 'ouses, so why think the worse of the Club?'

'You're a philosopher, Williamson.' Wimsey climbed the short flight of marble steps and turned into the bar. 'It's narrowin' down,' he muttered to himself. 'Between ten-fifteen and twelve-thirty. Looks as if it was goin' to be a close run for the Dormer stakes. But – dash it all! Let's hear what Penberthy has to say.'

The doctor was already standing at the bar with a whisky-and-soda before him. Wimsey demanded a Worthington and dived into his subject without more ado.

'Look here,' he said, 'I just wanted a word with you about old Fentiman. Frightfully confidential, and all that. But it seems the exact time of the poor old blighter's departure has become an important item. Question of succession. Get me? They don't want a row made. Asked me, as friend of the family and all that, don't y' know, to barge round and ask questions. Obviously, you're the first man to come to. What's your opinion? Medical opinion, apart from anything else?'

Penberthy raised his eyebrows.

'Oh, there's a question, is there? Thought there might be. That lawyer-fellow, what's-his-name, was here the other day, trying to pin me down. Seemed to think one can say to a minute when a man died by looking at his back teeth. I told him it wasn't possible. Once give these

29

birds an opinion, and the next thing is, you find yourself in a witness-box, swearing to it.'

'I know. But one gets a general idea.'

'Oh, yes. Only you have to check up your ideas by other things – facts, and so on. You can't just theorise.'

'Very dangerous things, theories. F'r instance – take this case. I've seen one or two stiff 'uns in my short life, and if I'd started theorisin' about this business, just from the look of the body, d'you know what I'd have said?'

'God knows what a layman would say about a medical question!' retorted the doctor, with a sour little grin.

'Hear, hear! Well, I should have said he'd been dead a long time.'

'That's pretty vague.'

'You said yourself that *rigor* was well advanced. Give it, say, six hours to set in, and – when did it pass off?'

'It was passing off then – I remarked upon it at the time.'

'So you did. I thought *rigor* usually lasted twenty-four hours or so.'

'It does, sometimes. Sometimes it goes off quickly. Quick come, quick go, as a rule. Still, I agree with you that, in the absence of other evidence, I should have put the death rather earlier than ten o'clock.'

'You admit that?'

'I do. But we know he came in not earlier than a quarter-past ten.'

'You've seen Williamson, then?'

'Oh, yes. I thought it better to check up on the thing as far as possible. So I can only suppose that, what with the death being sudden, and what with the warmth of the room – he was very close to the fire, you know – the

30

whole thing came on and worked itself off very quickly.'

'H'm! Of course, you knew the old boy's constitution very well?'

'Oh, rather. He was very frail. Heart gets a bit worn-out when you're over the four-score and ten, you know. I should never have been surprised at his dropping down anywhere. And then he'd had a bit of a shock, you see.'

'What was that?'

'Seeing his sister the afternoon before. They told you about that, I imagine, since you seem to know all about the business. He came along to Harley Street afterwards and saw me. I told him to go to bed and keep quiet. Arteries very strained, and pulse erratic. He was excited – naturally. He ought to have taken a complete rest. As I see it, he must have insisted on getting up, in spite of feeling groggy, walked here – he *would* do it – and collapsed straight away.'

'That's all right, Penberthy, but when – just when – did it happen?'

'Lord knows! I don't. Have another?'

'No, thanks; not for the moment. I say, I suppose you are perfectly satisfied about it all?'

'Satisfied?' The doctor stared at him. 'Yes, of course. If you mean satisfied as to what he died of, of course I'm satisfied. I shouldn't have given a certificate if I hadn't been satisfied.'

'Nothing about the body struck you as queer?'

'What sort of thing?'

'You know what I mean as well as I do,' said Wimsey, suddenly turning and looking the other straight in the face. The change in him was almost startling – it was as if a steel blade had whipped

31

suddenly out of its velvet scabbard. Penberthy met his eye, and nodded slowly.

'Yes, I do know what you mean. But not here. We'd better go up to the library. There won't be anybody there.'

5

—AND FINDS THE CLUB SUIT BLOCKED

THERE never was anybody in the library at the Bellona. It was a large, quiet, pleasant room, with the book-shelves arranged in bays, each of which contained a writing-table and three or four chairs. Occasionally someone would wander in to consult *The Times Atlas*, or a work on Strategy and Tactics, or to hunt up an ancient Army List, but for the most part it was deserted. Sitting in the farthest bay, immured by books and silence, confidential conversation could be carried on with all the privacy of the confessional.

'Well, now,' said Wimsey, 'what about it?'

'About—?' prompted the doctor, with professional caution.

'About that leg?'

'I wonder if anybody else noticed that,' said Penberthy.

'I doubt it. I did, of course. But then, I make that kind of thing my hobby. Not a popular one, perhaps – an ill-favoured thing, but mine own. In fact, I've got rather a turn for corpses. But not knowin' quite what it meant, and seein' you didn't seem to want to call attention to it, I didn't put myself forward.'

'No – I wanted to think it over. You see, it suggested, at the first blush, something rather—'

'Unpleasant,' said Wimsey. 'If you knew how often I'd heard that word in the last two days! Well, let's face it. Let's admit, straight away that, once *rigor* sets in, it stays in till it starts to pass off, and that, when it *does* start to go, it usually begins with the face and jaw, and not suddenly in one knee-joint. Now Fentiman's jaw and neck were as rigid as wood – I felt 'em. But the left leg swung loose from the knee. Now how do you explain that?'

'It is extremely puzzling. As no doubt you are aware, the obvious explanation would be that the joint had been forcibly loosened by somebody or something, after *rigor* had set in. In that case, of course, it wouldn't stiffen up again. It would remain loose until the whole body relaxed. But how it happened—'

'That's just it. Dead people don't go about jamming their legs into things and forcing their own joints. And surely, if anybody had found the body like that, he would have mentioned it. I mean, can you imagine one of the waiter-johnnies, for instance, finding an old gentleman stiff as a poker in the best armchair and then just givin' him a dose of knee-jerks and leavin' him there?'

'The only thing I could think of,' said Penberthy, 'was that a waiter or somebody had found him, and tried to move him – and then got frightened and barged off without saying anything. It sounds absurd. But people do do odd things, especially if they're scared.'

'But what was there to be scared of?'

'It might seem alarming to a man in a very nervous state. We have one or two shell-shock cases here that I wouldn't answer for in an emergency. It would be worth considering, perhaps, if anyone had shown special signs of agitation or shock that day.'

'That's an idea,' said Wimsey slowly. 'Suppose – suppose, for instance, there was somebody connected in some way with the General who was in an unnerved state of mind – and suppose he came suddenly on this

34

stiff corpse. You think he might – possibly – lose his head?'

'It's certainly possible. I can imagine that he might behave hysterically, or even violently, and force the knee-joint back with some unbalanced idea of straightening the body and making it look more seemly. And then, you know, he might just run away from the thing and pretend it hadn't happened. Mind you, I'm not saying it was so, but I can easily see it happening. And that being so, I thought it better to say nothing about it. It would be a very unpl – distressing thing to bring to people's notice. And it might do untold harm to the nervous case to question him about it. I'd rather let sleeping dogs lie. There was nothing wrong about the death, that's definite. As for the rest – our duty is to the living; we can't help the dead.'

'Quite. Tell you what, though, I'll have a shot at finding out whether – we may as well say what we mean – whether George Fentiman was alone in the smoking-room at any time during the day. One of the servants may have noticed. It seems the only possible explanation. Well, thanks very much for your help. Oh, by the way, you said at the time that the *rigor was passing off when we found the body* – was that just camouflage, or does it still hold good?'

'It was just beginning to pass off in the face and jaw, as a matter of fact. It had passed away completely by midnight.'

'Thanks. That's another fact, then. I like facts, and there are annoyin'ly few of them in this case. Won't you have another whisky?'

'No, thanks. Due at my surgery. See you another time. Cheerio!'

Wimsey remained for a few moments after he had

gone, smoking meditatively. Then he turned his chair to the table, took a sheet of paper from the rack and began to jot down a few notes of the case with his fountain pen. He had not got far, however, before one of the Club servants entered, peering into all the bays in turn, looking for somebody.

'Want me, Fred?'

'Your lordship's man is here, my lord, and says you may wish to be advised of his arrival.'

'Quite right. I'm just coming.' Wimsey took up the blotting-pad to blot his notes. Then his face changed. The corner of a sheet of paper protruded slightly. On the principle that nothing is too small to be looked at, Wimsey poked an inquisitive finger between the leaves, and extracted the paper. It bore a few scrawls relating to sums of money, very carelessly and shakily written. Wimsey looked at it attentively for a moment or two, and shook the blotter to see if it held anything further. Then he folded the sheet, handling it with extreme care by the corners, put it in an envelope and filed it away in his note-case. Coming out of the library, he found Bunter waiting in the hall, camera and tripod in hand.

'Ah, here you are, Bunter. Just a minute, while I see the Secretary.' He looked in at the office, and found Culyer immersed in some accounts.

'Oh, I say, Culyer – 'morning and all that – yes, disgustingly healthy, thanks, always am – I say, you recollect old Fentiman poppin' off in that inconsiderate way a little time ago?'

'I'm not likely to forget it,' said Culyer, with a wry face. 'I've had three notes of complaint from Wetheridge – one, because the servants didn't notice the matter earlier, set of inattentive rascals and all that; two, because the undertaker's men had to take the coffin past his door and disturbed him; three, because somebody's lawyer came along and asked him questions – together with distant allusions to the telephones being out of order and a shortage of soap in the bathroom. Who'd be a secretary?'

'Awfully sorry for you,' said Wimsey, with a grin. 'I'm not here to make trouble. *Au contraire*, as the man said in the Bay of Biscay when they asked if he'd dined. Fact is, there's a bit of a muddle about the exact minute when the old boy passed out – mind you, this is in strict confidence – and I'm havin' a look into it. Don't want a fuss made, but I'd like a few photographs of the place, just to look at in absence and keep the lie of the land under my hawk-like optic, what? I've got my man here with a camera. D'you mind pretendin' he's the bloke from the *Twaddler* or the *Picture News*, or something, and givin' him your official blessin' while he totters round with the doings?'

'Mysterious idiot – of course, if you like. Though how photographs of the place today are going to give you a line on the time of a death which happened ten days ago, I don't pretend to understand. But, I say – it's all fair and above board? We don't want any—'

'Of course not. That's the idea. Strictest confidence – any sum up to £50,000 on your note of hand alone, delivered in plain vans, no reference needed. Trust little Peter.'

'Oh, right-o! What d'you want done?'

'I don't want to go round with Bunter. Give the show away. May he be called in here?'

'Certainly.'

A servant was sent to fetch Bunter, who came in looking imperturbably prim and point-device. Wimsey looked him over and shook his head.

'I'm sorry, Bunter, but you don't look in the least like the professional photographer from the *Twaddler*. That dark-grey suit is all right, but you haven't got quite the air of devil-may-care seediness that marks the giants of Fleet Street. D'you mind stickin' all those dark-slides into one pocket and a few odd lenses and doodahs into the other, and rufflin' your manly locks a trifle? That's better. Why have you no pyro stains on the right thumb and forefinger?'

'I attribute it, my lord, principally to the circumstance that I prefer metol-quinol for the purpose of development.'

'Well, you can't expect an outsider to grasp a thing like that. Wait a minute. Culyer, you seem to have a fairly juicy pipe there. Give us a cleaner.'

Wimsey thrust the instrument energetically through the stem of the pipe, bringing out a revolting collection of brown, oily matter.

'Nicotine poisoning, Culyer – that's what you'll die of if you aren't jolly careful. Here you are, Bunter. Judiciously smeared upon the fingertips, that should give quite the right effect. Now, look here, Mr Culyer here will take you round. I want a shot of the smoking-room from the entrance, a close-up of the fireplace, showing General Fentiman's usual chair, and another shot from the door of the ante-room that leads into the library. Another shot through the ante-room into the library, and some careful studies of the far bay of the library from all points of view. After that, I want two or three views of the hall, and a shot of the cloak-room; get the attendant there to show you which was General Fentiman's customary peg, and take care that that gets into the picture. That's all for the moment, but you can take anything else that seems necessary for the purpose of camouflage. And I want all the detail you can possibly get in, so stop down to whatever it is and take as long as you like. You'll find me knocking about somewhere when you've finished, and you'd better get some more plates in, because we're going on to another place.'

'Very good, my lord.'

'Oh, and, Culyer, by the way. Dr Penberthy sent a female in to lay the General out, didn't he? D'you happen to remember when she arrived?'

'About nine o'clock the next morning, I think.'

'Have you got her name, by any chance?'

'I don't think so. But I know she came from Merritt's, the undertakers – round Shepherd's Market way. They'd probably put you on to her.'

'Thanks frightfully, Culyer. I'll make myself scarce now. Carry on, Bunter.'

Wimsey thought for a moment; then strolled across to the smoking-room, exchanged a mute greeting with one or two of the assembled veterans, picked up the *Morning Post*, and looked round for a seat. The great armchair with ears still stood before the fire, but some dim feeling of respect for the dead had left it vacant. Wimsey sauntered over to it, and dropped lazily into its well-sprung depths. A veteran close at hand looked angrily at him, and rustled *The Times* loudly. Wimsey ignored these signals, barricading himself behind his paper. The veteran sank back again, muttering something about 'young men' and 'no decency'. Wimsey sat on unmoved, and paid no attention, even when a man from the *Twaddler* came in, escorted by the secretary, to take photographs of the smoking-room. A few sensitives retired before this attack. Wetheridge waddled away with a grumbling protest into the library. It gave Wimsey considerable satisfaction to see the relentless camera pursue him into that stronghold.

It was half-past twelve before a waiter approached Lord Peter to say that Mr Culyer would be glad to speak to him for a moment. In the office, Bunter reported his job done, and was dispatched to get some lunch and a fresh supply of plates. Wimsey presently went down to the dining-room, where he found Wetheridge already established, getting the first cut off the saddle of mutton, and grumbling at the wine. Wimsey went deliberately over, greeted him heartily, and sat down at the same table.

Wetheridge said it was beastly weather. Wimsey agreed amiably. Wetheridge said it was scandalous, seeing what one paid for one's food in this place, that one couldn't get anything fit to eat. Wimsey, who was adored by *chef* and waiters alike for his appreciation of good food, and had been sent the choicest cut without having to ask for it, sympathised with this sentiment too. Wetheridge said he had been chased all over the Club that morning by an infernal photographer fellow, and that one got no peace these days with all this confounded publicity. Wimsey said it was all done for advertisement, and that advertisement was the curse of the age. Look at the papers – nothing but advertisements from cover to cover. Wetheridge said that in his time, by gad, a respectable Club would have scorned advertisements, and that he could remember the time when newspapers were run by gentlemen for gentlemen. Wimsey said that nothing was what it had been; he thought it must be due to the War.

'Infernal slackness, that's what it is,' said Wetheridge. 'The service in this place is a disgrace. That fellow Culyer doesn't know his job. This week it's the soap. Would you

believe it, there was none – actually none – in the bathroom yesterday. Had to ring for it. Made me late for
dinner. Last week it was the telephone. Wanted to get
through a man down in Norfolk. Brother was a friend of
mine – killed on the last day of the War, half an hour
before the guns stopped firing – damnable shame –
always ring up on Armistice Day, say a few words, don't
you know – hr'rm!'

Wetheridge, having unexpectedly displayed this softer
side of his character, relapsed into a snorting silence.

'Couldn't you get through, sir?' inquired Wimsey, with
feeling. Anything that had happened at the Bellona Club
on Armistice Day was of interest to him.

'I got *through* all right,' said Wetheridge morosely.
'But, confound it all, I had to go down to the cloak-room
to get a call from one of the boxes there. Didn't want to
hang about the entrance. Too many imbeciles coming in
and out. Exchanging silly anecdotes. Why a solemn
national occasion should be an excuse for all these fools
meeting and talking rot, I don't know.'

'Beastly annoyin'. But why didn't you tell 'em to put
the call through to the box by the library?'

'Aren't I telling you? The damned thing was out of
order. Damned great notice stuck across it as cool as you
please – "Instrument out of order". Just like that. No
apology. Nothing. Sickening, I call it. I told the fellow at
the switchboard it was a disgrace. And all he said was, he
hadn't put the notice up, but he'd draw attention to the
matter.'

'It was all right in the evening,' said Wimsey, 'because I
saw Colonel Marchbanks using it.'

'I know it was. And then, dashed if we didn't get the
fool thing ringing, ringing at intervals all the next morning. Infuriating noise. When I told Fred to stop it, he just

41

said it was the Telephone Company testing the line. They've no business to make a row like that. Why can't they test it quietly, that's what I want to know?'

Wimsey said telephones were an invention of the devil. Wetheridge grumbled his way through to the end of lunch, and departed. Wimsey returned to the entrance-hall, where he found the assistant commissionaire on duty, and introduced himself.

Weston, however, was of no assistance. He had not noticed General Fentiman's arrival on the eleventh. He was not acquainted with many of the members, having only just taken over his new duties. He thought it odd that he should not have noticed so very venerable a gentleman, but the fact remained that he had not. He regretted it extremely. Wimsey gathered that Weston was annoyed at having lost a chance of reflected celebrity. He had missed his scoop, as the reporters say.

Nor was the hall-porter any more helpful. The morning of November 11th had been a busy one. He had been in and out of his little glass pigeon-hole continually, shepherding guests into various rooms to find the members they wanted, distributing letters and chatting to country members who visited the Bellona seldom and liked to 'have a chat with Piper' when they did. He could not recollect seeing the General. Wimsey began to feel that there must have been a conspiracy to overlook the old gentleman on the last morning of his life.

'You don't think he never was here at all, do you, Bunter?' he suggested. 'Walkin' about invisible and tryin' hard to communicate, like the unfortunate ghost in that story of somebody or other's?'

Bunter was inclined to reject the psychic view of the case.

42

'The General must have been here in the body, my lord, because there *was* the body.'

'That's true,' said Wimsey. 'I'm afraid we can't explain away the body. S'pose that means I'll have to question every member of this beastly Club separately. But just at the moment I think we'd better go round to the General's flat and hunt up Robert Fentiman. Weston, get me a taxi, please.'

6

A CARD OF RE-ENTRY

THE door of the little flat in Dover Street was opened by an elderly manservant, whose anxious face bore signs of his grief at his master's death. He informed them that Major Fentiman was at home and would be happy to receive Lord Peter Wimsey. As he spoke, a tall, soldierly man of about forty-five came out from one of the rooms and hailed his visitor cheerily.

'That you, Wimsey? Murbles told me to expect you. Come in. Haven't seen you for a long time. Hear you're turning into a regular Sherlock. Smart bit of work that was you put in over your brother's little trouble. What's all this? Camera? Bless me, you're going to do our little job in the professional manner, eh? Woodward, see that Lord Peter's man has everything he wants. Have you had lunch? Well, you'll have a spot of something, I take it, before you start measuring up the footprints. Come along. We're a bit at sixes and sevens here, but you won't mind.'

He led the way into the small, austerely-furnished sitting-room.

'Thought I might as well camp here for a bit, while I get the old man's belongings settled up. It's going to be a deuce of a job, though, with all this fuss about the will. However, I'm his executor, so all this part of it falls to me in any case. It's very decent of you to lend us a hand. Queer old girl, Great Aunt Dormer. Meant well, you know, but made it damned awkward for everybody. How are you getting along?'

Wimsey explained the failure of his researches at the Bellona.

'Thought I'd better get a line on it at this end,' he added. 'If we know exactly what time he left here in the morning, we ought to be able to get an idea of the time he got to the Club.'

Fentiman screwed his mouth into a whistle.

'But, my dear old egg, didn't Murbles tell you the snag?'

'He told me nothing. Left me to get on with it. What *is* the snag?'

'Why, don't you see, the old boy never came home that night.'

'Never came home? Where was he, then?'

'Dunno. That's the puzzle. All we know is — Wait a minute, this is Woodward's story; he'd better tell you himself, Woodward!'

'Yes, sir.'

'Tell Lord Peter Wimsey the story you told me — about that telephone call, you know.'

'Yes, sir. About nine o'clock—'

'Just a moment,' said Wimsey, 'I do like a story to begin at the beginning. Let's start with the morning — the mornin' of November 10th. Was the General all right that morning? Usual health and spirits, and all that?'

'Entirely so, my lord. General Fentiman was accustomed to rise early, my lord, being a light sleeper, as was natural at his great age. He had his breakfast in bed at a quarter to eight — tea and buttered toast, with a hegg lightly boiled, as he did every day in the year. Then he got up, and I helped him to dress — that would be about half-past eight to nine, my lord. Then he took a little rest, after the exertion of dressing, and at a quarter to ten I fetched his hat, overcoat, muffler and stick, and saw him start off to walk to the Club. That was his daily routine. He seemed in very good spirits – and in his usual health. Of course, his heart was always frail, my lord, but he seemed no different from ordinary.'

'I see. And in the ordinary way he'd just sit at the Club all day and come home – when, exactly?'

'I was accustomed to having his evening meal ready for him at half-past seven precisely, my lord.'

'Did he always turn up to time?'

'Invariably so, my lord. Everythink as regular as on parade. That was the General's way. About three o'clock in the afternoon there was a ring on the telephone. We had the telephone put in, my lord, on account of the General's heart, so that we could always call up a medical man in case of emergency.'

'Very right, too,' put in Robert Fentiman.

'Yes, sir. General Fentiman was good enough to say, sir, he did not wish me to have the heavy responsibility of looking after him alone in case of illness. He was a very kind, thoughtful gentleman.' The man's voice faltered.

'Just so,' said Wimsey. 'I'm sure you must be very sorry to lose him, Woodward. Still, one couldn't expect otherwise, you know. I'm sure you looked after him splendidly. What was it happened about three o'clock?'

'Why, my lord, they rang up from Lady Dormer's to say as how her ladyship was very ill, and would General Fentiman please come at once if he wanted to see her alive. So I went down to the Club myself. I didn't like to telephone, you see, because General Fentiman was a little hard of hearing – though he had his faculties wonderful well for a gentleman of his age – and he never liked the telephone. Besides, I was afraid of the shock it might be to him, seeing his heart was so weak – which, of course, at his age you couldn't hardly expect otherwise – so that was why I went myself.'

'That was very considerate of you.'

'Thank you, my lord. Well, I see General Fentiman, and I give him the message – careful like, and breaking it gently, as you might say, I could see he was took aback a bit, but he just sits thinking for a few minutes, and then he says, 'Very well, Woodward, I will go. It is certainly my duty to go.' So I wraps him up careful, and gets him into a taxi, and he says, 'You needn't come with me, Woodward. I don't quite know how long I shall stay there. They will see that I get home quite safely.' So I told the man where to take him and came back to the flat. And that, my lord, was the last time I see him.'

Wimsey made a sympathetic clucking sound.

'Yes, my lord. When General Fentiman didn't return at his usual time, I thought he was maybe staying to dine at Lady Dormer's, and took no notice of it. However, at half-past eight I began to be afraid of the night air for it was very cold that day, my lord, if you remember. At nine o'clock I was just thinking of calling up the house-hold at Lady Dormer's to ask when he was to be expected home, when the phone rang.'

'At nine exactly?'

'About nine. It might have been a little later, but not more than a quarter-past at latest. It was a gentleman spoke to me. He said, "Is that General Fentiman's flat?" I said, "Yes; who is it, please?" And he said, "Is that Woodward?" giving my name, just like that, and I said, "Yes." And he said, "Oh, Woodward, General Fentiman wishes me to tell you not to wait up for him, as he is spending the night with me." So I said, "Excuse me, sir, who is it speaking, please?" And he said, "Mr Oliver." So I asked him to repeat the name, not having heard it

47

before, and he said, "Oliver" – it came over very plain – "Mr Oliver," he said; "I'm an old friend of General Fentiman's, and he is staying tonight with me, as we have some business to talk over." So I said, "Does the General require anything, sir?" thinking, you know, my lord, as he might wish to have his sleeping-suit and his tooth-brush or somethink of that, but the gentleman said no, he had got everything necessary and I was not to trouble myself. Well, of course, my lord, as I explained to Major Fentiman, I didn't like to take upon myself to ask questions, being only in service, my lord; it might seem taking a liberty. But I was very much afraid of the excitement and staying up late being too much for the General, so I went so far as to say I hoped General Fentiman was in good health and not tiring of himself, and Mr Oliver laughed and said he would take very good care of him and send him to bed straight away. And I was just about to make so bold as to ask him where he lived, when he rang off. And that was all I knew till I heard next day of the General being dead, my lord.'

'There now,' said Robert Fentiman. 'What do you think of that?'

'Odd,' said Wimsey, 'and most unfortunate as it turns out. Did the General often stay out at night, Woodward?'

'Never, my lord. I don't recollect such a thing happening once in five or six years. In the old days, perhaps, he'd visit friends occasionally, but not of late.'

'And you'd never heard of this Mr Oliver?'

'No, my lord.'

'His voice wasn't familiar?'

I couldn't say but what I might have heard it before, my lord, but I find it very difficult to recognise voices on the telephone. But I thought at the time it might be one of the gentlemen from the Club.'

'Do *you* know anything about the man, Fentiman?'

'Oh, yes – I've met him. At least, I suppose it's the same man. But I know nothing about him. I fancy I ran across him once in some frightful crush or other, a public dinner, or something of that kind, and he said he knew my grandfather. And I've seen him lunching at Gatti's and that sort of thing. But I haven't the remotest idea where he lives or what he does.'

'Army man?'

'No – something in the engineering line, I fancy.'

'What's he like?'

'Oh, tall, thin, grey hair and spectacles. About sixty-five to look at. He may be older – must be, if he's an old friend of grandfather's. I gathered he was retired from whatever it is he did, and lived in some suburb, but I'm hanged if I can remember which.'

'Not very helpful,' said Wimsey. 'D'you know, occasionally I think there's quite a lot to be said for women?'

'What's that got to do with it?'

'Well, I mean all this easy, uninquisitive way men have of makin' casual acquaintances is very fine and admirable and all that – but look how inconvenient it is! Here you are. You admit you've met this bloke two or three times, and all you know about him is that he is tall and thin and retired into some unspecified suburb. A woman, with the same opportunities, would have found out his address and occupation, whether he was married, how many children he had, with their names and what they did for a living, what his favourite author was, what food he liked best, the name of his tailor, dentist and boot-maker, when he knew your grandfather and what he thought of him – screeds of useful stuff!'

'So she would,' said Fentiman, with a grin, 'That's why I've never married.'

49

'I quite agree,' said Wimsey, 'but the fact remains that as a source of information you're simply a washout. Do, for goodness' sake, pull yourself together and try to remember something a bit more definite about the fellow. It may mean half a million to you to know what time grandpa set off in the morning from Tooting Bec or Finchley, or wherever it was. If it was a distant suburb, it would account for his arriving rather late at the Club – which is rather in your favour, by the way.'

'I suppose it is. I'll do my best to remember. But I'm not sure that I ever knew.'

'It's awkward,' said Wimsey. 'No doubt the police could find the man for us, but it's not a police case. And I don't suppose you particularly want to advertise.'

'Well – it may come to that. But, naturally, we're not keen on publicity if we can avoid it. If only I could remember exactly what work he said he'd been connected with!'

'Yes – or the public dinner or whatever it was where you first met him. One might get hold of a list of the guests.'

'My dear Wimsey – that was two or three years ago!'

'Or maybe they know the blighter at Gatti's.'

'That's an idea, I've met him there several times. Tell you what, I'll go along there and make inquiries, and if they don't know him, I'll make a point of lunching there pretty regularly. He's almost bound to turn up again.'

'Right. You do that. And meanwhile, do you mind if I have a look round the flat?'

'Rather not. D'you want me? Or would you rather have Woodward? He really knows a lot more about things.'

'Thanks. I'll have Woodward. Don't mind me. I shall just be fussing about.'

'Carry on, by all means. I've got one or two drawers full of papers to go through. If I come across anything bearing on the Oliver bloke I'll yell out to you.'

'Right.'

Wimsey went out, leaving him to it, and joined Woodward and Bunter, who were conversing in the next room. A glance told Wimsey that this was the General's bedroom.

On a table beside the narrow iron bedstead was an old-fashioned writing-desk. Wimsey took it up, weighed it in his hands a moment and then took it to Robert Fentiman in the other room.

'Have you opened this?' he asked.

'Yes – only old letters and things.'

'You didn't come across Oliver's address, I suppose?'

'No. Of course I looked for that.'

'Looked anywhere else? Any drawers? Cupboards? That sort of thing?'

'Not so far,' said Fentiman, rather shortly.

'No telephone memorandum or anything – you've tried the telephone book, I suppose?'

'Well, no – I can't very well ring up perfect strangers and—'

'And sing 'em the Froth-Blowers' Anthem? Good God, man, anybody'd think you were chasing a lost umbrella, not half a million of money. The man rang you up, so he may very well be on the phone himself. Better let Bunter tackle the job. He has an excellent manner on the line; people find it a positive pleasure to be tr-r-roubled by him.'

Robert Fentiman greeted his feeble pleasantry with an indulgent grin, and produced the telephone directory, to which Bunter immediately applied himself. Finding two and a half columns of Olivers, he removed the receiver and started to work steadily through them in rotation. Wimsey returned to the bedroom. It was in apple-pie order – the bed neatly made, the wash-hand apparatus set in order, as though the occupant might return at any moment, every speck of dust removed – a tribute to Woodward's reverent affection, but a depressing sight for an investigator. Wimsey sat down and let his eye rove slowly from the hanging wardrobe, with its polished doors, over the orderly line of boots and shoes arranged on their trees on a small shelf, the dressing-table, the washstand, the bed and the chest of drawers which, with the small bedside table and a couple of chairs, comprised the furniture.

'Did the General shave himself, Woodward?'

'No, my lord; not latterly. That was my duty, my lord.'

'Did he brush his own teeth, or dental plate, or whatever it was?'

'Oh, yes, my lord. General Fentiman had an excellent set of teeth for his age.'

Wimsey fixed his powerful monocle into his eye and carried the toothbrush over to the window. The result of the scrutiny was unsatisfactory. He looked around again.

'Is that his walking-stick?'

'Yes, my lord.'

'May I see it?'

Woodward brought it across, carrying it, after the manner of a well-trained servant, by the middle. Lord Peter took it from him in the same manner, suppressing a slight, excited smile. The stick was a heavy malacca, with a thick crutch-handle of polished ivory, suitable for sustaining the feeble steps of old age. The monocle came into play again, and this time its owner gave a chuckle of pleasure.

'I shall want to take a photograph of this stick presently, Woodward, Will you be very careful to see that it is not touched by anybody beforehand?'

'Certainly, my lord.'

Wimsey stood the stick carefully in its corner again, and then, as though it had put a new train of ideas into his mind, walked across to the shoe-shelf.

'Which were the shoes General Fentiman was wearing at the time of his death?'

'These, my lord.'

'Have they been cleaned since?'

Woodward looked a trifle stricken.

'Not to say cleaned, my lord. I just wiped them over with a duster. They were not very dirty, and somehow – I hadn't the heart – if you'll excuse me, my lord.'

'That's very fortunate.'

Wimsey turned them over and examined the soles very carefully, both with the lens and with the naked eye. With a small pair of tweezers, taken from his pocket, he delicately removed a small fragment of pile – apparently from a thick carpet – which was clinging to a projecting brad, and stored it carefully away in an envelope. Then, putting the right shoe aside, he subjected the left to a prolonged scrutiny, especially about the inner edge of the sole. Finally he asked for a sheet of paper, and wrapped the shoe up as tenderly as though it had been a piece of priceless Waterford glass.

'I should like to see all the clothes General Fentiman was wearing that day – the outer garments, I mean – hat, suit, overcoat, and so on.'

The garments were produced, and Wimsey went over every of them with the same care and patience, watched by Woodward with flattering attention.

'Have they been brushed?'

'No, my lord – only shaken out.' This time Woodward

offered no apology, having grasped dimly that polishing and brushing were not acts which called for approval under these unusual circumstances.

'You see,' said Wimsey, pausing for a moment to note an infinitesimally small ruffling of the threads on the left-hand trouser leg, 'we might be able to get some sort of a clue from the dust on the clothes, if any – to show us where the General spent the night. If – to take a rather unlikely example – we were to find a lot of sawdust, for instance, we might suppose that he had been visiting a carpenter. Or a dead leaf might suggest a garden or a common, or something of that sort, While a cobweb might mean a wine-cellar, or – or a potting-shed and so on. You see?'

'Yes, my lord' (rather doubtfully).

'You don't happen to remember noticing that little tear – well, it's hardly a tear – just a little roughness. It might bave caught on a nail.'

'I can't say I recollect it, my lord. But I might have over-looked it.'

'Of course. It's probably of no importance. Well – lock the things up carefully. It's just possible I might have to have the dust extracted and analysed. Just a moment. Has anything been removed from these clothes? The pockets were emptied, I suppose?'

'Yes, my lord.'

'There was nothing unusual in them?'

'No, my lord. Nothing but what the General always took out with him. Just his handkerchief, keys, money and cigar-case.'

'H'm. How about the money?'

'Well, my lord – I couldn't say exactly as to that. Major Fentiman has got it all. There was two pound notes in his note-case, I remember. I believe he had two pounds ten when he went out, and some loose silver in his trouser-pocket. He'd have paid his taxi-fare and his lunch at the Club out of the ten-shilling note.'

'That shows he didn't pay for anything unusual, then, in the way of train or taxis backwards and forwards, or dinner, or drinks.'

'No, my lord.'

'But naturally, this Oliver fellow would see to all that. Did the General have a fountain pen?'

'No, my lord. He did very little writing, my lord. I was accustomed to write any necessary letters to tradesmen, and so on.'

'What sort of nib did he use, when he did write?'

'A "J" pen, my lord. You will find it in the sitting-room. But mostly I believe he wrote his letters at the Club. He had a very small private correspondence – it might be a letter or so to the bank or to his man of business, my lord.'

'I see. Have you his cheque-book?'

'Major Fentiman has it, my lord.'

'Do you remember whether the General had it with him when he last went out?'

'No, my lord. It was kept in his writing-desk as a rule. He would write the cheques for the household here, my lord, and give them to me. Or occasionally he might take the book down to the Club with him.'

'Ah! well, it doesn't look as though the mysterious Mr Oliver was one of those undesirable blokes who demand money. Right you are, Woodward. You're perfectly certain that you removed nothing whatever from those clothes except what was in the pockets?'

'I am quite positive of that, my lord.'

'That's very odd,' said Wimsey, half to himself. 'I'm not sure that it isn't the oddest thing about the case.'

'Indeed, my lord? Might I ask why?'

'Why,' said Wimsey, 'I should have expected –' he checked himself. Major Fentiman was looking in at the door.

'What's odd, Wimsey?'

'Oh, just a little thing struck me,' said Wimsey vaguely. 'I expected to find something among those clothes which isn't there. That's all.'

'Impenetrable sleuth,' said the major, laughing. 'What are you driving at?'

'Work it out for yourself, my dear Watson,' said his lordship, grinning like a dog. 'You have all the data. Work it out for yourself, and let me know the answer.'

Woodward, a trifle pained by this levity, gathered up the garments and put them away in the wardrobe.

'How's Bunter getting on with those calls?'

'No luck, at present.'

'Oh! – well, he'd better come in now and do some photographs. We can finish the telephoning at home. Bunter! Oh, and, I say, Woodward – d'you mind if we take your fingerprints?'

'Fingerprints, my lord?'

'Good God, you're not trying to fasten anything on Woodward?'

'Fasten what?'

'Well – I mean, I thought it was only burglars and people who had fingerprints taken.'

'Not exactly. No – I want the General's fingerprints, really, to compare them with some others I got at the Club. There's a very fine set on that walking-stick of his, and I want Woodward's, just to make sure I'm not getting the two sets mixed up. I'd better take yours, too. It's just possible you might have handled the stick without noticing.'

'Oh, I get you, Steve. I don't think I've touched the thing, but it's as well to make sure, as you say. Funny sort of business, what? Quite the Scotland Yard touch. How d'you do it?'

'Bunter will show you.'

Bunter immediately produced a small inking-pad and roller, and a number of sheets of smooth, white paper. The fingers of the two candidates were carefully wiped with a clean cloth, and pressed first on the pad and then on the paper. The impressions thus obtained were labelled and put away in envelopes, after which the handle of the walking-stick was lightly dusted with grey powder, bringing to light an excellent set of prints of a right-hand set of fingers, superimposed here and there, but quite identifiable. Fentiman and Woodward gazed fascinated at this entertaining miracle.

'Are they all right?'

'Perfectly so, sir; they are quite unlike either of the other two specimens.'

'Then presumably they're the General's. Hurry up and get a negative.'

Bunter set up the camera and focused it.

'Unless,' observed Major Fentiman, 'they are Mr Oliver's. That would be a good joke, wouldn't it?'

'It would, indeed,' said Wimsey, a little taken aback. 'A very good joke – on somebody. And for the moment, Fentiman, I'm not sure which of us would do the laughing.'

7

THE CURSE OF SCOTLAND

WHAT with telephone calls and the development of photographs, it appeared obvious that Bunter was booked for a busy afternoon. His master, therefore, considerately left him in possession of the flat in Piccadilly, and walked abroad to divert himself in his own peculiar way.

His first visit was to one of those offices which undertake to distribute advertisements to the press. Here he drew up an advertisement addressed to taxi-drivers and arranged for it to appear, at the earliest possible date, in all the papers which men of that profession might be expected to read. Three drivers were requested to communicate with Mr J. Murbles, Solicitor, of Staple Inn, who would recompense them amply for their time and trouble. First: any driver who remembered taking up an aged gentleman from Lady Dormer's house in Portman Square or the near vicinity on the afternoon of November 10th. Secondly: any driver who recollected taking up an aged gentleman at or near Dr Penberthy's house in Harley Street at some time in the afternoon or evening of November 10th. And thirdly: any driver who had deposited a similarly aged gentleman at the door of the Bellona Club between 10 and 12.30 in the morning of November 11th.

'Though probably,' thought Wimsey, as he footed the bill for the insertions, to run for three days unless cancelled, 'Oliver had a car and ran the old boy up himself. Still, it's just worth trying.'

He had a parcel under his arm, and his next proceeding was to hail a cab and drive to the residence of Sir James Lubbock, the well-known analyst. Sir James was fortunately at home and delighted to see Lord Peter. He was a square-built man, with a reddish face and strongly-curling grey hair, and received his visitor in his laboratory, where he was occupied in superintending a Marsh's test for arsenic.

'D'ye mind just taking a pew for a moment, while I finish this off?'

Wimsey took the pew and watched, interested, the flame from the Bunsen burner playing steadily upon the glass tube, and the dark brown deposit slowly forming and deepening at the narrow end. From time to time the analyst poured down the thistle-funnel a small quantity of a highly disagreeable-looking liquid from a stoppered phial; once his assistant came forward to add a few more drops of what Wimsey knew must be hydrochloric acid. Presently, the disagreeable liquid having all been transferred to the flask, and the deposit having deepened almost to black at its densest part, the tube was detached and taken away, and the burner extinguished, and Sir James Lubbock, after writing and signing a brief note, turned round and greeted Wimsey cordially.

'Sure I am not interrupting you, Lubbock?'

'Not a scrap. We've just finished. That was the last mirror. We shall be ready in good time for our appearance in court. Not that there's much doubt about it. Enough of the stuff to kill an elephant. Considering the obliging care we take in criminal prosecutions to inform the public at large that two or three grains of arsenic will successfully account for an unpopular individual, however tough, it's surprising how wasteful people are with their drugs. You can't teach 'em. An office-boy who was as incompetent as the average murderer would be sacked with a kick in the bottom. Well, now! and what's your little trouble?'

'A small matter,' said Wimsey, unrolling his parcel and producing General Fentiman's left boot; 'it's cheek to come to you about it. But I want very much to know what this is, and as it's strictly a private matter, I took the liberty of bargin' round to you in a friendly way. Just along the inside of the sole, there – there on the edge.'

'Blood?' suggested the analyst, grinning.

'Well, no – sorry to disappoint you. More like paint, I fancy.'

Sir James looked closely at the deposit with a powerful lens.

'Yes; some sort of brown varnish. Might be off a floor or a piece of furniture. Do you want an analysis?'

'If it's not too much trouble.'

'Not at all. I think we'll get Saunders to do it; he has made rather a speciality of this kind of thing. Saunders, would you scrape this off carefully and see what it is? Get a slide of it, and make an analysis of the rest, if you can. How soon is it wanted?'

'Well, I'd like it as soon as possible. I don't mean within the next five minutes.'

'Well, stay and have a spot of tea with us, and I dare say we can get something ready for you by then. It doesn't look anything out-of-the-way. Knowing your tastes, I'm still surprised it isn't blood. Have you no blood in prospect?'

'Not that I know of. I'll stay to tea with pleasure, if you're certain I'm not being a bore.'

'Never that. Besides, while you're here, you might give

me your opinion on those old medical books of mine. I don't suppose they're particularly valuable, but they're quaint. Come along.'

Wimsey passed a couple of hours agreeably with Lady Lubbock and crumpets and a dozen or so anti-quated anatomical treatises. Presently Saunders re-turned with his report. The deposit was nothing more nor less than an ordinary brown paint and varnish of a kind well known to joiners and furniture makers. It was a modern preparation, with nothing unusual about it; one might find it anywhere. It was not a floor-varnish one would expect to meet it on a door or partition or something of that sort. The chemical formula followed.

'Not very helpful, I'm afraid,' said Sir James.

'You never know your luck,' replied Wimsey. 'Would you be good enough to label the slide and sign your name to it, and to the analysis, and keep them both by you for reference in case they're wanted?'

'Sure thing. How do you want 'em labelled?'

'Well – put down "Varnish from General Fentiman's left boot", and "Analysis of varnish from General Fen-timan's left boot", and the date, and I'll sign it, and you and Saunders can sign it, and then I think we shall be all right.'

'Fentiman? Was that the old boy who died suddenly the other day?'

'It was. But it's no use looking at me with that childlike air of intelligent taking-notice, because I haven't got any gory yarn to spin. It's only a question of where the old man spent the night, if you *must* know.'

'Curiouser and curiouser, Never mind, it's nothing to do with me. Perhaps when it's all over you'll tell me what it's about. Meanwhile the labels shall go on. You, I take it, are ready to witness to the identity of the boot, and I can witness to having seen the varnish on the boot, and Saunders can witness that he removed the varnish from the boot and analysed it and that this is the varnish he analysed. All according to Cocker. Here you are. Sign here and here, and that will be eight-and-sixpence, please.'

'It might be cheap at eight-and-sixpence,' said Wimsey. 'It might even turn out to be cheap at eight hundred and sixty quid – or eight thousand and sixty.'

Sir James Lubbock looked properly thrilled.

'You're only doing it to annoy, because you know it teases. Well, if you must be sphinx-like, you must. I'll keep these things under lock and key for you. Do you want the boot back?'

'I don't suppose the executor will worry. And a fellow looks such a fool carrying a boot about. Put it away with the other things till called for, there's a good man.'

So the boot was put away in a cupboard, and Lord Peter was free to carry on with his afternoon's entertainment.

His first idea was to go on up to Finsbury Park, to see the George Fentimans. He remembered in time, however, that Sheila would not yet be home from her work – she was employed as cashier in a fashionable tea-shop – and further (with a forethought rare in the well-to-do) that if he arrived too early he would have to be asked to supper, and that there would be very little supper and that Sheila would be worried about it and George annoyed. So he turned in to one of his numerous clubs, and had a sole Colbert very well cooked, with a bottle of Liebfraumilch; an apple charlotte and light savoury to follow, and black coffee and a rare old brandy to top up with – a simple and satisfactory meal which left him in the best of tempers.

The George Fentimans lived in two ground-floor rooms, with use of kitchen and bathroom, in a semi-detached house with a blue-and-yellow fanlight over the door and Madras muslin over the windows. They were really furnished apartments, but the landlady always referred to them as a flat, because that meant that tenants had to do their own work and provide their own service. The house felt stuffy as Lord Peter entered it, because somebody was frying fish in oil at no great distance, and a slight unpleasantness was caused at the start by the fact that he had rung only once, thus bringing up the person in the basement, whereas a better-instructed caller would have rung twice, to indicate that he wanted the ground floor.

Hearing explanations in the hall, George put his head out off the dining-room and said, 'Oh! hallo!'

'Hallo!' said Wimsey, trying to find room for his belongings on an overladen hat-stand, and eventually disposing of them on the handle of a perambulator. 'Thought I'd just come and look you up. Hope I'm not in the way.'

'Of course not. Jolly good of you to penetrate to this ghastly hole. Come in. Everything's in a beastly muddle as usual, but when you're poor you have to live like pigs. Sheila, here's Lord Peter Wimsey – you have met, haven't you?'

'Yes, of course. How nice of you to come round. Have you had dinner?'

'Yes, thanks.'

'Coffee?'

'No, thanks, really – I've only just had some.'

'Well,' said George, 'there's only whisky to offer you.'

63

'Later on, perhaps, thanks, old man. Not just now. I've had a brandy. Never mix grape and grain.'

'Wise man,' said George, his brow clearing, since, as a matter of fact, there was no whisky nearer than the public house, and acceptance would have meant six-and-six, at least, besides the exertion of fetching it.

Sheila Fentiman drew an armchair forward, and herself sat down on a low pouffe. She was a woman of thirty-five or so, and would have been very good-looking but for an appearance of worry and ill health that made her look older than her age.

'It's a miserable fire,' said George gloomily. 'Is this all the coal there is?'

'I'm sorry,' said Sheila; 'she didn't fill it up properly this morning.'

'Well, why can't you see that she does? It's always happening. If the scuttle isn't absolutely empty she seems to think she needn't bother about filling it up.'

'I'll get some.'

'No, it's all right. I'll go. But you ought to tell her about it.'

'I will – I'm always telling her.'

'The woman's no more sense than a hen. No – don't you go, Sheila – I won't have you carrying coal.'

'Nonsense,' said his wife, rather acidly. 'What a hypocrite you are, George. It's only because there's somebody here that you're so chivalrous all at once.'

'Here, let me,' said Wimsey desperately, 'I like fetching coal. Always loved coal as a kid. Anything grubby or noisy. Where is it? Lead me to it!'

Mrs Fentiman released the scuttle, for which George and Wimsey politely struggled. In the end they all went out together to the inconvenient bin in the backyard, Wimsey quarrying the coal, George receiving it in the scuttle, and the lady lighting them with a long candle, insecurely fixed in an enamel candlestick several sizes too large.

'And tell Mrs Crickett,' said George, irritably sticking to his grievance, 'that she must fill that scuttle up properly every day.'

'I'll try. But she hates being spoken to. I'm always afraid she'll give warning.'

'Well, there are other charwomen, I suppose?'

'Mrs Crickett is very honest.'

'I know; but that's not everything. You could easily find one if you took the trouble.'

'Well, I'll see about it. But why don't *you* speak to Mrs Crickett? I'm generally out before she gets here.'

'Oh, yes, I know. You needn't keep on rubbing it in about your having to go out to work. You don't suppose I *enjoy* it, do you? Wimsey can tell you how I feel about it.'

'Don't be so silly, George. Why is it, Lord Peter, that men are so cowardly about speaking to servants?'

'It's the woman's job to speak to servants,' said George, 'no business of mine.'

'All right – I'll speak, and you'll have to put up with the consequences.'

'There won't *be* any consequences, my dear, if you do it tactfully. I can't think why you want to make all this fuss.'

'Righto! I'll be as tactful as I can. You don't suffer from charladies, I suppose Lord Peter?'

'Good lord, no!' interrupted George. 'Wimsey lives decently. They don't know the dignified joys of hard-upness in Piccadilly.'

'I'm rather lucky,' said Wimsey, with that apologetic air which seems forced on anybody accused of too much wealth. 'I have an extraordinarily faithful and intelligent man who looks after me like a mother.'

'Dare say he knows when he's well off,' said George disagreeably.

'I dunno. I believe Bunter would stick to me whatever happened. He was my N.C.O. during part of the War, and we went through some roughish bits together, and after the whole thing was over I hunted him up and took him on. He was in service before that, of course, but his former master was killed and the family broken up, so he was quite pleased to come along. I don't know what I should do without Bunter now.'

'Is that the man who takes the photographs for you when you are on a crime-hunt?' suggested Sheila, hurriedly seizing on this, as she hoped, non-irritant topic.

'Yes. He's a great hand with a camera. Only drawback is that he's occasionally immured in the dark-room and I'm left to forage for myself. I've got a telephone extension through to him. "Bunter?" – "Yes, my lord!" – "Where are my dress studs?" – "In the middle section of the third small right-hand drawer of the dressing cabinet, my lord." – "Bunter!" – "Yes, my lord." – "Where have I put my cigarette-case?" – "I fancy I observed it last on the piano, my lord." – "Bunter!" – "Yes, my lord!" – "I've got into a muddle with my white tie." – "Indeed, my lord!" – "Well, can't you do anything about it?" – "Excuse me, my lord, I am engaged in the development of a plate." – "To hell with the plate!" – "Very good, my lord." – "Bunter – stop – don't be precipitate – finish the plate and then come and tie my tie." – "Certainly, my lord." And then I have to sit about miserably till the infernal plate is fixed, or whatever it is. Perfect slave in my own house – that's what I am.'

Sheila laughed.

'You look a very happy and well-treated slave. Are you investigating anything just now?'

'Yes. In fact – there you are again – Bunter has retired into photographic life for the evening. I haven't a roof to cover me. I have been wandering round like the what-d'you-call-it bird, which has no feet—'

'I'm sorry you were driven to such desperation as to seek asylum in our poverty-stricken hovel,' said George with a laugh.

Wimsey began to wish he had not come, Mrs Fentiman looked vexed.

'You needn't answer that,' she said, with an effort to be light; 'there *is* no answer.'

'I'll send it to Aunt Judith of *Rosie's Weekly Bits*,' said Wimsey. 'A makes a remark to which there is no answer. What is B to do?'

'Sorry,' said George, 'my conversation doesn't seem to be up to standard. I'm forgetting all my civilised habits. You'd better go on and pay no attention to me.'

'What's the mystery on hand now?' asked Sheila, taking her husband at his word.

'Well, actually it's about this funny business of the old General's will,' said Wimsey. 'Murbles suggested I should have a look into the question of the survivorship.'

'Oh, do you think you can really get it settled?'

'I hope so very much. But it's a very fine-drawn business – may resolve itself into a matter of seconds. By the way, Fentiman, were you in the Bellona smoking-room at all during the morning of Armistice Day?'

'So *that's* what you've come about. Why didn't you say so? No, I wasn't And what's more, I don't know anything at all about it. And why that infuriating old hag of a Dormer woman couldn't make a decent, sensible will while she was about it, I don't know. Where was the sense of leaving all those wads of money to the old man, when she knew perfectly well he was liable to peg out at any moment. And then, if he did die, handing the whole lot over to the Dorland girl, who hasn't an atom of claim on it? She might have had the decency to think about Robert and us a bit.'

'Considering how rude you were to her and Miss Dorland, George, I wonder she even left you the seven thousand.'

'What's seven thousand to her? Like a five-pound note to an ordinary person. An insult, I call it. I dare say I was rude to her, but I jolly well wasn't going to have her think I was sucking up to her for her money.'

'How inconsistent you are, George. If you didn't want the money, why grumble about not getting it?'

'You're always putting me in the wrong. You know I don't mean that. I *didn't* want the money – but the Dorland girl was always hinting that I did, and I ticked her off. I didn't know anything about the confounded legacy, and I didn't want to. All I mean is that if she did want to leave anything to Robert and me, she might have made it more than a rotten seven thousand apiece.'

'Well! don't grumble at it. It would be uncommonly handy at the moment.'

'I know – isn't that exactly what I'm saying? And now the old fool makes such a silly will that I don't know whether I'm to get it or not. I can't even lay hands on the old Governor's two thousand. I've got to sit here and twiddle my thumbs while Wimsey goes round with a tape measure and a tame photographer to see whether I'm entitled to my own grandfather's money!'

'I know it's frightfully trying, darling. But I expect it'll all come right soon, It wouldn't matter if it weren't for Douga MacStewart.'

'Who's Dougal MacStewart?' inquired Wimsey, suddenly alert. 'One of our old Scottish families, by the name. I fancy I have heard of him. Isn't he an obliging, helpful kind of chap, with a wealthy friend in the City?'

'Frightfully obliging,' said Sheila grimly. 'He simply forces his acquaintance on one. He—'

'Shut up, Sheila,' interrupted her husband rudely. 'Lord Peter doesn't want to know all the sordid details of our private affairs.'

'Knowing Dougal,' said Wimsey, 'I dare say I could give a guess at them. Some time ago you had a kind offer of assistance from our friend MacStewart. You accepted it to the mild tune of – what was it?'

'Five hundred,' said Sheila.

'Five hundred. Which turned out to be three-fifty in cash and the rest represented by a little honorarium to his friend in the City who advanced the money in so trustful a manner without security. When was that?'

'Three years ago – when I started that teashop in Kensington.'

'Ah, yes. And when you couldn't quite manage that sixty cent per month, or whatever it was, owing to trade depression, the friend in the City was obliging enough to add the interest to the principal, at great inconvenience to himself – and so forth. The MacStewart way is familiar to me. What's the dem'd total now, Fentiman, just out of curiosity?'

'Fifteen hundred by the thirtieth,' growled George, 'if you must know.'

'I warned George –' began Sheila unwisely.

'Oh, you always know what's best. Anyhow, it was your tea business. I told you there was no money in it, but women always think they can run things on their own nowadays.'

'I know, George. But it was MacStewart's interest that swallowed up the profits. You know I wanted you to borrow the money from Lady Dormer.'

'Well, I wasn't going to, and that's flat. I told you so at the time.'

'Well, but look here,' said Wimsey, 'You're perfectly all right about MacStewart's fifteen hundred, anyway, whichever way the thing goes. If General Fentiman died before his sister, you get seven thousand; if he died after her, you're certain of his two thousand, by the will. Besides, your brother will no doubt make a reasonable arrangement about sharing the money he gets as residuary legatee. Why worry?'

'Why? Because here's this infernal rigmarole tying the thing up and hanging it out till God knows when, and I can't touch anything.'

'I know, I know,' said Wimsey patiently; 'but all you've got to do is to go to Murbles and get him to advance you the money on your expectations. You can't get away with less than two thousand, whatever happens, so he'll be perfectly ready to do it. In fact, he's more or less bound to settle your just debts for you, if he's asked.'

'That's just what I've been telling you, George,' said Mrs Fentiman eagerly.

'Of course, you *would* be always telling me things. You never make a mistake, do you? And suppose the thing goes into court and we get let in for thousands of pounds in fees and things, Mrs Clever, eh?'

'I should leave it to your brother to go into court, if necessary,' said Wimsey sensibly. 'If he wins, he'll have plenty of cash for fees, and if he loses, you'll still have your seven thousand. You go to Murbles – he'll fix you up. Or, tell you what! – I'll get hold of friend MacStewart and see if I can't arrange to get the debt transferred to me. He won't consent, of course, if he knows it's me, but I can probably do it through Murbles. Then we'll threaten to fight him on the ground of extortionate interest and so on. We'll have some fun with it.'

'Dashed good of you, but I'd rather not, thanks.'

'Just as you like. But, anyway, go to Murbles. He'll get it squared up for you. Anyhow, I don't think there will be any litigation about the will. If we can't get to the bottom of the survivorship question, I should think you and Miss Dorland would be far better advised to come to a settlement out of court. It would probably be the fairest way in any case. Why don't you?'

'Why? Because the Dorland female wants her pound of flesh. That's why!'

'Does she? What kind of woman is she?'

'One of these modern, Chelsea women. Ugly as sin and hard as nails. Paints things – ugly, skinny prostitutes with green bodies and no clothes on. I suppose she thinks if she can't be a success as a woman she'll be a half-baked intellectual. No wonder a man can't get a decent job these days, with these hard-mouthed, cigarette-smoking females all over the place, pretending they're geniuses and business women and all the rest of it.'

'Oh, come, George! Miss Dorland isn't doing anybody out of a job; she couldn't just sit there all day being Lady Dormer's companion. What's the harm in her painting things?'

'Why couldn't she be a companion? In the old days, heaps of unmarried women were companions, and let me tell you, my dear girl, they had a much better time than they have now, with all this jazzing and short skirts and pretending to have careers. The modern girl hasn't a scrap of decent feeling or sentiment about her. Money –

money and notoriety – that's all she's after. That's what we fought the War for – and that's what we've come back to!'

'George, do keep to the point. Miss Dorland doesn't jazz—'

'I am keeping to the point. I'm talking about modern women. I don't say Miss Dorland in particular. But you *will* go taking everything personally. That's just like a woman. You can't argue about things in general – you always have to bring it down to some one little personal instance. You will side-track.'

'I wasn't side-tracking. We started to talk about Miss Dorland.'

'You said a person couldn't just be somebody's companion, and I said that in the old days plenty of nice women were companions and had a jolly good time—'

'I don't know about that.'

'Well, I do. They did. And they learnt to be decent companions to their husbands, too. Not always flying off to offices and clubs and parties like they are now. And if you think men like that sort of thing, I can tell you candidly, my girl, they don't. They hate it.'

'Does it matter? I mean, one doesn't have to bother so much about husband-hunting today.'

'Oh, no! Husbands don't matter at all, I suppose, to you advanced women. Any man will do, as long as he's got money—'

'Why do you say "you" advanced women! I didn't say *I* felt that way about it. I don't *want* to go out to work—'

'There you go. Taking everything to yourself. I *know* you don't want to work. I know it's only because of the damned rotten position I'm in. You needn't keep on about it. I know I'm a failure. Thank your stars, Wimsey, that when you marry you'll be able to support your wife.'

'George, you've no business to speak like that. I didn't mean that at all. You said—'

'I know what I said, but you took it all the wrong way. You always do. It's no good arguing with a woman. No – that's enough. For God's sake don't start all over again. I want a drink. Wimsey, you'll have a drink. Sheila, tell that girl of Mrs Munns's to go round for half a bottle of Johnny Walker.'

'Couldn't you get it yourself, dear? Mrs Munns doesn't like us sending her girl. She was frightfully disagreeable last time.'

'How can I go? I've taken my boots off. You do make such a fuss about nothing. What does it matter if old Mother Munns does kick up a shindy? She can't eat you.'

'No,' put in Wimsey. 'But think of the corrupting influence of the jug-and-bottle department on Mrs Munns's girl. I approve of Mrs Munns. She has a motherly heart. I myself will be the St George to rescue Mrs Munns's girl from the "Blue Dragon". Nothing shall stop me. No, don't bother to show me the way. I have a peculiar instinct about pubs. I can find one blindfold in a pea-souper with both hands tied behind me.'

Mrs Fentiman followed him to the front door.

'You mustn't mind what George says tonight. His tummy is feeling rotten and it makes him irritable. And it has been so worrying about this wretched money business.'

'That's all right,' said Wimsey. 'I know exactly. You should see me when my tummy's upset. Took a young woman out the other night – lobster mayonnaise, meringues and sweet champagne – her choice – oh, lord!'

He made an eloquent grimace and departed in the direction of the public house.

When he returned, George Fentiman was standing on the doorstep.

'I say, Wimsey – I do apologise for being so bloody rude. It's my filthy temper. Rotten bad form. Sheila's gone up to bed in tears, poor kid. All my fault. If you knew how this damnable situation gets on my nerves – though I know there's no excuse—'

''S quite all right,' said Wimsey. 'Cheer up. It'll all come out in the wash.'

'My wife –' began George again.

'She's damned fine, old man. But what it *is*, you both want a holiday.'

'We do, badly. Well, never say die. I'll see Murbles, as you suggest, Wimsey.'

Bunter received his master that evening with a prim smirk of satisfaction.

'Had a good day, Bunter?'

'Very gratifying indeed, I thank your lordship. The prints on the walking-stick are indubitably identical with those on the sheet of paper you gave me.'

'They are, are they? That's something. I'll look at 'em tomorrow, Bunter – I've had a tiring evening.'

8

LORD PETER LEADS THROUGH STRENGTH

At eleven o'clock the next morning, Lord Peter Wimsey, unobtrusively attired in a navy-blue suit and dark grey tie, suitable for a house of mourning, presented himself at the late Lady Dormer's house in Portman Square.

'Is Miss Dorland at home?'

'I will inquire, sir.'

'Kindly give her my card and ask if she can spare me a few moments.'

'Certainly, my lord. Will your lordship be good enough to take a seat?'

The man departed, leaving his lordship to cool his heels in a tall, forbidding room, with long crimson curtains, a dark red carpet and mahogany furniture of repellent appearance. After an interval of nearly fifteen minutes, he reappeared, bearing a note upon a salver. It was briefly worded:

> Miss Dorland presents her compliments to Lord Peter Wimsey and regrets that she is not able to grant an interview. If, as she supposes, Lord Peter has come to see her as the representative of Major and Captain Fentiman, Miss Dorland requests that he will address himself to Mr Pritchard, solicitor, of Lincoln's Inn, who is dealing, on her behalf, with all matters connected with the will of the late Lady Dormer.

'Dear me!' said Wimsey to himself, 'this looks almost like a snub. Very good for me, no doubt. Now I wonder

–' He read the note again. 'Murbles must have been rather talkative. I suppose he told Pritchard he was putting me on to it. Very indiscreet of Murbles and not like him.'

The servant still stood mutely by, with an air of almost violently disassociating himself from all commentary.

'Thank you,' said Wimsey. 'Would you be good enough to say to Miss Dorland that I am greatly obliged to her for this information.'

'Very good, my lord.'

'And perhaps you would kindly call me a taxi.'

'Certainly, my lord.'

Wimsey entered the taxi with all the dignity he could summon, and was taken to Lincoln's Inn.

Mr Pritchard was nearly as remote and snubbing in his manner as Miss Dorland. He kept Lord Peter waiting for twenty minutes and received him glacially, in the presence of a beady-eyed clerk.

'Oh, good morning,' said Wimsey affably. 'Excuse my callin' on you like this. More regular to do it through Murbles, I s'pose – nice old boy, Murbles, isn't he? But I always believe in goin' as direct to the point as may be. Saves time, what?'

Mr Pritchard bowed his head and asked how he might have the pleasure of serving his lordship.

'Well, it's about this Fentiman business. Survivorship and all that. Nearly said survival. Appropriate, what? You might call the old General a survival, eh?'

Mr Pritchard waited without moving.

'I take it Murbles told you I was lookin' into the business what? Tryin' to check up on the time-table and all that?'

Mr Pritchard said neither yea nor nay, but placed his fingers together and sat patiently.

'It's a bit of a problem, you know. Mind if I smoke? Have one yourself?'

'I am obliged to you, I never smoke in business hours.'

'Very proper. Much more impressive. Puts the wind up the clients what? Well, now, I just thought I'd let you know that it's likely to be a close-ish thing. Very difficult to tell to a minute or so, don't you know. May turn out one way – may turn out the other – may turn out completely bafflin' and all that. You get me?'

'Indeed?'

'Oh, yes, absolutely. P'raps you'd like to hear how far I've got.' And Wimsey recounted the history of his researches at the Bellona, in so far as the evidence of the commissionaires and the hall-porter were concerned. He said nothing of his interview with Penberthy, nor of the odd circumstances connected with the unknown Oliver, confining himself to stressing the narrowness of the time-limits between which the General must be presumed to have arrived at the Club. Mr Pritchard listened without comment. Then he said:

'And what, precisely, have you come to suggest?'

'Well, what I mean to say is, don't you know, wouldn't it be rather a good thing if the parties could be got to come to terms? Give and take, you see – split the doings and share the proceeds? After all, half a million's a goodish bit of money – quite enough for three people to live on in a quiet way, don't you think? And it would save an awful lot of trouble and – ahem! – lawyers' fees and things.'

'Ah!' said Mr Pritchard. 'I may say that I have been expecting this. A similar suggestion was made to me earlier by Mr Murbles, and I then told him that my client preferred not to entertain the idea. You will permit me to add, Lord Peter, that the reiteration of this proposal by you, after your employment to investigate the fact of the case in the interests of the other party, has a highly suggestive appearance. You will excuse me, perhaps, if I warn you further that your whole course of conduct in this matter seems to me open to a very undesirable construction.'

Wimsey flushed.

'You will perhaps permit *me*, Mr Pritchard, to inform you that I am not "employed" by anybody. I have been requested by Mr Murbles to ascertain the facts. They are rather difficult to ascertain, but I have learnt one very important thing from you this afternoon. I am obliged to you for your assistance. Good morning.'

The beady-eyed clerk opened the door with immense politeness.

'Good morning,' said Mr Pritchard.

'Employed, indeed,' muttered his lordship wrathfully. 'Undesirable construction. I'll construct him. That old brute knows something, and if he knows something, that shows there's something to be known. Perhaps he knows Oliver; I shouldn't wonder. Wish I'd thought to spring the name on him and see what he said. Too late now. Never mind, we'll get Oliver. Bunter didn't have any luck with those phone calls, apparently. I think I'd better get hold of Charles.'

He turned into the nearest telephone-booth and gave the number of Scotland Yard. Presently an official voice replied, of which Wimsey inquired whether Detective-Inspector Parker was available. A series of clicks proclaimed that he was being put through to Mr Parker, who presently said; 'Hallo!'

'Hallo, Charles! This is Peter Wimsey. Look here, I want you to do something for me. It isn't a criminal job, but it's important. A man calling himself Oliver rang up a number in Mayfair at a little after nine on the night of November 10th. Do you think you could get that call traced for me?'

'Probably. What was the number?'

Wimsey gave it.

'Right you are, old chap. I'll have it looked up and let you know. How goes it? Anything doing?'

'Yes – rather a cosy little problem – nothing for you people – as far as I know, that is. Come round one evening and I'll tell you about it, unofficially.'

'Thanks very much. Not for a day or two, though. We're run off our feet with this crate business.'

'Oh, I know – the gentleman who was sent from Sheffield to Euston in a crate, disguised as York hams. Splendid. Work hard and you will be happy. No, thanks, my child, I don't want another twopenn'orth – I'm spending the money on sweets. Cheerio, Charles!'

The rest of the day Wimsey was obliged to pass in idleness, so far as the Bellona Club affair was concerned. On the following morning he was rung up by Parker.

'I say – that phone call you asked me to trace.'

'Yes?'

'It was put through at 9.13 p.m. from a public call-box at Charing Cross Underground Station.'

'Oh, hell – the operator didn't happen to notice the bloke, I suppose?'

'There isn't an operator. It's one of those automatic boxes.'

'Oh! – may the fellow who invented them fry in oil. Thanks frightfully, all the same. It gives us a line on the direction, anyhow.'

'Sorry I couldn't do better for you. Cheerio!'

'Oh, cheer-damnably-ho!' retorted Wimsey crossly, slamming the receiver down. 'What is it, Bunter?'

'A district messenger; with a note, my lord.'

'Ah – from Mr Murbles. Good. This may be something. Yes. Tell the boy to wait; there's an answer.' He scribbled quickly. 'Mr Murbles has got an answer to that cabman advertisement, Bunter. There are two men turning up at six o'clock, and I'm arranging to go down and interview them.'

'Very good, my lord.'

'Let's hope that means we get a move on. Get me my hat and coat – I'm running round to Dover Street for a moment.'

Robert Fentiman was there when Wimsey called, and welcomed him heartily.

'Any progress?'

'Possibly a little this evening. I've got a line on those cabmen. I just came round to ask if you could let me have a specimen of old Fentiman's fist.'

'Certainly. Pick what you like. He hasn't left much about. Not exactly the pen of a ready writer. There are a few interesting notes of his early campaigns, but they're rather antiques by this time.'

'I'd rather have something quite recent.'

'There's a bundle of cancelled cheques here, if that would do.'

'It would do particularly well – I want something with figures in it if possible. Many thanks. I'll take these.'

'How on earth is his handwriting going to tell you when he pegged out?'

'That's my secret, dash it all! Have you been down to Gatti's?'

'Yes. They seem to know Oliver fairly well by sight, but that's all. He lunched there fairly often, say once a week or so, but they don't remember seeing him since the eleventh. Perhaps he's keeping under cover. However, I'll haunt the place a bit and see if he turns up.'

'I wish you would. His call came from a public box, so that line of inquiry peters out.'

'Oh, bad luck!'

'You've found no mention of him in any of the General's papers?'

'Not a thing, and I've gone through every bit and scrap of writing in the place. By the way, have you seen. George lately?'

'Night before last. Why?'

'He seems to me to be in rather a queer state. I went round last night and he complained of being spied on or something.'

'Spied on?'

'Followed about. Watched. Like the blighters in the 'tec stories. Afraid all this business is getting on his nerves. I hope he doesn't go off his rocker or anything. It's bad enough for Sheila as it is. Decent little woman.'

'Thoroughly decent,' agreed Wimsey, 'and very fond of him.'

'Yes. Works like billy-o to keep the home together and all that. Tell you the truth, I don't know how she puts up with George. Of course, married couples are always sparring and so on, but he ought to behave before other people. Dashed bad form, being rude to your wife in public. I'd like to give him a piece of my mind.'

'He's in a beastly galling position,' said Wimsey. 'She's his wife and she's got to keep him, and I know he feels it very much.'

'Do you think so? Seems to me he takes it rather as a matter of course. And whenever the poor little woman reminds him of it, he thinks she's rubbing it in.'

'Naturally, he hates being reminded of it. And I've

heard Mrs Fentiman say one or two sharp things to him.'

'I dare say. Trouble with George is, he can't control himself. He never could. A fellow ought to pull himself together and show a bit of gratitude. He seems to think that because Sheila has to work like a man she doesn't want the courtesy and – you know, tenderness and so on – that a woman ought to get.'

'It always gives me the pip,' said Wimsey, 'to see how rude people are when they're married. I suppose it's inevitable. Women are funny. They don't seem to care half so much about a man's being honest and faithful – and I'm sure your brother's all that – as for their opening doors and saying "thank you". I've noticed it lots of times.'

'A man ought to be just as courteous after marriage as he was before,' declared Robert Fentiman virtuously.

'So he ought, but he never is. Possibly there's some reason we don't know about,' said Wimsey. 'I've asked people, you know – my usual inquisitiveness – and they generally just grunt and say that *their* wives are sensible and take their affection for granted. But I don't believe women ever get sensible, not even through prolonged association with their husbands.'

The two bachelors wagged their heads solemnly.

'Well, I think George is behaving like a sweep,' said Robert, 'but perhaps I'm hard on him. We never did get on very well. And anyhow, I don't pretend to understand women. Still, this persecution-mania, or whatever it is, is another thing. He ought to see a doctor.'

'He certainly ought. We must keep an eye on him. If I see him at the Bellona I'll have a talk to him and try and get out of him what it's all about.'

'You won't find him at the Bellona. He's avoided it since all this unpleasantness started. I think he's out hunting for jobs. He said something about one of those motor people in Great Portland Street wanting a salesman. He can handle a car pretty well, you know.'

'I hope he gets it. Even if it doesn't pay very well it would do him a world of good to have something to do with himself. Well, I'd better be amblin' off. Many thanks, and let me know if you get hold of Oliver.'

'Oh, rather!'

Wimsey considered a few moments on the doorstep, and then drove straight down to New Scotland Yard, where he was soon ushered into Detective-Inspector Parker's office.

Parker, a square-built man in the late thirties, with the nondescript features which lend themselves so excellently to detective purposes, was possibly Lord Peter's most intimate – in some ways his only intimate – friend. The two men had worked out many cases together and each respected the other's qualities, though no two characters could have been more widely different. Wimsey was the Roland of the combination – quick, impulsive, careless, and an artistic Jack-of-all-trades. Parker was the Oliver – cautious, solid, painstaking, his mind a blank to art and literature, and exercising itself, in spare moments, with Evangelical theology. He was the one person who was never irritated by Wimsey's mannerisms, and Wimsey repaid him with a genuine affection foreign to his usually detached nature.

'Well, how goes it?'

'Not so bad. I want you to do something for me.'

'Not really?'

'Yes, really, blast your eyes. Did you ever know me when I didn't! I want you to get hold of one of your handwriting experts to tell me if these two fists are the same.'

He put on the table, on the one hand the bundle of used cheques, and on the other the sheet of paper he had taken from the library at the Bellona Club.

Parker raised his eyebrows.

'That's a very pretty set of fingerprints you've been pulling up there. What is it? Forgery?'

'No. Nothing of that sort. I just want to know whether the same bloke who wrote these cheques made the notes too.'

Parker rang a bell, and requested the attendance of Mr Collins.

'Nice fat sums involved, from the looks of it,' he west on, scanning the sheet of notes appreciatively. '£150,000 to R., £300,000 to G. – lucky G. – who's G.? £20,000 here and £50,000 there. Who's your rich friend, Peter?'

'It's that long story I was going to tell you about when you'd finished your crate problem.'

'Oh, is it? Then I'll make a point of solving the crate without delay. As a matter of fact, I'm rather expecting to hear something about it before long. That's why I'm here, dancing attendance on the phone. Oh, Collins, this is Lord Peter Wimsey, who wants very much to know whether these two handwritings are the same.'

The expert took up the paper and the cheques, and looked them over attentively.

'Not a doubt about it, I should say, unless the forgery has been astonishingly well done. Some of the figures, especially, are highly characteristic. The fives, for instance, and the threes, and the fours, made all of a piece with the two little loops. It's a very old-fashioned hand-writing, and made by a very old man, in not too good health, especially this sheet of notes. Is that the old Fentiman who died the other day?'

'Well, it is, but you needn't shout about it. It's just a private matter.'

'Just so. Well, I should say you need have no doubt about the authenticity of that bit of paper, if that's what you are thinking of.'

'Thanks. That's precisely what I do want to know. I don't think there's the slightest question of forgery or anything. In fact, it was just whether we could look on these rough notes as a guide to his wishes. Nothing more.'

'Oh, yes, if you rule out forgery, I'd answer for it any day that the same person wrote all these cheques and the notes.'

'That's fine. That checks up the results of the finger-print test too. I don't mind telling you, Charles,' he added, when Collins had departed, 'that this case is getting damned interesting.'

At this point the telephone rang, and Parker, after listening for some time, ejaculated, 'Good work!' and then, turning to Wimsey:

'That's our man. They've got him. Excuse me if I rush off. Between you and me, we've pulled this off rather well. It may mean rather a big thing for me. Sure we can't do anything else for you? Because I've got to get to Sheffield. See you tomorrow or next day.'

He caught up his coat and hat and was gone. Wimsey made his own way out and sat for a long time at home, with Bunter's photographs of the Bellona Club before him, thinking.

At six o'clock, he presented himself at Mr Murbles's chambers in Staple Inn. The two taxi-drivers had already arrived and were seated, well on the edges of their chairs, politely taking old sherry with the solicitor.

'Ah!' said Mr Murbles, 'this is a gentleman who is

interested in the inquiry we are making. Perhaps you would have the goodness to repeat to him what you have already told me. I have ascertained enough,' he added, turning to Wimsey, 'to feel sure that these are the right drivers, but I should like you to put any questions you wish yourself. This gentleman's name is Swain, and his story should come first, I think.'

'Well, sir,' said Mr Swain, a stout man of the old type of driver, 'you was wanting to know if anybody picked up an old gent in Portman Square the day before Armistice Day rahnd abaht the afternoon. Well, sir, I was goin' slow through the Square at 'arf-past four, or it might be a quarter to five on that 'ere day, when a footman comes out of a 'ouse – I couldn't say the number for certain, but it was on the east side of the Square as might be abaht the middle – and 'e makes a sign for me to stop. So I draws up, and presently a very old gent comes out. Very thin, 'e was, an' muffled up, but I see 'is legs and they was very thin and 'e looked abaht a 'undred an' two by 'is face, and walked with a stick. 'E was upright, for such a very old gent, but 'e moved slow and rather feeble. An old military gent, I thought 'e might be – 'e 'ad that way of speakin', if you understand me, sir. So the footman tells me to drive 'im to a number in 'Arley Street.

'Do you remember it?'

Swain mentioned a number which Wimsey recognised as Penberthy's.

'So I drives 'im there. And 'e asks me to ring the bell for 'im, and when the young man comes to the door to ask if the doctor could please see General Fenton, or Fenni-more, or some such name, sir.'

'Was it Fentiman, do you think?'

'Well, yes, it might 'ave been Fentiman. I think it was. So the young man comes back and says, "yes certingly," so I 'elps the old gent aht. Very faint, 'e seemed, and a very bad colour, sir, breathing 'eavy and blue-like abaht the lips. Pore old b———, I thinks, beggin' yer pardon, sir, 'e won't be 'ere long, I thinks. So we 'elps him up the steps into the 'ouse and 'e gives me my fare and a shilling for myself, and that's the last I see of 'im, sir.'

'That fits in all right with what Penberthy said,' agreed Wimsey. 'The General felt the strain of his interview with his sister and went straight round to see him. Right. Now, how about this other part of the business?'

'Well,' said Mr Murbles, 'I think this gentleman, whose name is – let me see – Hinkins – yes. I think Mr Hinkins picked up the General when he left Harley Street.'

'Yes, sir,' agreed the other driver, a smartish-looking man with a keen profile and a sharp eye. 'A very old gentleman, like what we've 'eard described, took my taxi at this same number in 'Arley Street, at 'alf-past five. I remember the day very well, sir; November 10th it was, and I remember it because, after I done taking him where I'm telling you, my magneto started to give trouble, and I didn't 'ave the use of the bus on Armistice Day, which was a great loss to me, because that's a good day as a rule. Well, this old military gentleman gets in, with his stick and all, just as Swain says, only I didn't notice him looking particularly ill, though I see he was pretty old. Maybe the doctor would have given him something to make him better.'

'Very likely,' said Mr Murbles.

'Yes, sir. Well, he gets in, and he says, 'Take me to Dover Street,' he says, but if you was to ask me the number, sir, I'm afraid I don't rightly remember, because, you see we never went there after all.'

'Never went there?' cried Wimsey.

'No, sir. Just as we was comin' out into Cavendish Square, the old gentleman puts his head out and says, 'Stop!' So I stops, and I see him wavin' his hand to a gentleman on the pavement. So this other one comes up, and they has a few words together and then the old—'

'One moment. What was this other man like?'

'Dark and thin, sir, and looked about forty. He had on a grey suit and overcoat and a soft hat, with a dark handkercher round his throat. Oh, yes, and he had a small, black moustache. So the old gentleman says, "Cabman," he says just like that, "cabman, go back up to Regent's Park and drive round till I tell you to stop." So the other gentleman gets in with him, and I goes back and drives round the Park, quiet-like, because I guessed they wanted to 'ave a bit of a talk. So I goes twice round, and as we was going round the third time, the younger gentleman sticks 'is 'ed out and says, "Put me down at Gloucester Gate." So I puts him down there, and the old gentleman says, "Good-bye, George, bear in mind what I have said." So the gentleman says, "I will, sir," and I see him cross the road, like as if he might be going up Park Street.'

Mr Murbles and Wimsey exchanged glances.

'And then where did you go?'

'Then, sir, the fare says to me, "Do you know the Bellona Club in Piccadilly?" he says. So I says, "Yes, sir."'

'The Bellona Club?'

'Yes, sir.'

'What time was that?'

'It might be getting on for half-past six, sir. I'd been driving very slow, as I tells you, sir. So I takes him to the Club, like he said, and in he goes, and that's the last I see of him, sir.'

'Thanks very much,' said Wimsey. 'Did he seem to be at all upset or agitated when he was talking to the man he called George?'

'No, sir, I couldn't say that. But I thought he spoke a bit sharp-like. What you might call telling him off, sir.'

'I see. What time did you get to the Bellona?'

'I should reckon it was about twenty minutes to seven, sir, or just a little bit more. There was a tidy bit of traffic about. Between twenty and ten to seven, as near as I can recollect.'

'Excellent. Well, you have both been very helpful. That will be all today, but I'd like you to leave your names and addresses with Mr Murbles, in case we might want some sort of a statement from either of you later on. And – er—'

A couple of Treasury notes crackled, Mr Swain and Mr Hinkins made suitable acknowledgement and departed, leaving their addresses behind them.

'So he went back to the Bellona Club. I wonder what for?'

'I think I know,' said Wimsey. 'He was accustomed to do any writing or business there, and I fancy he went back to put down some notes as to what he meant to do with the money his sister was leaving him. Look at this sheet of paper, sir. That's the General's handwriting, as I've proved this afternoon, and those are his fingerprints. And the initials "R" and "G" probably stand for Robert and George, and these figures for the various sums he meant to leave them.'

'That appears quite probable. Where did you find this?'

'In the end bay of the library at the Bellona, sir, tucked inside the blotting-paper.'

'The writing is very weak and straggly.'

'Yes – quite tails off, doesn't it. As though he had come

over faint and couldn't go on. Or perhaps he was only tired. I must go down and find out if anybody saw him there that evening. But Oliver, curse him! is the man who knows. If only we could get hold of Oliver.'

'We've had no answer to our third question in the advertisement. I've had letters from several drivers who took old gentlemen to the Bellona that morning, but none of them corresponds with the General. Some had check overcoats, and some had whiskers and some had bowler hats or beards – whereas the General was never seen without his silk hat and had, of course, his old-fashioned long military moustache.'

'I wasn't hoping for very much from that. We might put in another ad. in case anybody picked him up from the Bellona on the evening or night of the 10th, but I've got a feeling that this infernal Oliver probably took him away in his own car. If all else fails, we'll have to get Scotland Yard on to Oliver.'

'Make careful inquiries at the Club, Lord Peter. It now becomes more than possible that somebody saw Oliver there and noticed them leaving together.'

'Of course. I'll go along there at once. And I'll put the advertisement in as well. I don't think we'll rope in the B.B.C. It is so confoundedly public.'

'That,' said Mr Murbles, with a look of horror, 'would be most undesirable.'

Wimsey rose to go. The solicitor caught him at the door.

'Another thing we ought really to know,' he said, 'is what General Fentiman was saying to Captain George.'

'I've not forgotten that,' said Wimsey, a little uneasily. 'We shall have – oh, yes – certainly – of course, we shall have to know that.'

'Look here, Wimsey,' said Captain Culyer of the Bellona Club, 'aren't you ever going to get finished with this investigation or whatever it is? The members are complaining, really they are, and I can't blame them. They find your everlasting questions an intolerable nuisance, old boy, and I can't stop them from thinking there must be something behind it. People complain that they can't get attention from the porters or the waiters, because you're everlastingly there chatting, and if you're not there, you're hanging round the bar, eavesdropping. If this is your way of conducting an inquiry tactfully, I wish you'd do it tactlessly. It's becoming thoroughly unpleasant. And no sooner do you stop it, than the other fellow begins.'

'What other fellow?'

'That nasty little skulking bloke who's always turning up at the service door and questioning the staff.'

'I don't know anything about *him*,' replied Wimsey; 'I never heard of him. I'm sorry I'm being a bore and all that, though I swear I couldn't be worse than some of your other choice specimens in that line, but I've hit a snag. This business – quite in your ear, old bean – isn't as straightforward as it looks on the surface. That fellow Oliver whom I mentioned to you—'

'He's not known here, Wimsey.'

'No, but he may have been here.'

'If nobody saw him, he can't have been here.'

91

'Well, then, where did General Fentiman go to when he left? And when did he leave? That's what I want to know. Dash it all, Culyer, the old boy's a landmark. We know he came back here on the evening of the 10th – the driver brought him to the door, Rogers saw him come in and two members noticed him in the smoking-room just before seven. I have a certain amount of evidence that he went into the library. And he can't have stayed long, because he had his outdoor things with him. Somebody *must* have seen him leave. It's ridiculous. The servants aren't all blind. I don't like to say it, Culyer, but I can't help thinking that somebody has been bribed to hold his tongue . . . Of course, I knew that would annoy you, but how can you account for it? Who's this fellow you say has been hangin' round the kitchen?'

'I came across him one morning when I'd been down to see about the wine. By the way, there's a case of Margaux come in which I'd like your opinion on some day. The fellow was talking to Babcock, the wine steward, and I asked him pretty sharply what he wanted. He thanked me, and said he had come from the railway to inquire after a packing-case that had gone astray, but Babcock, who is a very decent fellow, told me afterwards that he had been working the pump-handle about old Fentiman, and I gathered he had been pretty liberal with his cash. I thought you were up to your tricks again.'

'Is the fellow a sahib?'

'Good God, no! Looks like an attorney's clerk or something. A nasty little tout.'

'Glad you told me. I shouldn't wonder if he's the snag I'm up against. Probably Oliver coverin' his tracks.'

'Do you suspect this Oliver of something wrong?'

'Well – I rather think so. But I'm damned if I know

quite what. I think he knows something about old Fentiman that we don't. And of course he knows how he spent
the night, and that's what I'm after.'

'What the devil does it matter how he spent the night?
He can't have been very riotous, at his age.'

'It might throw some light on the time he arrived in the
morning, mightn't it?'

'Oh – Well, all I can say is, I hope to God you'll hurry
up and finish with it. This Club's becoming a perfect
bear-garden. I'd almost rather have the police in.'

'Keep hopin'. You may get 'em yet.'

'You don't mean that, seriously?'

'I'm never serious. That's what my friends dislike
about me. Honestly, I'll try and make as little row as I
can. But if Oliver is sending his minions to corrupt your
staff and play Old Harry with my investigations, it's
going to make it damned awkward. I wish you'd let me
know if the fellow turns up again. I'd like to cast my eye
over him.'

'All right, I will. And do clear out now, there's a good
fellow.'

'I go,' said Wimsey, 'my tail well tucked down between
my legs and a flea in each ear. Oh! by the way—'

'*Well?*' (in an exasperated tone.)

'When did you last see George Fentiman?'

'Not for donkey's years. Not since it happened.'

'I thought not. Oh, and by the way—'

'*Yes?*'

'Robert Fentiman was actually staying in the Club at
the time, wasn't he?'

'Which time?'

'The time it happened, you ass.'

'Yes, he was. But he's living at the old man's place
now.'

'I know, thanks. But I wondered whether – Where does he live when he isn't in town?'

'Out at Richmond, I think. In rooms, or something.'

'Oh, does he? Thanks very much. Yes, I really will go. In fact, I've practically gone.'

He went. He never stopped going till he came to Finsbury Park. George was out, and so, of course, was Mrs Fentiman, but the charwoman said she had heard the Captain mention he was going down to Great Portland Street. Wimsey went in pursuit. A couple of hours spent lounging round showrooms and talking to car-demonstrators, nearly all of whom were, in one manner or another, his dear old pals, resulted in the discovery that George Fentiman was being taken on by the Walmisley-Hubbard outfit for a few weeks to show what he could do.

'Oh, he'll do you all right,' said Wimsey; 'he's a damn' fine driver. Oh, lord, yes! *He's* all right.'

'He looks a bit nervy,' said the particular dear old pal attached to the Walmisley-Hubbard show. 'Wants bucking up, what? That reminds me. What about a quick one?'

Wimsey submitted to a mild quick one and then wandered back to look at a new type of clutch. He spun out this interesting interview till one of the Walmisley-Hubbard 'shop buses' came in with Fentiman at the wheel.

'Hallo!' said Wimsey; 'trying her out?'

'Yes. I've got the hang of her all right.'

'Think you could sell her?' asked the old pal.

'Oh, yes. Soon learn to show her off. She's a jolly decent bus.'

'That's good. Well, I expect you're about ready for a quick one. How about it, Wimsey?'

They had a quick one together. After this, the dear old pal remembered that he must buzz off because he'd promised to hunt up a customer.

'You'll turn up tomorrow, then?' he said to George. 'There's an old bird down at Malden wants to have a trial trip. I can't go, so you can have a shot at him. All right?'

'Perfectly.'

'Righty-ho! I'll have the bus ready for you at eleven. Cheer-most-frightfully-ho! So long.'

'Little sunbeam about the house, isn't he?' said Wimsey.

'Rather. Have another?'

'I was thinking, how about lunch? Come along with me if you have nothing better to do.'

George accepted and put forward the names of one or two restaurants.

'No,' said Wimsey, 'I've got a fancy to go to Gatti's today, if you don't mind.'

'Not at all; that will do splendidly. I've seen Murbles, by the by, and he's prepared to deal with the MacStewart man. He thinks he can hold him off till it's all settled up – if it ever *is* settled.'

'That's good,' said Wimsey, rather absently.

'And I'm damned glad about this chance of a job,' went on George. 'If it turns out any good, it'll make things a lot easier – in more than one way.'

Wimsey said heartily that he was sure it would, and then relapsed into a silence unusual with him, which lasted all the way to the Strand.

At Gatti's he left George in a corner while he went to have a chat with the head-waiter, emerging from the interview with a puzzled expression which aroused even George's curiosity, full as he was of his own concerns.

'What's up? Isn't there anything you can bear to eat?'

'It's all right. I was just wondering whether to have *moules marinières* or not.'

'Good idea.'

Wimsey's face cleared, and for some time they absorbed mussels from the shell with speechless, though not altogether silent, satisfaction.

'By the way,' said Wimsey suddenly, 'you never told me that you had seen your grandfather the afternoon before he died.'

George flushed. He was struggling with a particularly elastic mussel, firmly rooted to the shell, and could not answer for a moment.

'How on earth – confound it all, Wimsey, are *you* behind this infernal watch that's being kept on me?'

'Watch?'

'Yes, I said watch. I call it a damn' rotten thing to do. I never thought for a moment you had anything to do with it.'

'I haven't. Who's keeping a watch on you?'

'There's a fellow following me about. A spy. I'm always seeing him. I don't know whether he's a detective or what. He looks like a criminal. He came down in the bus with me from Finsbury Park this morning. He was after me all day yesterday. He's probably about now. I won't have it. If I catch sight of him again I shall knock his dirty little head off. Why should I be followed and spied on? I haven't done anything. And now *you* begin.'

'I swear I've nothing to do with anybody following you about. Honestly, I haven't. I wouldn't employ a man, anyway, who'd let a bloke see that he was being followed. No. When I start huntin' you, I shall be as silent and stealthy as a gas-leak. What's this incompetent bloodhound like to look at?'

'Looks like a tout. Small, thin, with his hat pulled down over his eyes and an old raincoat with the collar turned up. And a very blue chin.'

'Sounds like a stage detective. He's a silly ass, anyway.'

'He gets on my nerves.'

'Oh, all right. Next time you see him punch his head.'

'But what does he want?'

'How should I know? What have you been doing?'

'Nothing, of course. I tell you, Wimsey, I believe there's some sort of conspiracy going on to get me into trouble, or do away with me, or something. I can't stand it. It's simply damnable. Suppose this fellow starts hanging round the Walmisley-Hubbard place. Look nice, won't it, for their salesman to have a 'tec on his heels all the time? Just as I hoped things were coming right—'

'Bosh!' said Wimsey. 'Don't let yourself get rattled. It's probably all imagination, or just a coincidence.'

'It isn't. I wouldn't mind betting he's outside in the street now.'

'Well, then, we'll settle his hash when we get outside. Give him in charge for annoying you. Look here forget him for a bit. Tell me about the old General. How did he seem that last time you saw him?'

'Oh, he seemed fit enough. Crusty, as usual.'

'Crusty, was he? What about?'

'Private matters,' said George sullenly.

Wimsey cursed himself for having started his questions tactlessly. The only thing now was to retrieve the situation as far as possible.

'I'm not at all sure,' he said, 'that relations shouldn't all be painlessly put away after three-score and ten. Or at any rate segregated. Or have their tongues sterilised, so that they can't be poisonously interferin'.'

'I wish they were,' growled George. 'The old man –

damn it all, I know he was in the Crimea, but he's no idea what a real war's like. He thinks things can go on just as they did half a century ago. I dare say he never did behave as I do. Anyway, I know he never had to go to his wife for his pocket-money, let alone having the inside gassed out of him. Coming preaching to me – and I couldn't say anything, because he was so confoundedly old, you know.'

'Very trying,' murmured Wimsey sympathetically.

'It's all so damned unfair,' said George. 'Do you know,' he burst out, the sense of grievance suddenly overpowering his wounded vanity, 'the old devil actually threatened to cut me out of the miserable little bit of money he had to leave me if I didn't "reform my domestic behaviour"? That's the way he talked. Just as if I was carrying on with another woman or something. I know I did have an awful row with Sheila one day, but of course I didn't mean half I said. She knows that, but the old man took it all seriously.'

'Half a moment,' broke in Wimsey. 'Did he say all this to you in the taxi that day?'

'Yes, he did. A long lecture, all about the purity and courage of a good woman, driving round and round Regent's Park. I had to promise to turn over a new leaf and all that. Like being back at one's prep school.'

'But didn't he mention anything about the money Lady Dormer was leaving to him?'

'Not a word. I don't suppose he knew about it.'

'I think he did. He'd just come from seeing her, you know, and I've a very good idea she explained matters to him then.'

'Did she? Well, that rather explains it. I thought he was being very pompous and stiff about it. He said what a responsibility money was, you know, and how he would like to feel that anything he left to me was being properly used, and all that. And he rubbed it in about my not having been able to make good for myself – that was what got my goat – and about Sheila. Said I ought to appreciate a good woman's love more, my boy, and cherish her, and so on. As if I needed him to tell me that. But, of course, if he knew he was in the running for this half-million it makes rather a difference. By Jove, yes! I expect he would feel a bit anxious at the idea of leaving it all to a fellow he looked on as a waster.'

'I wonder he didn't mention it.'

'You didn't know grandfather. I bet he was thinking over in his mind whether it wouldn't be better to give my share to Sheila, and he was sounding me, to see what sort of disposition I'd got. The old fox! Well, I did my best to put myself in a good light, of course, because just at the moment I didn't want to lose my chance of his two thousand. But I don't think he found me satisfactory. I say,' went on George, with rather a sheepish laugh, 'perhaps it's just as well he popped off when he did. He might have cut me off with a shilling, eh?'

'Your brother would have seen you through in any case.'

'I suppose he would. Robert's quite a decent sort, really, though he does get on one's nerves so.'

'Does he?'

'He's so thick-skinned; the regular unimaginative Briton. I believe Robert would cheerfully go through another five years of war and think it all a very good rag. Robert was proverbial, you know, for never turning a hair. I remember Robert, at that ghastly hole at Carency, where the whole ground was rotten with corpses – ugh! – potting those swollen great rats for a penny a time, and laughing at them. Rats. Alive and putrid with what

99

they'd been feeding on. Oh, yes. Robert was thought a damn' good soldier.'

'Very fortunate for him,' said Wimsey.

'Yes. He's the same sort as grandfather. They liked each other. Still, grandfather was very decent about me. A beast, as the schoolboy said, but a just beast. And Sheila was a great favourite of his.'

'Nobody could help liking her,' said Wimsey politely.

Lunch ended on a more cheerful note than it had begun. As they came out into the street, however, George Fentiman glanced round uneasily. A small man in a buttoned-up overcoat and with a soft hat pulled down over his eyes, was gazing into the window of a shop near at hand.

George strode up to him.

'Look here, you!' he said. 'What the devil do you mean by following me about? You clear off, d'you hear?'

'I think you are mistaken, sir,' said the man, quietly enough. 'I have never seen you before.'

'Haven't you, by Jove? Well, *I've* seen *you* hanging about, and if you do it any more I'll give you something to remember me by. D'you hear?'

'Hallo!' said Wimsey, who had stopped to speak to the commissionaire, 'what's up – Here, you, wait a moment!'

But at sight of Wimsey the man had slipped like an eel among the roaring Strand traffic, and was lost to view.

George Fentiman turned to his companion triumphantly.

'Did you see that? The lousy little beggar! Made off like a shot when I threatened him. That's the fellow who's been dogging me about for three days.'

'I'm sorry,' said Wimsey, 'but it was not your prowess, Fentiman. It was my awful aspect that drove him away. What is it about me? Have I a front like Jove to threaten and command? Or am I wearing a repulsive tie?'

'He's gone, anyway.'

'I wish I'd had a better squint at him. Because I've got a sort of idea that I've seen those lovely features before, and not so long ago, either. Was this the face that launched a thousand ships? No, I don't think it was that.'

'All I can say is,' said George, 'that if I see him again I'll put such a face on him that his mother won't know him.'

'Don't do that. You might destroy a clue. I – wait a minute – I've got an idea. I believe it must be the same man who's been haunting the Bellona and asking questions. Oh, Hades! and we've let him go. And I'd put him down in my mind as Oliver's minion. If ever you see him again, Fentiman, freeze on to him like grim death. I want to talk to him.'

10

LORD PETER FORCES A CARD

'Hallo!'

'Is that you, Wimsey? Hallo! I say, is that Lord Peter Wimsey! Hallo! I must speak to Lord Peter Wimsey! Hallo!'

'All right. I've said hallo. Who're you? And what's the excitement?'

'It's me. Major Fentiman. I say – *is* that Wimsey?'

'Yes. Wimsey speaking. What's up?'

'I can't hear you.'

'Of course you can't if you keep on shouting. This is Wimsey. Good morning. Stand three inches from the mouthpiece and speak in an ordinary voice. Do not say hallo! To recall the operator depress the receiver *gently* two or three times.'

'Oh, shut up! Don't be an ass. I've seen Oliver!'

'Have you? Where?'

'Getting into a train at Charing Cross.'

'Did you speak to him?'

'No – it's maddening. I was just getting my ticket when I saw him passing the barrier. I tore down after him. Some people got in my way, curse them. There was a Circle train standing at the platform. He bolted in and they clanged the doors. I rushed on, waving and shouting, but the train went out. I cursed like anything.'

'I bet you did. How very sickening.'

'Yes, wasn't it? I took the next train—'

'What for?'

'Oh, I don't know. I thought I might spot him on a platform someplace.'

'What a hope! You didn't think to ask where he'd booked for?'

'No. Besides, he probably got the ticket from an automatic.'

'Probably. Well, it can't be helped, that's all. He'll probably turn up again. You're sure it was he?'

'Oh, dear, yes. I couldn't be mistaken. I'd know him anywhere. I thought I'd just let you know.'

'Thanks awfully. It encourages me extremely. Charing Cross seems to be a haunt of his. He phoned from there on the evening of the tenth, you know.'

'So he did.'

'I'll tell you what we'd better do, Fentiman. The thing is getting rather serious. I propose that you should go and keep an eye on Charing Cross Station. I'll get hold of a detective—'

'A police detective?'

'Not necessarily. A private one would do. You and he can go along and keep watch on the station for, say, a week. You must describe Oliver to the detective as best you can, and you can watch turn and turn about.'

'Hang it all, Wimsey – it'll take a lot of time. I've gone back to my rooms at Richmond. And besides, I've got my own duties to do.'

'Yes – well, while you're on duty the detective must keep watch.'

'It's a dreadful grind, Wimsey.' Fentiman's voice sounded dissatisfied.

'It's half a million of money. Of course, if you're not keen—'

'I *am* keen. But I don't believe anything will come of it.'

'Probably not; but it's worth trying. And in the meantime I'll have another watch kept at Gatti's.'

'At Gatti's?'

'Yes. They know him there. I'll send a man down—'

'But he never comes there now.'

'Oh, but he may come again. There's no reason why he shouldn't. We know now that he's in town, and not gone out of the country or anything. I'll tell the management that he's wanted for an urgent business matter, so as not to make unpleasantness.'

'They won't like it.'

'Then they'll have to lump it.'

'Well, all right. But, look here – *I'll* do Gatti's.'

'That won't do. We want you to identify him at Charing Cross. The waiter or somebody can do the identifying at Gatti's. You say they know him?'

'Yes, of course they do. But –'

'But what? – By the way, which waiter is it you spoke to? I had a talk with the head man there yesterday, and he didn't seem to know anything about it.'

'No – it wasn't the head waiter. One of the others. The plump, dark one.'

'All right. I'll find the right one. Now, will you see to the Charing Cross end?'

'Of course – if you really think it's any good.'

'Yes, I do. Right you are. I'll get hold of the 'tec and send him along to you, and you can arrange with him.'

'Very well.'

'Cheerio!'

Lord Peter rang off and sat for a few moments, grinning to himself. Then he turned to Bunter.

'I don't often prophesy, Bunter, but I'm going to do it now. Your fortune told by hands or cards. Beware of the dark stranger. That sort of thing.'

'Indeed, my lord?'

'Cross the gipsy's palm with silver. I see Mr Oliver. I see him taking a journey in which he will cross water. I see trouble. I see the ace of spades – upside-down, Bunter.'

'And what then, my lord?'

'Nothing. I look into the future and I see a blank. The gipsy has spoken.'

'I will bear it in mind, my lord.'

'Do. If my prediction is not fulfilled, I will give you a new camera. And now I'm going round to see that fellow who calls himself Sleuths Incorporated, and get him to put a good man on to keep watch at Charing Cross. And after that I'm going down to Chelsea, and I don't quite know when I shall be back. You'd better take the afternoon off. Put me out some sandwiches or something, and don't wait up if I'm late.'

Wimsey disposed quickly of his business with Sleuths Incorporated, and then made his way to a pleasant little studio overlooking the river at Chelsea. The door, which bore a neat label, 'Miss Marjorie Phelps', was opened by a pleasant-looking young woman with curly hair and a blue overall heavily smudged with clay.

'Lord Peter! How nice of you! Do come in.'

'Shan't I be in the way?'

'Not a scrap. You don't mind if I go on working?'

'Rather not.'

'You could put the kettle on and find some food if you liked to be really useful. I just want to finish up this figure.'

'That's fine. I took the liberty of bringing a pot of Hybla honey with me.'

'What sweet ideas you have! I really think you are one of the nicest people I know. You don't talk rubbish about art, and you don't want your hand held, and your mind always turns on eating and drinking.'

'Don't speak too soon. I don't want my hand held, but I did come here with an object.'

'Very sensible of you. Most people come without any.'

'And stay interminably.'

'They do.'

Miss Phelps cocked her head on one side and looked critically at the little dancing lady she was modelling. She had made a line of her own in pottery figurines, which sold well and were worth the money.

'That's rather attractive,' said Wimsey.

'Rather pretty-pretty. But it's a special order, and one can't afford to be particular. I've done a Christmas present for you, by the way. You'd better have a look at it, and if you think it offensive we'll smash it together. It's in that cupboard.'

Wimsey opened the cupboard and extracted a little figure about nine inches high. It represented a young man in a flowing dressing-gown, absorbed in the study of a huge volume held on his knee. The portrait was life-like. He chuckled.

'It's damned good, Marjorie. A very fine bit of modelling. I'd love to have it. You aren't multiplying it too often, I hope? I mean, it won't be on sale at Selfridge's?'

'I'll spare you that. I thought of giving one to your mother.'

'That'll please her no end. Thanks ever so. I shall look forward to Christmas for once. Shall I make some toast?'

'Rather!'

Wimsey squatted happily down before the gas fire, while the modeller went on with her work. Tea and figurine were ready almost at the same moment, and

Miss Phelps, flinging off her overall, threw herself luxuriously into a battered armchair by the hearth.

'And what can I do for you?'

'You can tell me all you know about Miss Ann Dorland.'

'Ann Dorland? Great heavens! You haven't fallen for Ann Dorland, have you? I've heard she's coming into a lot of money.'

'You have a perfectly disgusting mind, Miss Phelps. Have some more toast. Excuse my licking my fingers. I have not fallen for the lady. If I had, I'd manage my affairs without assistance. I haven't even seen her. What's she like?'

'To look at?'

'Among other things.'

'Well, she's rather plain. She has dark, straight hair, cut in a bang across the forehead and bobbed – like a Flemish page. Her forehead is broad and she has a square sort of face and a straight nose – quite good. Also, her eyes are good – grey, with nice heavy eyebrows, not fashionable a bit. But she has a bad skin and rather sticky-out teeth. And she's dumpy.'

'She's a painter, isn't she?'

'M'm – well! she paints.'

'I see. A well-off amateur with a studio.'

'Yes. I will say that old Lady Dormer was very decent to her. Ann Dorland, you know, is some sort of far-away distant cousin on the female side of the Fentiman family, and when Lady Dormer first got to hear of her she was an orphan and incredibly poverty-stricken. The old lady liked to have a bit of young life about the house, so she took charge of her, and the wonderful thing is that she didn't try to monopolise her. She let her have a big place for a studio and bring in any friends she liked and go about as she chose – in reason, of course.'

'Lady Dormer suffered a good deal from oppressive relations in her own youth,' said Wimsey.

'I know, but most old people seem to forget that. I'm sure Lady Dormer had time enough. She must have been rather unusual. Mind you, I didn't know her very well, and I don't really know a great deal about Ann Dorland. I've been there, of course. She gave parties – rather incompetently. And she comes round to some of our studios from time to time. But she isn't really one of us.'

'Probably one has to be really poor and hard-working to be that.'

'No. You, for instance, fit in quite well on the rare occasions when we have the pleasure. And it doesn't matter not being able to paint. Look at Bobby Hobart and his ghastly daubs – he's a perfect dear and everybody loves him. I think Ann Dorland must have a complex of some kind. Complexes explain so much, like the blessed word hippopotamus.'

Wimsey helped himself lavishly to honey and looked receptive.

'I think really,' went on Miss Phelps, 'that Ann ought to have been something in the City. She has brains, you know. She'd run anything awfully well. But she isn't creative. And then, of course, so many of our little lot seem to be running love-affairs. And a continual atmosphere of hectic passion is very trying if you haven't got any of your own.'

'Has Miss Dorland a mind above hectic passion?'

'Well, no. I dare say she would quite have liked – but nothing ever came of it. Why are you interested in having Ann Dorland analysed?'

'I'll tell you some day. It isn't just vulgar curiosity.'

'No, you're very decent as a rule, or I wouldn't be telling you all this. I think, really, Ann has a sort of fixed idea that she couldn't ever possibly attract anyone, and so she's either sentimental and tiresome, or rude and snubbing, and our crowd does hate sentimentality and simply can't bear to be snubbed. Ann's rather pathetic, really. As a matter of fact, I think she's gone off art a bit. Last time I heard about her, she had been telling someone she was going in for social service, or sick-nursing, or something of that kind. I think it's very sensible. She'd probably get along much better with the people who do that sort of thing. They're so much more solid and polite.'

'I see. Look here, suppose I ever wanted to run across Miss Dorland accidentally on purpose – where should I be likely to find her?'

You *do* seem thrilled about her! I think I should try the Rushworths. They go in rather for science and improving the submerged tenth and things like that. Of course, I suppose Ann's in mourning now, but I don't think that would necessarily keep her away from the Rushworths'. Their gatherings aren't precisely frivolous.'

'Thanks very much. You're a mine of valuable information. And, for a woman, you don't ask many questions.'

'Thank you for those few kind words, Lord Peter.'

'I am now free to devote my invaluable attention to *your* concerns. What is the news? And who is in love with whom?'

'Oh, life is a perfect desert. Nobody is in love with me, and the Schlitzers have had a worse row than usual and separated.'

'No!'

'Yes. Only, owing to financial considerations, they've got to go on sharing the same studio – you know, that big room over the mews. It must be very awkward, having to

109

eat and sleep and work in the same room with somebody you're being separated from. They don't even speak, and it's very awkward when you call on one of them and the other has to pretend not to be able to see or hear you.'

'I shouldn't think one could keep it up under those circumstances.'

'It's difficult. I'd have had Olga here, only she is so dreadfully bad-tempered. Besides, neither of them will give up the studio to the other.'

'I see. But isn't there any third party in the case?'

Yes – Ulric Fiennes, the sculptor, you know. But he can't have her at his place because his wife's there, and he's really dependent on his wife, because his sculpting doesn't pay. And besides, he's at work on that colossal group for the Exhibition and he can't move it; it weighs about twenty tons. And if he went off and took Olga away, his wife would lock him out of the place. It's very inconvenient being a sculptor. It's like playing the double-bass; one's so handicapped by one's luggage.'

'True. Whereas, when you run away with me, we'll be able to put all the pottery shepherds and shepherdesses in a handbag.'

'Of course. What fun it will be. Where shall we run to?'

'How about starting tonight and getting as far as Oddenino's and going on to a show – if you're not doing anything?'

'You are a lovable man, and I shall call you Peter. Shall we see "Betwixt and Between"?'

'The thing they had such a job to get past the censor? Yes, if you like. Is it particularly obscene?'

'No, epicene, I fancy.'

'Oh, I see. Well, I'm quite agreeable. Only I warn you that I shall make a point of asking you the meaning of all the risky bits in a very audible voice.'

'That's your idea of amusement, is it?'

'Yes. It does make them so wild. People say "Hush!" and giggle, and if I'm lucky I end up with a gorgeous row in the bar.'

'Then I won't risk it. No. I'll tell you what I'd really love. We'll go and see "George Barnwell" at the Elephant and have a fish-and-chips supper afterwards.'

This was agreed upon, and was voted in retrospect a most profitable evening. It finished up with grilled kippers at a friend's studio in the early hours. Lord Peter returned home to find a note upon the hall table.

'MY LORD,

'The person from Sleuths Incorporated rang up today that he was inclined to acquiesce in your lordship's opinion, but that he was keeping his eye upon the party and would report further tomorrow. The sandwiches are on the dining-room table, if your lordship should require refreshment.

'Yours obediently,
'M. BUNTER.'

'Cross the gipsy's palm with silver,' said his lordship happily, and rolled into bed.

11

LORD PETER CLEARS TRUMPS

'SLEUTHS INCORPORATED'S' report, when it came, might be summed up as: 'Nothing doing and Major Fentiman convinced that there never will be anything doing; opinion shared by Sleuths Incorporated.' Lord Peter's reply was: 'Keep on watching and something will happen before the week is out.'

His lordship was justified.

On the fourth evening, 'Sleuths Incorporated' reported again. The particular sleuth in charge of the case had been duly relieved by Major Fentiman at 6 p.m. and had gone to get his dinner. On returning to his post an hour later, he had been presented with a note left for him with the ticket collector at the stairhead. It ran:

'Just seen Oliver getting into taxi. Am following. Will communicate to refreshment-room.

'FENTIMAN.'

The sleuth had perforce to return to the refreshment-room and hang about waiting for a further message. 'But all the while, my lord, the second man I put on as instructed by you, my lord, was a-following the Major unbeknownst.' Presently a call was put through from Waterloo. 'Oliver is on the Southampton train. I am following.' The sleuth hurried down to Waterloo, found the train gone and followed on by the next. At Southampton he made inquiries and learned that a gentleman answering to Fentiman's description had made a violent disturbance as the Havre boat was just starting, and had been summarily ejected at the insistence of an elderly man whom he appeared to have annoyed or attacked in some way. Further investigation among the Port authorities made it clear that Fentiman had followed this person down, made himself offensive on the train and had been warned off by the guard, collared his prey again on the gangway and tried to prevent him from going aboard. The gentleman had produced his passport and *pièces d'identité*, showing him to be a retired manufacturer of the name of Postlethwaite, living at Kew. Fentiman had insisted that he was, on the contrary, a man called Oliver, address and circumstances unknown, whose testimony was wanted in some family matter. As Fentiman was unprovided with a passport and appeared to have no official authority for stopping and questioning travellers, and as his story seemed vague and his manner agitated, the local police had decided to detain Fentiman. Postlethwaite was allowed to proceed on his way, after leaving his address in England and his destination, which, as he contended, and as he produced papers and correspondence to prove, was Venice.

The sleuth went round to the police station, where he found Fentiman, apoplectic with fury, threatening proceedings for false imprisonment. He was able to get him released, however, on bearing witness to Fentiman's identity and good faith, and after persuading him to give a promise to keep the peace. He had then reminded Fentiman that private persons were not entitled to assault or arrest peaceable people against whom no charge could be made, pointing out to him that his proper course, when Oliver denied being Oliver, would have been to follow on quietly and keep a watch on him, while communicating with Wimsey or Mr Murbles or Sleuths

Incorporated. He added that he was himself now waiting at Southampton for further instructions from Lord Peter. Should he follow to Venice, or send his subordinate, or should he return to London? In view of the frank behaviour of Mr Postlethwaite, it seemed probable that a genuine mistake had been made as to identity, but Fentiman insisted that he was not mistaken.

Lord Peter, holding the trunk line, considered for a moment. Then he laughed.

'Where is Major Fentiman?' he asked.

'Returning to town, my lord. I have represented to him that I have now all the necessary information to go upon, and that his presence in Venice would only hamper my movements, now that he has made himself known to the party.'

'Quite so. Well, I think you might as well send your man on to Venice, just in case it's a true bill. And listen . . .' He gave some further instructions, ending with: 'And ask Major Fentiman to come and see me as soon as he arrives.'

'Certainly, my lord.'

'What price the gipsy's warning now?' said Lord Peter, as he communicated this piece of intelligence to Bunter.

Major Fentiman came round to the flat that afternoon, in a whirl of apology and indignation.

'I'm sorry, old man. It was damned stupid of me, but I lost my temper. To hear that fellow calmly denying that he had ever seen me or poor old grandfather, and coming out with his bits of evidence so pat, put my bristles up. Of course, I see now that I made a mistake. I quite realise that I ought to have followed him up quietly. But how was I to know that he wouldn't answer to his name?'

'But you ought to have guessed, when he didn't, that

either you had made a mistake or that he had some very good motive for trying to get away,' said Wimsey.

'I wasn't accusing him of anything.'

'Of course not, but he seems to have thought you were.'

'But why? – I mean, when I first spoke to him, I just said: "Mr Oliver, I think?" And he said: "You are mistaken." And I said: "Surely not. My name's Fentiman, and you knew my grandfather, old General Fentiman." And he said he hadn't the pleasure. So I explained that we wanted to know where the old boy had spent the night before he died, and he looked at me as if I was a lunatic. That annoyed me, and I said I knew he was Oliver, and then he complained to the guard. And when I saw him just trying to hop off like that, without giving us any help, and when I thought about that half-million, it made me so mad I just collared him. "Oh, no, you don't," I said – and that was how the fun began, don't you see.'

'I see perfectly,' said Wimsey. 'But don't *you* see, that if he really *is* Oliver and has gone off in that elaborate manner, with false passports and everything, he must have something important to conceal?'

Fentiman's jaw dropped.

'You don't mean – you don't mean there's anything funny about the death? Oh! surely not.'

'There must be something funny about Oliver, anyway, mustn't there? On your own showing.'

'Well, if you look at it that way, I suppose there must. I tell you what, he's probably got into some bother or other and is clearing out. Debt, or a woman, or something. Of course that must be it. And I was beastly inconvenient, popping up like that. So he pushed me off. I see it all now. Well, in that case, we'd better let him

115

rip. We can't get him back, and I dare say he won't be able to tell us anything after all.'

'That's possible, of course. But when you bear in mind that he seems to have disappeared from Gatti's, where you used to see him, almost immediately after the General's death, doesn't it look rather as though he was afraid of being connected up with that particular incident?'

Fentiman wriggled uncomfortably.

'Oh, but hang it all! What could he have to do with the old man's death?'

'I don't know. But I think we might try to find out.'

'How?'

'Well, we might apply for an exhumation order.'

'Dig him up!' cried Fentiman, scandalised.

'Yes. There was no post-mortem, you know.'

'No, but Penberthy knew all about it and gave the certificate.'

'Yes: but at that time there was no reason to suppose that anything was wrong.'

'And there isn't now.'

'There are a number of peculiar circumstances, to say the least.'

'There's only Oliver – and I may have been mistaken about him.'

'But I thought you were so sure?'

'So I was. But – this is preposterous, Wimsey! Besides, think what a scandal it would make!'

'Why should it? You are the executor. You can make a private application and the whole thing can be done quite privately.'

'Yes, but surely the Home Office would never consent, on such flimsy grounds.'

'I'll see that they do. They'll know I wouldn't be keen

on anything flimsy. Little bits of fluff were never in my line.'

'Oh, do be serious. What reason can we give?'

'Quite apart from Oliver, we can give a very good one. We can say that we want to examine the contents of the viscera to see how soon the General died after taking his last meal. That might be of great assistance in solving the question of the survivorship. And the law, generally speaking, is nuts on what they call the orderly devolution of property.'

'Hold on! D'you mean to say you can tell when a bloke died just by looking inside his tummy?'

'Not exactly, of course. But one might get an idea. If we found, that is, that he'd only that moment swallowed his brekker, it would show that he'd died not very long after arriving at the Club.'

'Good Lord! – that would be a poor look-out for me.'

'It might be the other way, you know.'

'I don't like it, Wimsey. It's very unpleasant. I wish to goodness we could compromise on it.'

'But the lady in the case won't compromise. You know that. We've got to get at the facts somehow. I shall certainly get Murbles to suggest the exhumation to Pritchard.'

'Oh, Lord! What'll *he* do?'

'Pritchard? If he's an honest man and his client's an honest woman, they'll support the application. If they don't I shall fancy they've something to conceal.'

'I wouldn't put it past them. They're a low-down lot. But they can't do anything without my consent, can they?'

'Not exactly – at least, not without a lot of trouble and publicity. But if *you're* an honest man, you'll give your consent. *You've* nothing to conceal, I suppose?'

'Of course not. Still, it seems rather—'

'They suspect us already of some kind of dirty work,'

117

persisted Wimsey. 'That brute Pritchard as good as told me so. I'm expecting every day to hear that he has suggested exhumation off his own bat. I'd rather we got in first with it.'

'If that's the case, I suppose we must do it. But I can't believe it'll do a bit of good, and it's sure to get round and make an upheaval. Isn't there some other way – you're so darned clever—'

'Look here, Fentiman. Do you want to get at the facts? Or are you out to collar the cash by hook or by crook? You may as well tell me frankly which it is.'

'Of course I want to get at the facts.'

'Very well; I've told you the next step to take.'

'Damn it all,' said Fentiman discontentedly; 'I suppose it'll have to be done, then. But I don't know whom to apply to or how to do it.'

'Sit down, then, and I'll dictate the letter for you.'

From this there was no escape, and Robert Fentiman did as he was told, grumbling.

'There's George. I ought to consult him.'

'It doesn't concern George, except indirectly. That's right. Now write to Murbles, telling him what you're doing and instructing him to let the other party know.'

'Oughtn't we to consult about the whole thing with Murbles first?'

'I've already consulted Murbles, and he agrees it's the thing to do.'

'These fellows would agree to anything that means fees and trouble.'

'Just so. Still, solicitors are necessary evils. Is that finished?'

'Yes.'

'Give the letters to me; I'll see they're posted. Now you needn't worry any more about it. Murbles and I will see to it all, and the detective-wallah is looking after Oliver all right, so you can run away and play.'

'You—'

'I'm sure you're going to say how good it is of me to take all this trouble. Delighted, I'm sure. It's of no consequence. A pleasure, in fact. Have a drink.'

The disconcerted Major refused the drink rather shortly, and prepared to depart.

'You mustn't think I'm not grateful, Wimsey, and all that. But it is rather unseemly.'

'With all your experience,' said Wimsey, 'you oughtn't to be so sensitive about corpses. We've seen many things much unseemlier than a nice, quiet little resurrection in a respectable cemetery.'

'Oh, I don't care twopence about the corpse,' retorted the Major, 'but the thing doesn't look well. That's all.'

'Think of the money,' grinned Wimsey, shutting the door of the flat upon him.

He returned to the library, balancing the two letters in his hand. 'There's many a man now walking the streets of London,' said he, 'through not clearing trumps. Take these letters to the post, Bunter. And Mr Parker will be dining here with me this evening. We will have a *perdrix aux choux* and a savoury to follow, and you can bring up two bottles of the Chambertin.'

'Very good, my lord.'

Wimsey's next proceeding was to write a little confidential note to an official whom he knew very well at the Home Office. This done, he returned to the telephone and asked for Penberthy's number.

'That you, Penberthy? . . . Wimsey speaking . . . Look here, old man, you know that Fentiman business? . . . Yes – well, we're applying for an exhumation.'

'For a *what*?'

'An exhumation. Nothing to do with your certificate. We know *that's* all right. It's just by way of getting a bit more information about when the beggar died.'

He outlined his suggestion.

'Think there's something in it?'

'There might be, of course.'

'Glad to hear you say that. I'm a layman in these matters, but it occurred to me as a good idea.'

'Very ingenious.'

'I always was a bright lad. You'll have to be present, of course.'

'Am I to do the autopsy?'

'If you like. Lubbock will do the analysis.'

'Analysis of what?'

'Contents of the doings. Whether he had kidneys on toast or eggs and bacon, and all that.'

'Oh, I see. I doubt if you'll get much from that, after all this time.'

'Possibly not, but Lubbock had better have a squint at it.'

'Yes, certainly. As I gave the certificate, it's better that my findings should be checked by somebody.'

'Exactly. I knew you'd feel that way. You quite understand about it?'

'Perfectly. Of course, if we'd had any idea there was going to be all this uncertainty, I'd have made a post-mortem at the time.'

'Naturally you would. Well, it can't be helped. All in the day's work. I'll let you know when it's to be. I suppose the Home Office will send somebody along. I thought I ought just to let you know about it.'

'Very good of you. Yes. I'm glad to know. Hope nothing unpleasant will come out.'

'Thinking of your certificate?'

'Oh, well – no – I'm not worrying much about that. Though you never know, of course. I was thinking of that *rigor*, you know. Seen Captain Fentiman lately?'

'Yes. I didn't mention—'

'No. Better not, unless it becomes absolutely necessary. Well, I'll hear from you later, then?'

'That's the idea. Good-bye.'

That day was a day of incident.

About four o'clock a messenger arrived, panting, from Mr Murbles. (Mr Murbles refused to have his chambers desecrated by a telephone.) Mr Murbles's compliments, and would Lord Peter be good enough to read this note and let Mr Murbles have an immediate answer.

The note ran:

'DEAR LORD PETER,

'In *re* Fentiman deceased. Mr Pritchard has called. He informs me that his client is now willing to compromise on a division of the money if the Court will permit. Before I consult my client, Major Fentiman, I should be greatly obliged by your opinion as to how the investigation stands at present.

Yours faithfully,
'JNO. MURBLES.'

Lord Peter replied as follows:

'DEAR MR MURBLES,

'*Re* Fentiman deceased. Too late to compromise now, unless you are willing to be party to a fraud. I warned you, you know. Robert has applied for exhumation. Can you dine with me at 8?

'P. W.'

Having sent this off, his lordship rang for Bunter.

'Bunter, as you know, I seldom drink champagne. But I am inclined to do so now. Bring a glass for yourself as well.'

The cork popped merrily, and Lord Peter rose to his feet.

'Bunter,' said he, 'I give you a toast: The triumph of Instinct over Reason!'

12

LORD PETER TURNS A TRICK

DETECTIVE-INSPECTOR PARKER came to dinner encircled in a comfortable little halo of glory. The Crate Mystery had turned out well, and the Commissioner had used expressions suggestive of promotion in the immediate future. Parker did justice to his meal and, when the party had adjourned to the library, gave his attention to Lord Peter's account of the Bellona affair with the cheerful appreciation of a connoisseur sampling a vintage port. Mr Murbles, on the other hand, grew more and more depressed as the story was unfolded.

'And what do you think of it?' inquired Wimsey.

Parker opened his mouth to reply, but Mr Murbles was beforehand with him.

'This Oliver appears to be a very elusive person,' said he.

'Isn't he?' agreed Wimsey dryly. 'Almost as elusive as the famous Mrs Harris. Would it altogether surprise you to learn that when I asked a few discreet questions at Gatti's, I discovered not only that nobody there had the slightest recollection of Oliver, but that no inquiries about him had ever been made by Major Fentiman?'

'Oh, dear me!' said Mr Murbles.

'You forced Fentiman's hand very ingeniously by sending him down with your private sleuth to Charing Cross,' remarked Parker approvingly.

'Well, you see, I had a feeling that unless we did something pretty definite, Oliver would keep vanishing and reappearing like the Cheshire Cat, whenever our investigations seemed to be taking an awkward turn.'

'You are intimating, if I understand you rightly,' said Mr Murbles, 'that this Oliver has no real existence.'

'Oliver was the carrot on the donkey's nose,' said Peter, 'my noble self being cast for the part of the donkey. Not caring for the rôle, I concocted a carrot of my own, in the person of Sleuths Incorporated. No sooner did my trusting sleuth depart to his lunch than, lo, and behold! the hue and cry is off again after Oliver. Away goes friend Fentiman – and away goes Sleuth Number Two, who was there all the time, neatly camouflaged, to keep his eye on Fentiman. Why Fentiman should have gone to the length of assaulting a perfect stranger and accusing him of being Oliver, I don't know. I fancy his passion for thoroughness made him overreach himself a bit there.'

'But what exactly has Major Fentiman been doing?' asked Mr Murbles. 'This is a very painful business, Lord Peter. It distresses me beyond words. Do you suspect him of – er—'

'Well,' said Wimsey, 'I knew *something* odd had happened, you know, as soon as I saw the General's body – when I pulled the *Morning Post* away so easily from under his hands. If he had really died clutching it, the *rigor* would have made his clutch so tight that one would have had to prise the fingers open to release it. And then, that knee-joint!'

'I didn't quite follow about that.'

'Well, you know that when a man dies, *rigor* begins to set in after a period of some hours, varying according to the cause of death, temperature of the room and a lot of other conditions. It starts in the face and jaw, and extends gradually over the body. Usually it lasts about twenty-four hours and then passes off again in the same order in which it started. But if, during the period of rigidity, you loosen one of the joints by main force, then it doesn't stiffen again, but remains loose. Which is why, in a hospital, if the nurses have carelessly let a patient die and stiffen with his knees up, they call in the largest and fattest person on the staff to sit on the corpse's knees and break the joints loose again.'

Mr Murbles shuddered distastefully.

'So that, taking the loose knee-joint and the general condition of the body together, it was obvious from the start that somebody had been tampering with the General. Penberthy knew that too, of course, only, being a doctor, he wasn't going to make any indiscreet uproar if he could avoid it. It doesn't pay, you know.'

'I suppose not.'

'Well, then, you came round to me, sir, and insisted on making the uproar. I warned you, you know, to let sleeping dogs lie.'

'I wish you had spoken more openly.'

'If I had, would you have cared to hush the matter up?'

'Well, well,' said Mr Murbles, polishing his eyeglasses.

'Just so. The next step was to try and find out what had actually happened to the General on the night of the 10th and morning of the 11th. And the moment I got round to his flat I was faced with two entirely contradictory pieces of evidence. First, there was the story about Oliver, which appeared more or less reasonable upon the face of it. And secondly, there was Woodward's evidence about the clothes.'

'What about them?'

'I asked him, you remember, whether anything at all had been removed from the clothes after he had fetched them away from the cloak-room at the Bellona, and he said, nothing. His memory as to other points seemed pretty reliable, and I felt sure that he was honest and straightforward. So I was forced to the conclusion that, wherever the General had spent the night, he had certainly never set foot in the street the next morning.'

'Why?' asked Mr Murbles. 'What did you expect to find on the clothes?'

'My dear sir, consider what day it was. November 11th. Is it conceivable that, if the old man had been walking in the streets as a free agent on Armistice Day, he would have gone into the Club without his Flanders poppy? A patriotic, military old bird like that? It was really unthinkable.'

'Then where was he? And how did he get into the Club? He was there, you know.'

'True; he *was* there – in a state of advanced *rigor*. In fact, according to Penberthy's account – which, by the way, I had checked by the woman who laid out the body later – the *rigor* was even then beginning to pass off. Making every possible allowance for the warmth of the room and so on, he must have been dead long before ten in the morning, which was his usual time for going to the Club.'

'But, my dear lad, bless my soul, that's impossible. He couldn't have been carried in there dead. Somebody would have noticed it.'

'So they would. And the odd thing is that nobody ever saw him arrive at all. What is more, nobody saw him leave for the last time on the previous evening. General Fentiman – one of the best-known figures in the Club. And he seems to have become suddenly invisible. That won't do, you know.'

'What is your idea, then? That he slept the night in the Club?'

'I think he slept a very peaceful and untroubled sleep that night – in the Club.'

'You shock me inexpressibly,' said Mr Murbles. 'I understand you to suggest that he died—'

'Some time the previous evening. Yes.'

'But he couldn't have sat there all night in the smoking-room. The servants would have been bound to – er – notice him.'

'Of course. But it was to somebody's interest to see that they didn't notice. Somebody who wanted it thought that he hadn't died till the following day, after the death of Lady Dormer.'

'Robert Fentiman.'

'Precisely.'

'But how did Robert know about Lady Dormer?'

'Ah! That is a point I'm not altogether happy about. George had an interview with General Fentiman after the old man's visit to his sister. George denies that the General mentioned anything to him about the will, but then, if George was in the plot he naturally would deny it. I am rather concerned about George.'

'What had he to gain?'

'Well, if George's information was going to make a difference of half a million to Robert, he would naturally expect to be given a share of the boodle, don't you think?'

Mr Murbles groaned.

'Look here,' broke in Parker, 'this is a very pretty theory, Peter, but, allowing that the General died, as you say, on the evening of the 10th, where was the body? As Mr Murbles says, it would have been a trifle noticeable if left about.'

'No, no,' said Mr Murbles, seized with an idea. 'Repellent as the whole notion is to me, I see no difficulty about that. Robert Fentiman was at that time living in the Club. No doubt the General died in Robert's bed-room and was concealed there till the next morning!'

Wimsey shook his head. 'That won't work. I think the General's hat and coat and things were in Robert's bedroom, but the corpse couldn't have been. Think, sir. Here is a photograph of the entrance-hall, with the big staircase running up in full view of the front door and the desk and the bar-entrance. Would you risk carrying a corpse downstairs in the middle of the morn-ing, with servants and members passing in and out continually? And the service stairs would be even worse. They are right round the other side of the building, with continual kitchen traffic going on all the time. No. The body wasn't in Robert's bedroom.'

'Where, then?'

'Yes, where? After all, Peter, we've got to make this story hold water.'

Wimsey spread the rest of the photographs out upon the table.

'Look for yourselves," he said. 'Here is the end bay of the library, where the General was sitting making notes about the money he was to inherit. A very nice, retired spot, invisible from the doorway, supplied with ink, blotter, writing-paper and every modern convenience, including the works of Charles Dickens elegantly bound in morocco. Here is a shot of the library taken from the smoking-room, clean through the ante-room and down the gangway – again a tribute to the convenience of the Bellona Club. Observe how handily the telephone cabi-net is situated, in case—'

'The telephone cabinet?'

'Which, you will remember, was so annoyingly la-belled "Out of Order" when Wetheridge wanted to telephone. I can't find anybody who remembers putting up that notice, by the way.'

'Good God, Wimsey! Impossible. Think of the risk.'

'What risk? If anybody opened the door, there was old General Fentiman, who had gone in, not seeing the notice, and died of fury at not being able to get his call. Agitation acting on a weak heart and all that. Not *very* risky, really. Unless somebody was to think to inquire about the notice, and probably it wouldn't occur to anyone in the excitement of the moment.'

'You're an ingenious beast, Wimsey.'

'Aren't I? But we can prove it. We're going down to the Bellona Club to prove it now. Half-past eleven. A nice, quiet time. Shall I tell you what we are going to find inside that cabinet?'

'Fingerprints?' suggested Mr Murbles eagerly.

'Afraid that's too much to hope for after all this time. What do you say, Charles?'

'I say we shall find a long scratch on the paint,' said Parker, 'where the foot of the corpse rested and stiffened in that position.'

'Holed it in one, Charles. And that, you see, was when the leg had to be bent with violence in order to drag the corpse out.'

'And as the body was in a sitting position,' pursued Parker, 'we shall, of course, find a seat inside the cabinet.'

'Yes, and, with luck, we *may* find a projecting nail or something which caught the General's trouser-leg when the body was removed.'

'And possibly a bit of carpet.'

'To match the fragment of thread I got off the corpse's right boot? I hope so.'

'Bless my soul,' said Mr Murbles. 'Let us go at once.

Really, this is most exciting. That is, I am profoundly grieved. I hope it is not as you say.'

They hastened downstairs and stood for a few moments waiting for a taxi to pass. Suddenly Wimsey made a dive into a dark corner by the porch. There was a scuffle, and out into the light came a small man, heavily muffled in an overcoat, with his hat thrust down to his eyebrows in the manner of a stage detective. Wimsey unbonneted him with the air of a conjuror producing a rabbit from a hat.

'So it's you, is it? I thought I knew your face. What the devil do you mean by following people about like this?'

The man ceased struggling and glanced sharply up at him with a pair of dark, beady eyes.

'Do you think it wise, my lord, to use violence?'

'Who is it?' asked Parker.

'Pritchard's clerk. He's been hanging around George Fentiman for days. Now he's hanging round me. He's probably the fellow that's been hanging round the Bellona. If you go on like this, my man, you'll find yourself hanging somewhere else one of these days. Now, see here. Do you want me to give you in charge?'

'That is entirely as your lordship pleases,' said the clerk, with a cunning sneer. 'There is a policeman just round the corner, if you wish to attract publicity.'

Wimsey looked at him for a moment, and then began to laugh.

'When did you last see Mr Pritchard? Come on, out with it! Yesterday? This morning? Have you seen him since lunch time?'

A shadow of indecision crossed the man's face.

'You haven't? I'm sure you haven't. Have you?'

'And why not, my lord?'

'You go back to Mr Pritchard,' said Wimsey impressively, and shaking his captive gently by the coat collar to add force to his words, 'and if he doesn't countermand your instructions and call you off this sleuthing business (which, by the way, you do very amateurishly), I'll give you a fiver. See? Now hop it. I know where to find you and you know where to find me. Good night and may Morpheus hover over your couch and bless your slumbers. Here's our taxi.'

13

SPADES ARE TRUMPS

It was close on one o'clock when the three men emerged from the solemn portals of the Bellona Club. Mr Murbles was very much subdued. Wimsey and Parker displayed the sober elation of men whose calculations have proved satisfactory. They had found the scratches. They had found the nail in the seat of the chair. They had even found the carpet. Moreover, they had found the origin of Oliver. Reconstructing the crime, they had sat in the end bay of the library, as Robert Fentiman might have sat, casting his eyes around him while he considered how he could best hide and cover up this extremely inopportune decease. They had noticed how the gilt lettering on the back of a volume caught the gleam from the shaded reading lamp. *Oliver Twist*. The names not consciously noted at the time, had yet suggested itself an hour or so later to Fentiman, when, calling up from Charing Cross, he had been obliged to invent a surname on the spur of the moment.

And, finally, placing the light, spare form of the unwilling Mr Murbles, in the telephone cabinet, Parker had demonstrated that a fairly tall and strong man could have extricated the body from the box, carried it into the smoking-room and arranged it in the armchair by the fire, all in something under four minutes.

Mr Murbles made one last effort on behalf of his client. 'There were people in the smoking-room all morning, my dear Lord Peter. If it were as you suggest, how could Fentiman have made sure of four, or even three minutes secure from observation while he brought the body in?'

'Were people there *all* morning, sir? Are you sure? Wasn't there just one period when one could be certain that everybody would be either out in the street or upstairs on the big balcony that runs along in front of the first-floor windows, looking out – and listening? It was Armistice Day, remember.'

Mr Murbles was horror-struck.

'The two minutes' silence? – God bless my soul! How abominable! How – how blasphemous! Really, I cannot find words. This is the most disgraceful thing I ever heard of. At the moment when all our thoughts should be concentrated on the brave fellows who laid down their lives for us – to be engaged in perpetrating a fraud – an irreverent crime—'

'Half a million is a good bit of money,' said Parker thoughtfully.

'Horrible!' said Mr Murbles.

'Meanwhile,' said Wimsey, 'what do you propose to do about it?'

'Do?' spluttered the old solicitor indignantly. 'Do? Robert Fentiman will have to confess to this disgraceful plot immediately. Bless my soul! To think that I should be mixed up in a thing like this! He will have to find another man of business in future. We shall have to explain matters to Pritchard and apologise. I really hardly know how to tell him such a thing.'

'I rather gather he suspects a good deal of it already,' said Parker mildly. 'Else why should he have sent that clerk of his to spy on you and George Fentiman? I dare say he has been keeping tabs on Robert, too.'

'I shouldn't wonder,' said Wimsey. 'He certainly treated

me like a conspirator when I called on him. The only thing that puzzles me now is why he should have suddenly offered to compromise.'

'Probably Miss Dorland lost patience, or they despaired of proving anything,' said Parker. 'While Robert stuck to that Oliver story, it would be very hard to prove anything.'

'Exactly,' said Wimsey. 'That is why I had to hang on so long, and press Robert so hard about it. I might suspect Oliver to be non-existent, but one can't prove a negative.'

'And suppose he still sticks to the story now?'

'Oh! I think we can put the wind up him all right,' said Wimsey. 'By the time we've displayed our proofs and told him exactly what he was doing with himself on November 10th and 11th, he'll have no more spirit in him than the Queen of Sheba.'

'It must be done at once,' said Mr Murbles. 'And of course this exhumation business will have to be stopped. I will go round and see Robert Fentiman tomorrow – this morning, that is.'

'Better tell him to trot round to your place,' said Wimsey. 'I'll bring all the evidence round there, and I'll have the varnish on the cabinet analysed and shown to correspond with the sample I took from the General's boots. Make it for two o'clock, and then we can all go round and interview Pritchard afterwards.'

Parker supported this suggestion. Mr Murbles was so wrought up that he would gladly have rushed away to confront Robert Fentiman immediately. It being, however, pointed out to him that Fentiman was in Richmond, that an alarm at this ungodly hour might drive him to do something desperate, and also that all three investigators needed repose, the old gentleman gave way and permitted himself to be taken home to Staple Inn.

Wimsey went round to Parker's flat in Great Ormond Street to have a drink before turning in, and the session was prolonged till the small hours had begun to grow into big hours and the early workmen were abroad.

Lord Peter, having set the springe for his woodcock, slept the sleep of the just until close upon eleven o'clock the next morning. He was aroused by voices without, and presently his bedroom door was flung open to admit Mr Murbles, of all people, in a high state of agitation, followed by Bunter, protesting.

'Hallo, sir!' said his lordship, much amazed. 'What's up?'

'We have been outwitted,' cried Mr Murbles, waving his umbrella, 'we have been forestalled! We should have gone to Major Fentiman last night. I wished to do so, but permitted myself to be persuaded against my better judgement. It will be a lesson to me.'

He sat down, panting a little.

'My dear Mr Murbles,' said Wimsey pleasantly, 'your method of recalling one to the dull business of the day is as delightful as it is unexpected. Anything better calculated to dispel that sluggish feeling I can scarcely imagine. But, pardon me – you are somewhat out of breath. Bunter! a whisky-and-soda for Mr Murbles.'

'Indeed no!' ejaculated the solicitor hurriedly. 'I couldn't touch it. Lord Peter—'

'A glass of sherry?' suggested his lordship helpfully.

'No, no – nothing, thanks. A shocking thing has occurred. We are left—'

'Better and better. A shock is exactly what I feel to need. My *café au lait*, Bunter – and you may turn the bath on. Now, sir – out with it. I am fortified against anything.'

'Robert Fentiman,' announced Mr Murbles impressively, 'has disappeared.'

He thumped his umbrella.

'Good God!' said Wimsey.

'He has gone,' repeated the solicitor. 'At ten o'clock this morning I attended in person at his rooms in Richmond – in *person* – in order to bring him the more effectually to a sense of his situation. I rang the bell, I asked for him. The maid told me he had left the night before. I asked where he had gone. She said she did not know. He had taken a suitcase with him. I interviewed the landlady. She told me that Major Fentiman had received an urgent message during the evening and had informed her that he was called away. He had not mentioned where he was going nor how soon he would return. I left a note addressed to him, and hastened back to Dover Street. The flat there was shut up and untenanted. The man Woodward was nowhere to be found. I then came immediately to you. And I find you—'

Mr Murbles waved an expressive hand at Wimsey, who was just taking from Bunter's hands a chaste silver tray, containing a Queen Anne coffee pot and milk jug and a small pile of correspondence.

'So you do,' said Wimsey. 'A depraved sight, I am afraid. H'm! It looks very much as though Robert had got wind of trouble and didn't like to face the music.'

He sipped his *café au lait* delicately, his rather bird-like face cocked sideways. 'But why worry? He can't have got very far.'

'He may have gone abroad.'

'Possibly. All the better. The other party won't want to take proceedings against him over there. Too much

136

bother – however spiteful they may feel. Hallo! Here's a writing I seem to recognise. Yes. It is my sleuth from Sleuths Incorporated. Wonder what *he* wants. I told him to go home and send the bill in – Whew!'

'What is it?'

'This is the bloke who chased Fentiman to Southampton. Not the one who went on to Venice after the innocent Mr Postlethwaite; the other. He's writing from Paris. He says:

'MY LORD,

'While making a few inquiries at Southampton pursuant to the investigation with which your lordship entrusted me (*What marvellous English these fellows write, don't they? Nearly as good as the regular police*), I came almost accidentally (*"almost" is good*) upon a trifling clue which led me to suppose that the party whom I was instructed by your lordship to keep under observation had been less in error than we were led to suppose, and had merely been misled by a confusion of identity natural in a gentleman not scientifically instructed in the art of following up suspected persons. In short (*thank God for that!*) in short, I believe that I have myself come upon the track of O. (*These fellows are amazingly cautious; he might just as well write Oliver and have done with it*), and have followed the individual in question to this place. I have telegraphed to the gentleman your friend (*I presume that means Fentiman*) to join me immediately with a view to identifying the party. I will of course duly acquaint your lordship with any further developments in the case, and believe me – (*and so forth*).'

'Well, I'm damned!'

'The man must be mistaken, Lord Peter.'

137

'I jolly well hope so,' said Wimsey, rather red in the face. 'It'll be a bit galling to have Oliver turning up, just when we've proved so conclusively that he doesn't exist. Paris! I suppose he means that Fentiman spotted the right man at Waterloo and lost him on the train or in the rush for the boat. And got hold of Postlethwaite instead. Funny. Meanwhile, Fentiman's off to France. Probably taken the 10.30 boat to Folkestone. I don't know how we're to get hold of him.'

'How very extraordinary!' said Mr Murbles. 'Where does that detective person write from?'

'Just "Paris",' said Wimsey. 'Bad paper and worse ink. And a small stain of *vin ordinaire*. Probably written in some little café yesterday afternoon. Not much hope there. But he's certain to let me know where they get to.'

'We must send someone to Paris immediately in search of them,' declared Mr Murbles.

'Why?'

'To fetch Major Fentiman back.'

'Yes, but look here, sir. If there really is an Oliver after all, it rather upsets our calculations, doesn't it?'

Mr Murbles considered this.

'I cannot see that it affects our conclusions as to the hour of the General's death,' he said.

'Perhaps not, but it considerably alters our position with regard to Robert Fentiman.'

'Ye-es. Yes, that is so. Though,' said Mr Murbles severely, 'I still consider that the story requires close investigation.'

'Agreed. Well, look here. I'll run over to Paris myself and see what I can do. And you had better temporise with Pritchard. Tell him that you think there will be no need to compromise and that we hope soon to be in possession of the precise facts. That'll show him we don't mean to have any truck with anythin' fishy. I'll learn him to cast nasturtiums at me.'

'And – oh, dear! there's another thing. We must try and get hold of Major Fentiman to stop this exhumation.'

'Oh, lord! – Yes. That's a bit awkward. Can't you stop it by yourself?'

'I hardly think I can. Major Fentiman has applied for it as executor and I cannot see what I can do in the matter without his signature. The Home Office would hardly—'

'Yes. I quite see that you can't mess about with the Home Office. Well, though, that's easy. Robert never was keen on the resurrection idea. Once we've got his address, he'll be only too happy to send you a chit to call the whole thing off. You leave it to me. After all, even if we don't find Robert for a few days and the old boy has to be dug up after all, it won't make things any worse. Will it?'

Mr Murbles agreed dubiously.

'Then I'll pull the old carcase together,' said Wimsey brightly, flinging the bedclothes aside and leaping to his feet, 'and toddle off to the City of Light. Will you excuse me for a few moments, sir? The bath awaits me. Bunter, put a few things into a suitcase and be ready to come with me to Paris.'

On second thoughts, Wimsey waited till the next day, hoping, as he explained, to hear from the detective. As nothing reached him, however, he started in pursuit, instructing the head office of Sleuths Incorporated to wire any information received to him at the Hotel Meurice. The next news that arrived from him was a card to Mr Murbles written on a P.L.M. express, which said simply:

'Quarry gone on to Rome. Hard on trail. – P.W.'

The next day came a foreign telegram:

'Making for Sicily. Faint but pursuing. – P.W.'

In reply to this, Mr Murbles wired:

'Exhumation fixed for day after tomorrow. Please make haste.'

To which Wimsey replied:

'Returning for exhumation. – P.W.'

He returned alone.

'Where is Robert Fentiman?' demanded Mr Murbles agitatedly.

Wimsey, his hair matted damply and his face white from travelling day and night, grinned feebly.

'I rather fancy,' he said in a wan voice, 'that Oliver is at his old tricks again.'

'Again?' cried Mr Murbles, aghast. 'But the letter from your detective was genuine.'

'Oh, yes – that was genuine enough. But even detectives can be bribed. Anyhow, we haven't seen hide nor hair of our friends. They've been always a little ahead. Like the Holy Grail, you know, "Fainter by day, but always in the night blood-red, and sliding down the blackened marsh, blood-red" – perfectly bloody, in fact. Well, here we are. When does the ceremony take place? Quietly, I take it. No flowers?'

The 'ceremony' took place, as such ceremonies do, under the discreet cover of darkness. George Fentiman, who, in Robert's absence, attended to represent the family, was nervous and depressed. It is trying enough to go to the funeral of one's friends and relations, amid the grotesque pomps of glass hearses, and black horses, and wreaths, and appropriate hymns 'beautifully' rendered by well-paid choristers, but, as George irritably remarked, the people who grumble over funerals don't realise their luck. However depressing the thud of earth on the coffin-lid may be, it is music compared to the rattle of gravel and thump of spades which herald a premature and unreverend resurrection, enveloped in clouds of formalin and without benefit of clergy.

Dr Penberthy also appeared abstracted and anxious to get the business over. He made the journey to the cemetery ensconced in the farthest corner of the big limousine, and discussed thyroid abnormalities with Dr Horner, Sir James Lubbock's assistant, who had come to help with the autopsy. Mr Murbles was, naturally, steeped in gloom. Wimsey devoted himself to his accumulated correspondence, out of which one letter only had any bearing on the Fentiman case. It was from Marjorie Phelps, and ran:

'If you want to meet Ann Dorland, would you care to come along to a "do" at the Rushworths' Wednesday week? It will be very deadly, because Naomi Rushworth's new young man is going to read a paper on ductless glands which nobody knows anything about. However, it appears that ductless glands will be "news" in next to no time – ever so much more up-to-date than vitamins – so the Rushworths are all over glands – in the social sense, I mean. Ann D. is certain to be there, because, as I told you, she is taking to this healthy-bodies-for-all stunt, or whatever it is, so you'd better come. It will be company for me! – and I've got to go, anyway, as I'm supposed to be a friend of Naomi's.

Besides, they say that if one paints or sculps or models, one ought to know all about glands, because of the way they enlarge your jaw and alter your face, or something. Do come, because if you don't I shall be fastened on by some deadly bore or other – and I shall have to hear all Naomi's raptures about the man, which will be too awful.'

Wimsey made a note to be present at this enlivening party, and looking round, saw that they were arriving at the Necropolis – so vast, so glittering with crystal-globed wreaths, so towering with sky-scraping monuments, that no lesser name would serve it. At the gate they were met by Mr Pritchard in person (acidulated in his manner and elaborately polite to Mr Murbles), and by the Home Office representative (suave and bland and disposed to see reporters lurking behind every tombstone). A third person, coming up, proved to be an official from the Cemetery Company, who took charge of the party and guided them along the neat gravelled walks to where digging operations were already in process.

The coffin, being at length produced and identified by its brass plate, was then carefully borne to a small out-building close at hand, which appeared to be a potting-shed in ordinary life, converted by a board and a couple of trestles into a temporary mortuary. Here a slight halt and confusion was caused by the doctors demanding in aggressively cheerful and matter-of-fact tones more light and space to work in. The coffin was placed on a bench; somebody produced a mackintosh sheet and spread it on the trestle table; lamps were brought and suitably grouped. After which the workmen advanced, a little reluctantly, to unscrew the coffin-lid, preceded by Dr Penberthy, scattering formalin from a spray, rather like an infernal thurifer at some particularly unwholesome sacrifice.

'Ah! very nice indeed,' said Dr Horner appreciatively, as the corpse was disengaged from the coffin and transferred to the table. 'Excellent. Not much difficulty over this job. That's the best of getting on to it at once. How long has he been buried, did you say? Three or four weeks? He doesn't look it. Will you make the autopsy or shall I? Just as you like. Very well. Where did I put my bag? Ah! Thank you, Mr – er – er –' (An unpleasantly-occupied pause, during which George Fentiman escaped, murmuring that he thought he'd have a smoke outside.) 'Undoubted heart trouble, of course. I don't see any unusual appearances, do you? . . . I suppose we'd better secure the stomach as it stands . . . Pass me the gut, would you? Thanks. D'you mind holding while I get this ligature on? Ta.' (Snip, snip.) 'The jars are just behind you. Thanks. Look out! You'll have it over. Ha! ha! that was a near thing. Reminds me of Palmer, you know – and Cook's stomach – always think that a very funny story, ha! ha! – I won't take all the liver – just a sample – it's only a matter of form – and sections of the rest – yes – better have a look at the brain while we are about it, I suppose. Have you got the large saw?'

'How callous these medical men seem,' murmured Mr Murbles.

'It's nothing to them,' said Wimsey. 'Horner does this kind of job several times a week.'

'Yes, but he need not be so noisy. Dr Penberthy behaves with decorum.'

'Penberthy runs a practice,' said Wimsey with a faint grin. 'He has to exercise a little restraint over himself. Besides, he knew old Fentiman, and Horner didn't.'

At length the relevant portions of General Fentiman's

anatomy having been collected into suitable jars and bottles, the body was returned to the coffin and screwed down. Penberthy came across to Wimsey and took his arm.

'We ought to be able to get a pretty good idea of what you want to know,' he said. 'Decomposition is very little advanced, owing to an exceptionally well-made coffin. By the way' (he dropped his voice), 'that leg, you know – did it ever occur to you – or rather, did you ever discover any explanation of that?'

'I *did* have an idea about it,' admitted Wimsey, 'but I don't yet know whether it was the right one. I shall probably know for certain in a day or two.'

'You think the body was interfered with?' said Penberthy, looking him steadily in the face.

'Yes, and so do you,' replied Wimsey, returning the gaze.

'I've had my suspicions all the time, of course. I told you so, you know. I wonder whether – you don't think I was wrong to give the certificate, do you?'

'Not unless you suspected anything wrong with the death itself,' said Wimsey. 'Have you and Horner noticed anything queer?'

'No. But – oh, well! having a patient dug up always makes me worried, you know. It's easy to make a mistake, and one looks an awful fool in court. I'd hate being made to look a fool just at present,' added the doctor with a nervous laugh. 'I'm thinking of – Great Scott, man! how you startled me!'

Dr Horner had brought a large, bony hand down on his shoulder. He was a red-faced, jovial man, and he smiled as he held up his bag before them.

'All packed up and ready,' he announced. 'Got to be getting back now, aha! Got to be getting back.'

144

'Have the witnesses signed the labels?' asked Penberthy, rather shortly.

'Yes, yes, quite all right. Both the solicitor johnnies, so they can't quarrel about *that* in the witness-box,' replied Horner. 'Come along, please – I've got to get off.'

They found George Fentiman outside, seated on a tombstone and sucking at an empty pipe.

'Is it all over?'

'Yes.'

'Have they found anything?'

'Haven't looked yet,' broke in Horner genially. 'Not at the part which interests *you*, that is. Leave that for my colleague Lubbock, you know. Soon give you an answer – say, in a week's time.'

George passed his handkerchief over his forehead, which was beaded with little drops of sweat.

'I don't like it,' he said 'But I suppose it had to be done. What was that? I thought – I'd swear I saw something moving over there.'

'A cat, probably,' said Penberthy; 'there's nothing to be alarmed at.'

'No,' said George; 'but sitting about here, one – fancies things.' He hunched his shoulders, squinting round at them with the whites of his eyeballs showing. 'Things,' he said; 'people – going to and fro . . . and walking up and down. Following one.'

14

GRAND SLAM IN SPADES

ON the seventh morning after the exhumation – which happened to be a Tuesday – Lord Peter walked briskly into Mr Murbles's chambers in Staple Inn, with Detective-Inspector Parker at his heels.

'Good morning,' said Mr Murbles, surprised.

'Good morning,' said Wimsey. 'Hark! hark! the lark at heaven's gate sings. He is coming, my own, my sweet, were it ever so airy a tread. He will be here in a quarter of an hour.'

'Who will?' demanded Mr Murbles, somewhat severely.

'Robert Fentiman.'

Mr Murbles gave a little ejaculation of surprise.

'I had almost given up hope in that direction,' he said.

'So had not I. I said to myself, he is not lost but gone before. And it was so. Charles, we will lay out the *pièces de conviction* on the table. The boots. The photographs. The microscopic slides showing the various specimens. The paper of notes from the library. The outer garments of the deceased. Just so. And *Oliver Twist*. Beautiful. Now, as Sherlock Holmes says, we shall look imposing enough to strike terror into the guilty breast, though armed in triple steel.'

'Did Fentiman return of his own accord?'

'Not altogether. He was, if I may so express myself, led. Almost, in fact, led on. O'er moor and fen, o'er crag and torrent till, don't you know. What is that noise in the outer room? It is – it is the cannon's opening roar.'

It was, indeed, the voice of Robert Fentiman, not in the best of tempers. In a few seconds he was shown in. He nodded curtly to Mr Murbles, who replied with a stiff bow, and then turned violently upon Wimsey.

'Look here, what's the meaning of all this? Here's that damned detective fellow of yours leading me a devil of a dance all over Europe and home again, and then this morning he suddenly turns round and tells me that you want to see me here with news about Oliver. What the devil do you know about Oliver?'

'Oliver?' said Wimsey. 'Oh, yes – he's an elusive personality. Almost as elusive in Rome as he was in London. Wasn't it odd, Fentiman, the way he always seemed to bob up directly your back was turned? Wasn't it funny, the way he managed to disappear from places the moment you set foot in 'em? Almost like the way he used to hang about Gatti's and then give you and me the slip. Did you have a jolly time abroad, old man? I suppose you didn't like to tell your companion that he and you were chasing a will-o'-the-wisp?'

Robert Fentiman's face was passing through phases ranging from fury to bewilderment and back again. Mr Murbles interrupted.

'Has this detective vouchsafed any explanation of his extraordinary behaviour, in keeping us in the dark for nearly a fortnight as to his movements?'

'I'm afraid I owe you the explanation,' said Wimsey airily. 'You see, I thought it was time the carrot was dangled before the other donkey. I knew that if we pretended to find Oliver in Paris, Fentiman would be in honour bound to chase after him. In fact, he was probably only too pleased to get away – weren't you, Fentiman?'

'Do you mean to say that you invented all this story about Oliver, Lord Peter?'

'I did. Not the original Oliver, of course, but the Paris Oliver. I told the sleuth to send a wire from Paris to summon our friend away and keep him away.'

'But why?'

'I'll explain that later. And of course you had to go, hadn't you, old man? Because you couldn't very well refuse to go without confessing that there was no such person as Oliver?'

'Damnation!' burst out Fentiman, and then suddenly began to laugh. 'You cunning little devil! I began to think there was something fishy about it, you know. When that first wire came I was delighted. Thought the sleuth-hound fellow had made a perfectly providential floater, don't you know. And the longer we kept toolin' round Europe the better I was pleased. But when the hare started to double back to England, home and beauty, I began to get the idea that somebody was pullin' my leg. By the way, was that why I was able to get all my *visas* with that uncanny facility at an unearthly hour over-night?'

'It was,' said Wimsey modestly.

'I might have known there was something wrong about it. You devil! Well – what now? If you've exploded Oliver, I suppose you've spilled all the rest of the beans, eh?'

'If you mean by that expression,' said Mr Murbles, 'that we are aware of your fraudulent and disgraceful attempt to conceal the true time of General Fentiman's decease, the answer is: Yes, we do know it. And I may say that it has come as a most painful shock to my feelings.'

Fentiman flung himself into a chair, slapping his thigh and roaring with laughter.

'I might have known you'd be on to it,' he gasped; 'but it was a damn' good joke, wasn't it? Good lord! I couldn't help chuckling to myself, you know. To think of all those refrigerated old imbeciles at the Club sittin' solemnly round there, and comin' in and noddin' to the old guv'nor like so many mandarins, when he was as dead as a door-nail all the time. That leg of his was a bit of a slip-up, of course, but that was an accident. Did you ever find out where he was all the time?'

'Oh, yes – pretty conclusively. You left your marks on the cabinet, you know.'

'No, did we? Hell!'

'Yes – and when you stuck the old boy's overcoat back in the cloakroom you forgot to stick a poppy in it.'

'Oh, lord! that *was* a bloomer. D'you know, I never thought of that. Oh, well, I suppose I couldn't hope to carry it off with a confounded bloodhound like you on the trail. But it was fun while it lasted. Even now, the thought of old Bunter solemnly callin' up two and a half columns of Olivers makes me shout with joy. It's almost as good as getting the half-million.'

'That reminds me,' said Wimsey. 'The one thing I don't know is how you knew about the half-million. Did Lady Dormer tell you about her will? Or did you hear of it from George?'

'George? Great Scott, no! George knew nothing about it. The old boy told me himself.'

'General Fentiman?'

'Of course. When he came back to the Club that night, he came straight up to see me.'

'And we never thought of that,' said Wimsey, crushed, 'Too obvious, I suppose.'

'You can't be expected to think of everything,' said Robert condescendingly. 'I think you did very well, take it all around. Yes – the old boy toddled up to me and told me all about it. He said I wasn't to tell George, because he wasn't quite satisfied with George – about Sheila, you know – and he wanted to think it over and see what was best to be done, in the way of making a new will, you see.'

'Just so. And he went down to the library to do it.'

'That's right; and I went down and had some grub. Well, then, afterwards I thought perhaps I hadn't said quite enough on behalf of old George. I mean, the guv'nor needed to have it pointed out to him that George's queerness was caused a great deal by bein' dependent on Sheila and all that, and if he had some tin of his own he'd be much better-tempered – you get me? So I hopped through to the library to find the guv' – and there he was – dead!'

'What time was that?'

'Somewhere round about eightish, I should think. Well, I was staggered. Of course, my first idea was to call for help, but it wasn't any go. He was quite dead. And then it jolly well came over me all at once how perfectly damnably we had missed the train. Just to think of that awful Dorland woman walking into all those thousands – I tell you, it made me so bally wild, I could have exploded and blown the place up! . . . And then, you know, I began to get a sort of creepy feeling, alone there with the body and nobody in the library at all. We seemed cut off from the world, as the writing fellows say. And then it just seemed to take hold of my mind, why should he have died like that? I did have a passing hope that the old girl might have pegged out first, and I was just going along to the telephone to find out, when –

thinking of the telephone cabinet, you see – the whole thing popped into my head ready-made, as you might say. In three minutes I'd lugged him along and stuck him up on the seat, and then I hopped back to write a label for the door. I say, I thought I was jolly smart to remember not to blot that label on the library blotting-paper.'

'Believe me,' said Wimsey, 'I appreciated that point.'

'Good. I'm glad you did. Well, it was pretty plain sailing after that. I got the guv'nor's togs from the cloakroom and took 'em up to my room, and then I thought about old Woodward sittin' up waitin' for him. So I trundled out and went down to Charing Cross – how do you think?'

'By bus?'

'Not quite as bad as that. By Underground. I did realise it wouldn't work to call a taxi.'

'You show quite a disposition for fraud, Fentiman.'

'Yes, don't I? – Well, all that was easy. I must say, I didn't pass a frightfully good night.'

'You'll take it more calmly another time.'

'Yes – it was my maiden effort in crime, of course. The next morning—'

'Young man,' said Mr Murbles, in an awful voice, 'we will draw a veil over the next morning. I have listened to your shameless statement with a disgust which words cannot express. But I cannot, and I will not, sit here and listen while you congratulate yourself, with a cynicism at which you should blush, on having employed those sacred moments when every thought should have been consecrated—'

'Oh, punk!' interrupted Robert rudely. 'My old pals are none the worse because I did a little bit of self-help. I know fraud isn't altogether the clean potato, but, dash it all! surely we have a better right to the old boy's money than that girl. I bet *she* never did anything in the Great War, daddy. Well, it's all gone bust – but it was a darn' good stunt while it lasted.'

'I perceive,' replied Mr Murbles icily, 'that any appeal to your better feelings would be waste of time. I imagine, however, you realise that fraud is a penal offence.'

'Yes – that's a nuisance, isn't it? What are we going to do about it? Do I have to go and eat humble pie to old Pritchard? Or does Wimsey pretend to have discovered something frightfully abstruse from looking at the body? – Oh, good lord, by the way – what's happened about that confounded exhumation stunt? I never thought a word more about it. I say, Wimsey, was that the idea? Did you know then that I'd been trying to work this stunt and was it your notion you could get me out of it?'

'Partly.'

'Damned decent of you. You know, I did tumble to it that you'd got a line on me when you sent me down with that detective fellow to Charing Cross. And, I say, you nearly had me there! I'd made up my mind to pretend to go after Oliver, you know – and then I spotted that second bloodhound of yours on the train with me. That gave me gooseflesh all over. The only thing I could think of – short of chucking up the whole show – was to accuse some harmless old bird of being Oliver – as a proof of good faith, don't you see.'

'That was it, was it? I thought you must have some reason.'

'Yes – and then, when I got that summons to Paris, I thought I must, somehow, have diddled the lot of you. But I suppose that was all arranged for. I say, Wimsey, why? Did you just want to get your own back, or what? Why did you want me out of England?'

'Yes, indeed, Lord Peter,' said Mr Murbles gravely, 'I

think you owe *me* at least some explanation on that point.'

'Don't you see,' said Wimsey, 'Fentiman was his grandfather's executor. If I got him out of the way, you couldn't stop the exhumation.'

'Ghoul!' said Robert. 'I believe you batten on corpses.'

Wimsey laughed, rather excitedly.

'Fentiman,' he said, 'what would you give at this moment for your chance of that half-million?'

'Chance?' cried Fentiman. 'There's no chance at all. What do you mean?'

Wimsey slowly drew a paper from his pocket.

'This came last night,' he said. 'And, by Jove, my lad, it's lucky for you that you had a good bit to lose by the old man's death. This is from Lubbock:

'DEAR LORD PETER,

'I am sending you a line in advance to let you know the result of the autopsy on General Fentiman. As regards the ostensible reason for the investigation, I may say that there was no food in the stomach and that the last meal had been taken several hours previously. The important point, however, is that, following your own rather obscurely-expressed suggestion, I tested the viscera for poison and discovered traces of a powerful dose of digitalin, swallowed not very long previous to decease. As you know, with a subject whose heart was already in a weak state, the result of such a dose could not but be fatal. The symptoms would be a slowing-down of the heart's action and collapse – practically indistinguishable from a violent heart-attack.

'I do not, of course, know what your attitude in this business is, though I congratulate you on the perspicacity which prompted you to suggest an analysis. In the

153

meanwhile, of course, you will realise that I am obliged to communicate the result of the autopsy to the public prosecutor.'

Mr Murbles sat petrified.

'My God!' cried Fentiman. And then again, 'My God! – Wimsey – if I'd known – if I'd had the faintest idea – I wouldn't have touched the body for twenty millions. Poison! Poor old blighter! What a damned shame! I remember now his saying that night he felt a bit sickish, but I never thought – I say, Wimsey – you do believe, don't you, that I hadn't the foggiest? I say – that awful female – I knew she was a wrong 'un. But poison! that is too thick. Good lord!'

Parker, who had hitherto preserved the detached expression of a friendly spectator, now beamed. 'Damn good, old man!' he cried, and smote Peter on the back. Professional enthusiasm overcame him. 'It's a real case,' he said, 'and you've handled it finely, Peter. I didn't know you had it in you to hang on so patiently. Forcing the exhumation on 'em through putting pressure on Major Fentiman was simply masterly! Pretty work! Pretty work!'

'Thank you, Charles,' said Wimsey dryly. 'I'm glad somebody appreciates me. Anyhow,' he added viciously, 'I bet that's wiped old Pritchard's eye.'

And at this remark, even Mr Murbles showed signs of returning animation.

154

15

SHUFFLE THE CARDS AND DEAL AGAIN

A HASTY consultation with the powers that be at Scotland Yard put Detective-Inspector Parker in charge of the Fentiman case, and he promptly went into consultation with Wimsey.

'What put you on to this poison business?' he asked.

'Aristotle, chiefly,' replied Wimsey. 'He says, you know, that one should always prefer the probable impossible to the improbable possible. It was possible, of course, that the General should have died off in that neat way at the most confusing moment. But how much nicer and more probable that the whole thing had been stage-managed. Even if it had seemed much more impossible I should have been dead nuts on murder. And there really was nothing impossible about it. Then there was Pritchard and the Dorland woman. Why should they have been so dead against compromise and so suspicious about things unless they had inside information from somewhere? After all, they hadn't seen the body as Penberthy and I did.'

'That leads on to the question of who did it. Miss Dorland is the obvious suspect, naturally.'

'She's got the biggest motive.'

'Yes. Well, let's be methodical. Old Fentiman was apparently as right as rain up till about half-past three when he started off for Portman Square, so that the drug must have been given him between then and eightish, when Robert Fentiman found him dead. Now who saw him between those two times?'

'Wait a sec. That's not absolutely accurate. He must have *taken* the stuff between those two times, but it might have been *given* him earlier. Suppose, for instance, somebody had dropped a poisoned pill into his usual bottle of soda-mints or whatever he used to take. That could have been worked at any time.'

'Well – not too early on, Peter. Suppose he had died a lot too soon and Lady Dormer had heard about it.'

'It wouldn't have made any difference. She wouldn't need to alter her will, or anything. The bequest to Miss Dorland would just stand as before.'

'Quite right. I was being stupid. Well, then, we'd better find out if he did take anything of that kind regularly. If he did, who would have had the opportunity to drop the pill in?'

'Penberthy, for one.'

'The doctor? – yes, we must stick him down as a possible, though he wouldn't have had the slightest motive. Still, we'll put him in the column headed Opportunity.'

'That's right, Charles. I do like your methodical ways.'

'Attraction of opposites,' said Parker, ruling a notebook into three columns. 'Opportunity: No. 1, Dr Penberthy. If the tablets or globules or whatever they were, were Penberthy's own prescription, he would have a specially good opportunity. Not so good, though, if they were the kind of things you get ready-made from the chemist in sealed bottles.'

'Oh, bosh! he could always have asked to have a squint at 'em to see if they were the right kind. I insist on having Penberthy in. Besides, he was one of the people who saw the General between the two critical hours –

during what we may call the administration period; so he had an extra amount of opportunity.'

'So he had. Well, I've put him down. Though there seems no reason for him –'

'I'm not going to be put off by a trifling objection like that. He had the opportunity, so down he goes. Well, then, Miss Dorland comes next.'

'Yes. She goes down under Opportunity and also under Motive. She certainly had a big interest in polishing off the old man; she saw him during the period of administration and she very likely gave him something to eat or drink while he was in the house. So she is a very likely subject. The only difficulty with her is the difficulty of getting hold of the drug. You can't get digitalin just by asking for it, you know.'

'N-no. At least, not by itself. You can get it mixed up with other drugs quite easily. I saw an ad. in the *Daily Views* only this morning, offering a pill with half a grain of digitalin in it.'

'Did you? where? – oh, that! Yes, but it's got nux vomica in it too, which is supposed to be an antidote. At any rate, it bucks the heart up by stimulating the nerves, so as to counteract the slowing down action of the digitalin.'

'H'm. Well, put down Miss Dorland under Means with a query mark. Oh! of course, Penberthy has to go down under Means, too. He is the one person who could get the stuff without any bother.'

'Right. Means: No. 1, Dr Penberthy. Opportunity: No. 1, Dr Penberthy, No. 2, Miss Dorland. We'll have to put in the servants at Lady Dormer's too, shan't we? Any of them who brought him food or drink, at any rate.'

'Put 'em in, by all means. They might have been in

collusion with Miss Dorland. And how about Lady Dormer herself?'

'Oh, come, Peter. There wouldn't be any sense in that.'

'Why not? She may have been planning revenge on her brother all these years, camouflaging her feelings under a pretence of generosity. It would be rather fun to leave a terrific legacy to somebody you loathed, and then, just when he was feelin' nice and grateful and all over coals of fire, poison him to make sure he didn't get it. We simply must have Lady Dormer. Stick her down under Opportunity and under Motives.'

'I refuse to do more than Opportunity and Motive (query).'

'Have it your own way, Well, now – there are our friends the two taxi-drivers.'

'I don't think you can be allowed those. It would be awfully hard work poisoning a fare, you know.'

'I'm afraid it would. I say! I've just got a rippin' idea for poisoning a taxi-man, though. You give him a dud half-crown, and when he bites it—'

'He dies of lead poisoning. That one's got whiskers on it.'

'Juggins. You poison the half-crown with prussic acid.'

'Splendid! And he falls down foaming at the mouth. That's frightfully brilliant. Do you mind giving your attention to the matter in hand?'

'You think we can leave out the taxi-drivers, then?'

'I think so.'

'Right-o! I'll let you have them. That brings us, I'm sorry to say, to George Fentiman.'

'You've got rather a weakness for George Fentiman, haven't you?'

'Yes – I like old George. He's an awful pig in some ways, but I quite like him.'

'Well, I don't know George, so I shall firmly put him down. Opportunity No. 3, he is.'

'He'll have to go down under Motive, too, then.'

'Why? What did he stand, to gain by Miss Dorland's getting the legacy?'

'Nothing – if he knew about it. But Robert says emphatically that he didn't know. So does George. And if he didn't, don't you see, the General's death meant that he would immediately step into that two thousand quid which Dougal MacStewart was being so pressing about.'

'MacStewart? – oh, yes – the money-lender. That's one up to you, Peter; I'd forgotten him. That certainly does put George on the last of the possibles. He was pretty sore about things too, wasn't he?'

'Very. And I remember his saying one rather unguarded thing at least down at the Club on the very day the murder – or rather, the death – was discovered.'

'That's in his favour, if anything,' said Parker cheerfully, 'unless he's very reckless indeed.'

'It won't be in his favour with the police,' grumbled Wimsey.

'My dear man!'

'I beg your pardon. I was forgetting for the moment. I'm afraid you are getting a little above your job, Charles. So much intelligence will spell either an Assistant Commissionership or ostracism if you aren't careful.'

'I'll chance that. Come on – get on with it. Who else is there?'

'There's Woodward. Nobody could have a better opportunity of tampering with the General's pill boxes.'

'And I suppose his little legacy might have been a motive?'

'Or he may have been in the enemy's pay. Sinister men-servants so often are, you know. Look what a boom there has been lately in criminal butlers and thefts by perfect servants.'

'That's a fact. And now, how about the people at the Bellona?'

'There's Wetheridge. He's a disagreeable devil. And he has always cast covetous eyes at the General's chair by the fire. I've seen him.'

'Be serious, Peter.'

'I'm perfectly serious. I don't like Wetheridge. He annoys me. And then we mustn't forget to put down Robert.'

'Robert? Why, he's the one person we can definitely cross off. He knew it was to his interest to keep the old man alive. Look at the pains he took to cover up the death.'

'Exactly. He is the Most Unlikely Person, and that is why Sherlock Holmes would suspect him at once. He was, by his own admission, the last person to see General Fentiman alive. Suppose he had a row with the old man and killed him, and then discovered, afterwards, about the legacy.'

'You're scintillating with good plots today, Peter. If they quarrelled, he might possibly have knocked his grandfather down – though I don't think he'd do such a rotten and unsportsmanlike thing – but he surely wouldn't have poisoned him.'

Wimsey sighed.

'There's something in what you say,' he admitted. 'Still, you never know. Now then, is there any name we've thought of which appears in all three columns of our list?'

'No, not one. But several appear in two.'

'We'd better start on those, then. Miss Dorland is the most obvious, naturally, and after her, George, don't you think?'

'Yes. I'll have a round-up among all the chemists who may possibly have supplied her with the digitalin. Who's her family doctor?'

'Dunno. That's your pigeon. By the way, I'm supposed to be meeting the girl at a cocoa party or something of the sort tomorrow. Don't pinch her before then if you can help it.'

'No; but it looks to me as though we might need to put a few questions. And I'd like to have a look round Lady Dormer's house.'

'For heaven's sake, don't be flat-footed about it, Charles. Use tact.'

'You can trust your father. And, I say, you might take me down to the Bellona in a tactful way. I'd like to ask a question or two there.'

Wimsey groaned.

'I shall be asked to resign if this goes on. Not that it's much loss. But it would please Wetheridge so much to see the back of me. Never mind. I'll make a Martha of myself. Come on.'

The entrance of the Bellona Club was filled with an unseemly confusion. Culyer was arguing heatedly with a number of men, and three or four members of the committee stood beside him with brows as black as thunder. As Wimsey entered, one of the intruders caught sight of him with a yelp of joy.

'Wimsey – Wimsey, old man! Here, be a sport and get us in on this. We've got to have the story some day. You probably know all about it, you old blighter.'

It was Salcombe Hardy, of the *Daily Yell*, large and untidy and slightly drunk as usual. He gazed at Wimsey with childlike blue eyes. Barton, of the *Banner*, red-haired and pugnacious, faced round promptly.

'Ah, Wimsey, that's fine. Give us a line on this, can't you? Do explain that if we get a story we'll be good and go.'

'Good lord!' said Wimsey; 'how do these things get into the papers?'

'I think it's rather obvious,' said Culyer acidly.

'It wasn't me,' said Wimsey.

'No, no,' put in Hardy. 'You mustn't think that. It was my stunt. In fact, I saw the whole show up at the Necropolis. I was on a family vault, pretending to be a recording angel.'

'You would be,' said Wimsey. 'Just a moment, Culyer.' He drew the secretary aside. 'See here, I'm damned annoyed about this, but it can't be helped. You can't stop these boys when they're after a story. And, anyway, it's all got to come out. It's a police affair now. This is Detective-Inspector Parker of Scotland Yard.'

'But what's the matter?' demanded Culyer.

'Murder's the matter, I'm afraid.'

'Oh, hell!'

'Sorry and all that. But you'd better grin and bear it. Charles, give these fellows as much story as you think they ought to have, and get on with it. And, Salcombe, if you'll call off your tripe-hounds, we'll let you have an interview and a set of photographs.'

'That's the stuff,' said Hardy.

'I'm sure,' agreed Parker pleasantly, 'that you lads don't want to get in the way, and I'll tell you all that's advisable. Show us a room, Captain Culyer, and I'll send out a statement and then you'll let us get to work.'

This was agreed and, a suitable paragraph having been provided by Parker, the Fleet Street gang departed, bearing Wimsey away with them like a captured Sabine maiden, to drink in the nearest bar, in the hope of acquiring picturesque details.

'But I wish you'd kept out of it, Sally,' mourned Peter.

'Oh, God,' said Salcombe, 'nobody loves us! It's a forsaken thing to be a poor bloody reporter.' He tossed a lank black lock of hair back from his forehead, and wept.

Parker's first and most obvious move was to interview Penberthy, whom he caught at Harley Street after surgery hours.

'Now I'm not going to worry you about that certificate, doctor,' he began pleasantly. 'We're all liable to make mistakes, and I understand that a death resulting from an overdose of digitalin would look very like a death from heart failure.'

'It would *be* a death from heart failure,' corrected the doctor patiently. Doctors are weary of explaining that heart failure is not a specific disease, like mumps or housemaid's knee. It is this incompatibility of outlook between the medical and the lay mind which involves counsel and medical witnesses in a fog of misunderstanding and mutual irritation.

'Just so,' said Parker. 'Now, General Fentiman had got heart disease already, hadn't he? Is digitalin a thing one takes for heart disease?'

'Yes; in certain forms of heart disease, digitalin is a very valuable stimulant.'

'Stimulant? I thought it was a depressant.'

'It acts as a stimulant at first; in later stages it depresses the heart's action.'

'Oh, I see.' Parker did not see very well, since, like most people, he had a vague idea that each drug has one simple effect appropriate to it, and is, specifically, a cure for something or the other. 'It first speeds up the heart and then slows it down.'

'Not exactly. It strengthens the heart's action by retarding the beat, so that the cavities can be more completely emptied and the pressure is relieved. We give it in certain cases of valvular disease – under proper safeguards, of course.'

'Were you giving it to General Fentiman?'

'I had given it him from time to time.'

'On the afternoon of November 10th – you remember that he came to you in consequence of a heart attack. Did you give him digitalin then?'

Dr Penberthy appeared to hesitate painfully for a moment. Then he turned to his desk and extracted a large book.

'I had better be perfectly frank with you,' he said. 'I did. When he came to me, the feebleness of the heart's action and the extreme difficulty in breathing suggested the urgent necessity of a cardiac stimulant. I gave him a prescription containing a small quantity of digitalin to relieve this condition. Here is the prescription. I will write it out for you.'

'A small quantity?' repeated Parker.

'Quite small, combined with other drugs to counteract the depressing after-effects.'

'It was not as large as the dose afterwards found in the body?'

'Good heavens, no – nothing like. In a case like General Fentiman's, digitalin is a drug to be administered with the greatest caution.'

'It would not be possible, I suppose, for you to have made a mistake in dispensing? To have given an overdose by error?'

'That possibility occurred to me at once, but as soon as

I heard Sir James Lubbock's figures, I realised that it was quite out of the question. The dose given was enormous: nearly two grains. But, to make quite certain, I have had my supply of the drug carefully checked, and it is all accounted for.'

'Who did that for you?'

'My trained nurse. I will let you have the books and chemists' receipts.'

'Thank you. Did your nurse make up the dose for General Fentiman?'

'Oh, no; it is a preparation I always keep by me, ready made up. If you like to see her, she will show it to you.'

'Thanks very much. Now, when General Fentiman came to see you, he had just had an attack. Could that have been caused by digitalin?'

'You mean, had he been poisoned before he came to me? Well, of course, digitalin is rather an uncertain drug.'

'How long would a big dose like that take to act?'

'I should expect it to take effect fairly quickly. In the ordinary way it would cause sickness and vertigo. But with a powerful cardiac stimulant like digitalin, the chief danger is that any sudden movement, such as springing suddenly to one's feet from a position of repose, is liable to cause sudden syncope and death. I should say that this was what occurred in General Fentiman's case.'

'And that might have happened at any time after the administration of the dose?'

'Just so.'

'Well, I'm very much obliged to you, Dr Penberthy. I will just see your dispenser and take copies of the entries in your books, if I may.'

This done, Parker made his way to Portman Square, still a little hazy in his mind as to the habits of the common foxglove when applied internally – a haziness which was in no way improved by a subsequent consultation of the 'Materia Medica', 'Pharmacopoeia', Dixon Mann, Taylor, Glaister, and others of those writers who had so kindly and helpfully published their conclusions on toxicology.

16

QUADRILLE

'MRS RUSHWORTH, this is Lord Peter Wimsey. Naomi, this is Lord Peter. He's fearfully keen on glands and things, so I've brought him along. And, Naomi, do tell me all about your news. Who is it? Do I know him?'

Mrs Rushworth was a long, untidy woman, with long, untidy hair wound into bell-pushes over her ears. She beamed short-sightedly at Peter.

'So glad to see you. So very wonderful about glands, isn't it? Dr Voronoff, you know, and those marvellous old sheep. Such a hope for all of us. Not that dear Walter is specially interested in rejuvenation. Perhaps life is long and difficult enough as it is, don't you think – so full of problems of one kind and another. And the Insurance companies have quite set their faces against it, or so I understand. That's natural, isn't it, when you come to think of it. But the effect on character is so interesting, you know. Are you devoted to young criminals, by any chance?'

Wimsey said that they presented a very perplexing problem.

'How very true. So perplexing. And just to think that we have been quite wrong about them all these thousands of years. Flogging and bread-and-water, you know, and Holy Communion, when what they really needed was a little bit of rabbit-gland or something to make them just as good as gold. Quite terrible, isn't it? And all those poor freaks in side-shows, too – dwarfs and giants, you know – all pineal or pituitary, and they come right again. Though I dare say they make a great deal more money as they are, which throws such a distressing light on unemployment, does it not?'

Wimsey said that everything had the defects of its qualities.

'Yes, indeed,' agreed Mrs Rushworth. 'But I think it is so infinitely more heartening to look at it from the opposite point of view. Everything has the qualities of its defects, too, has it not? It is so important to see these things in their true light. It will be such a joy for Naomi to be able to help dear Walter in this great work. I hope you will feel eager to subscribe to the establishment of the new Clinic.'

Wimsey asked, what new Clinic.

'Oh! hasn't Marjorie told you about it? The new Clinic to make everybody good by glands. That is what dear Walter is going to speak about. He is so keen, and so is Naomi. It was such a joy to me when Naomi told me that they were really engaged, you know. Not that her old mother hadn't suspected something, of course,' added Mrs Rushworth archly. 'But young people are so odd nowadays, and keep their affairs so much to themselves.'

Wimsey said that he thought both parties were heartily to be congratulated. And indeed, from what he had seen of Naomi Rushworth, he felt that she at least deserved congratulation, for she was a singularly plain girl, with a face like a weasel.

'You will excuse me if I run off and speak to some of these other people, won't you?' went on Mrs Rushworth. 'I'm sure you will be able to amuse yourself. No doubt you have many friends in my little gathering.'

Wimsey glanced round and was about to felicitate himself on knowing nobody, when a familiar face caught his eye.

'Why,' said he, 'there is Dr Penberthy.'

'Dear Walter!' cried Mrs Rushworth, turning hurriedly in the direction indicated. 'I declare, so he is. Ah, well – now we shall be able to begin. He should have been here before, but a doctor's time is never his own.'

'Penberthy!' said Wimsey half aloud; 'good lord!'

'Very sound man,' said a voice beside him. 'Don't think the worse of his work from seeing him in this crowd. Beggars in a good cause can't be choosers, as we parsons know too well.'

Wimsey turned to face a tall, lean man, with a handsome, humorous face, whom he recognised as a well-known slum padre.

'Father Whittington, isn't it?'

'The same. You're Lord Peter Wimsey, I know. We've got an interest in crime in common, haven't we? I'm interested in this glandular theory. It may throw a great light on some of our heart-breaking problems.'

'Glad to see there's no antagonism between religion and science,' said Wimsey.

'Of course not. Why should there be? We are all searching for Truth.'

'And all these?' asked Wimsey, indicating the curious crowd with a wave of the hand.

'In their way. They mean well. They do what they can, like the woman in the Gospels, and they are surprisingly generous. Here's Penberthy, looking for you, I fancy. Well, Dr Penberthy, I've come, you see, to hear you make mincemeat of original sin.'

'That's very open-minded of you,' said Penberthy,

with a rather strained smile. 'I hope you are not hostile. We've no quarrel with the Church, you know, if she'll stick to her business and leave us to ours.'

'My dear man, if you can cure sin with an injection, I shall be only too pleased. Only be sure you don't pump in something worse in the process. You know the parable of the swept and garnished house.'

'I'll be as careful as I can,' said Penberthy. 'Excuse me one moment. I say, Wimsey, you've heard all about Lubbock's analysis, I suppose?'

'Yes. Bit of a startler, isn't it?'

'It's going to make things damnably awkward for me, Wimsey. I wish to God you'd given me a hint at the time. Such a thing never once occurred to me.'

'Why should it? You were expecting the old boy to pop off from heart, and he did pop off from heart. Nobody could possibly blame you.'

'Couldn't they? That's all you know about juries. I wouldn't have had this happen, just at this moment, for a fortune. It couldn't have chosen a more unfortunate time.'

'It'll blow over, Penberthy. That sort of mistake happens a hundred times a week. By the way, I gather I'm to congratulate you. When did this get settled? You've been very quiet about it.'

'I was starting to tell you up at that infernal exhumation business, only somebody barged in. Yes. Thanks very much. We fixed it up – oh, about a fortnight or three weeks ago. You have met Naomi?'

'Only for a moment this evening. My friend Miss Phelps carried her off to hear all about you.'

'Oh, yes. Well, you must come along and talk to her. She's a sweet girl, and very intelligent. The old lady's a bit of a trial, I don't mind saying, but her heart's in the right place. And there's no doubt she gets hold of people whom it's very useful to meet.'

'I didn't know you were such an authority on Glands.'

'I only wish I could afford to be. I've done a certain amount of experimental work under Professor Sligo. It's the Science of the future, as they say in the press. There really isn't any doubt about that. It puts biology in quite a new light. We're on the verge of some really interesting discoveries, no doubt about it. Only, what with the antivivisectors and the parsons and the other old women, one doesn't make the progress one ought. Oh, lord – they're waiting for me to begin. See you later.'

'Half a jiff. I really came here – no, dash it, that's rude! But I'd no idea you were the lecturer till I spotted you. I originally came here (that sounds better) to get a look at Miss Dorland of Fentiman fame. But my trusty guide has abandoned me. Do you know Miss Dorland? Can you tell me which she is?'

'I know her to speak to. I haven't seen her this evening. She may not turn up, you know.'

'I thought she was very keen on – on glands and things.'

'I believe she is – or thinks she is. Anything does for these women as long as it's new – especially if it's sexual. By the way, I don't intend to be sexual.'

'Bless you for that. Well, possibly Miss Dorland will show up later.'

'Perhaps. But – I say, Wimsey. She's in rather a queer position, isn't she? She may not feel inclined to face it. It's all in the papers, you know.'

'Dash it, don't I know it? That inspired tippler, Salcombe Hardy, got 'old of it somehow. I think he bribes the cemetery officials to give him advance news of exhumations. He's worth his weight in pound notes to the *Yell*. Cheerio! Speak your bit nicely. You don't mind if I'm not in the front row, do you? I always take up a strategic position near the door that leads to the grub.'

Penberthy's paper struck Wimsey as being original and well delivered. The subject was not altogether unfamiliar to him, for Wimsey had a number of distinguished scientific friends who found him a good listener, but some of the experiments mentioned were new and the conclusions suggestive. True to his principles, Wimsey made a bolt for the supper-room while polite hands were still applauding. He was not the first, however. A large figure in a hard-worked-looking dress-suit was already engaged with a pile of savoury sandwiches and a whisky-and-soda. It turned at his approach and beamed at him from its liquid innocent blue eyes. Sally Hardy – never quite drunk and never quite sober – was on the job, as usual. He held out the sandwich plate invitingly.

'Damn' good, these are,' he said. 'What are you doing here?'

'What are you, if it comes to that?' asked Wimsey.

Hardy laid a fat hand on his sleeve.

'Two birds with one stone,' he said impressively. 'Smart fellow, that Penberthy. Glands are news, you know. He knows it. He'll be one of these fashionable practitioners' – Sally repeated this phrase once or twice, as it seemed to have got mixed up with the soda – 'before long. Doing us poor bloody journalists out of a job, like— and—.' (He mentioned two gentlemen whose signed contributions to popular dailies were a continual source of annoyance to the G.M.C.)

'Provided he doesn't damage his reputation over this Fentiman affair,' rejoined Wimsey, in a refined shriek

172

which did duty for a whisper amid the noisy stampede which had followed them up to the refreshment table.

'Ah! there you are,' said Hardy. 'Penberthy's news in himself. He's a story, don't you see. We'll have to sit on the fence a bit, of course, till we see which way the cat jumps. I'll have a par. about it at the end, mentioning that he attended old Fentiman. Presently we'll be able to work up a little thing on the magazine page about the advisability of a P.M. in all cases of sudden death. You know – even experienced doctors may be deceived. If he comes off very badly in cross-examination, there can be something about specialists not always being trustworthy – a kind word for the pore downtrodden G.P. and all that. Anyhow, he's worth a story. It doesn't matter what you say about him, provided you say something. You couldn't do us a little thing – about eight hundred words, could you – about *rigor mortis* or something? Only make it snappy.'

'I could not,' said Wimsey. 'I haven't time and I don't want the money. Why should I? I'm not a dean or an actress.'

'No, but you're news. You can give me the money, if you're so beastly flush. Look here, have you got a line on this case at all? That police friend of yours won't give anything away. I want to get something in before there's an arrest, because after that it's contempt. I suppose it's the girl you're after, isn't it? Can you tell me anything about her?'

'No – I came here tonight to get a look at her, but she hasn't turned up. I wish you could dig up her hideous past for me. The Rushworths must know something about her, I should think. She used to paint or something. Can't you get on to that?'

Hardy's face lighted up.

'Waffles Newton will probably know something,' he

said. 'I'll see what I can dig out. Thanks very much, old man. That's given me an idea. We might get one of her pictures on the back page. The old lady seems to have been a queer old soul. Odd will, wasn't it?'

'Oh, I can tell you all about that,' said Wimsey. 'I thought you probably knew.'

He gave Hardy the history of Lady Dormer as he had heard it from Mr Murbles. The journalist was enthralled.

'Great stuff!' he said. 'That'll get 'em. Romance there! This'll be a scoop for the *Yell*. Excuse me. I want to phone it through to 'em before somebody else gets it. Don't hand it out to any of the other fellows.'

'They can get it from Robert or George Fentiman,' warned Wimsey.

'Not much, they won't,' said Salcombe Hardy feelingly. 'Robert Fentiman gave old Barton of the *Banner* such a clip under the ear this morning that he had to go and see a dentist. And George has gone down to the Bellona, and they won't let anybody in. I'm all right on this. If there's anything I can do for you, I will, you bet. So long.'

He faded away. A hand was laid on Peter's arm.

'You're neglecting me shockingly,' said Marjorie Phelps. 'And I'm frightfully hungry. I've been doing my best to find things out for you.'

'That's top-hole of you. Look here. Come and sit out in the hall; it's quieter. I'll scrounge some grub and bring it along.'

He secured a quantity of curious little stuffed buns, four *petits-fours*, some dubious claret-cup and some coffee, and brought them with him on a tray, snatched while the waitress's back was turned.

'Thanks,' said Marjorie; 'I deserve all I can get for

having talked to Naomi Rushworth. I cannot like that girl. She hints things.'

'What, particularly?'

'Well, I started to ask about Ann Dorland. So she said she wasn't coming. So I said, "Oh, why?" and she said, "she *said* she wasn't well".'

'Who said?'

'Naomi Rushworth said Ann Dorland said she couldn't come because she wasn't well. But she said that was only an excuse, of course.'

'Who said?'

'Naomi said. So I said, was it? And she said yes, she didn't suppose she felt like facing people very much. So I said, "I thought you were such friends." So she said: "Well, we are, but of course Ann always was a little abnormal, you see." So I said that was the first I had heard of it. And she gave me one of her catty looks and said, "Well, there was Ambrose Ledbury, wasn't there? But, of course, you had other things to think of then, hadn't you?" The little beast. She means Komski. And, after all, everybody knows how obvious she's made herself over this man Penberthy.'

'I'm sorry, I've got mixed.'

'Well, I was rather fond of Komski. And I did almost promise to live with him, till I found that his last three women had all got fed up with him and left him, and I felt there must be something wrong with a man who continually got left, and I've discovered since that he was a dreadful bully when he dropped that touching lost-dog manner of his. So I was well out of it. Still, seeing that Naomi has been going about for the last year nearly, looking at Dr Penberthy like a female spaniel that thinks it's going to be whipped, I can't see why she need throw Komski in my face. And as for

Ambrose Ledbury, anybody might have been mistaken in him.'

'Who was Ambrose Ledbury?'

'Oh, he was the man who had that studio over Boulter's Mews. Powerfulness was his strong suit, and being above worldly considerations. He was rugged and wore homespun and painted craggy people in bedrooms, but his colour was amazing. He really could paint and so we could excuse a lot, but he was a professional heartbreaker. He used to gather people up hungrily in his great arms, you know – that's always rather irresistible. But he had no discrimination. It was just a habit, and his affairs never lasted long. But Ann Dorland was really rather overcome, you know. She tried the craggy style herself, but it wasn't at all her line – she hasn't any colour-sense, so there was nothing to make up for the bad drawing.'

'I thought you said she didn't have any affairs.'

'It wasn't an affair. I expect Ledbury gathered her up at some time or other when there wasn't anybody else handy, but he did demand good looks for anything serious. He went off to Poland a year ago with a woman called Natasha somebody. After that, Ann Dorland began to chuck painting. The trouble was, she took things seriously. A few little passions would have put her right, but she isn't the sort of person a man can enjoy flirting with. Heavy-handed. I don't think she would have gone on worrying about Ledbury if he hadn't happened to be the one and only episode. Because, as I say, she did make a few efforts, but she couldn't bring 'em off.'

'I see.'

'But that's no reason why Naomi should turn round like that. The fact is, the little brute's so proud of having landed a man – *and* an engagement ring – for herself, that she's out to patronise everybody else.'

'Oh?'

'Yes; besides, everything is looked at from dear Walter's point of view now, and naturally Walter isn't feeling very loving towards Ann Dorland.'

'Why not?'

'My dear man, you're being very discreet, aren't you? Naturally, everybody's saying that she did it.'

'Are they?'

'Who else could they think did it?'

Wimsey realised, indeed, that everybody must be thinking it. He was exceedingly inclined to think it himself.

'Probably that's why she didn't turn up.'

'Of course it is. She's not a fool. She must know.'

'That's true. Look here, will you do something for me? Something more, I mean?'

'What?'

'From what you say, it looks as though Miss Dorland might find herself rather short of friends in the near future. If she comes to you—'

'I'm not going to spy on her. Not if she had poisoned fifty old generals.'

'I don't want you to. But I want you to keep an open mind, and tell me what you think. Because I don't want to make a mistake over this. And I'm prejudiced. I want Miss Dorland to be guilty. So I'm very likely to persuade myself she is when she isn't. See?'

'Why do you want her to be guilty?'

'I oughtn't to have mentioned that. Of course, I don't want her found guilty if she isn't really.'

'All right. I won't ask questions. And I'll try and see Ann. But I won't try to worm anything out of her. That's definite. I'm standing by Ann.'

'My dear girl,' said Wimsey, 'you're not keeping an open mind. You think she did it.'

Marjorie Phelps flushed.

'I don't. Why do you think that?'

'Because you're so anxious not to worm anything out of her. Worming couldn't hurt an innocent person.'

'Peter Wimsey! You sit there, looking a perfectly well-bred imbecile, and then in the most underhand way you twist people into doing things they ought to blush for. No wonder you detect things. I will *not* do your worming for you!'

'Well, if you don't, I shall know your opinion, shan't I?'

The girl was silent for a moment. Then she said:

'It's all so beastly.'

'Poisoning is a beastly crime, don't you think?' said Wimsey.

He got up quickly. Father Whittington was approaching with Penberthy.

'Well,' said Lord Peter, 'have the altars reeled?'

'Dr Penberthy has just informed me that they haven't a leg to stand on,' replied the priest, smiling. 'We have been spending a pleasant quarter of an hour abolishing good and evil. Unhappily, I understand his dogma as little as he understands mine. But I exercised myself in Christian humility. I said I was willing to learn.'

Penberthy laughed.

'You don't object, then, to my casting out devils with a syringe,' he said, 'when they have proved obdurate to prayer and fasting?'

'Not at all. Why should I? So long as they *are* cast out. And provided you are certain of your diagnosis.'

Penberthy crimsoned and turned away sharply.

'Oh, lord!' said Wimsey. 'That was a nasty one. From a Christian priest, too!'

'What have I said?' cried Father Whittington, much disconcerted.

'You have reminded Science,' said Wimsey, 'that only the Pope is infallible.'

17

PARKER PLAYS A HAND

'Now, Mrs Mitcham,' said Inspector Parker affably. He was always saying 'Now, Mrs Somebody', and he always remembered to say it affably. It was part of the routine.

The late Lady Dormer's housekeeper bowed frigidly, to indicate that she would submit to questioning.

'We want just to get the exact details of every little thing that happened to General Fentiman the day before he was found dead. I am sure you will help us. Do you recollect exactly what time he got here?'

'It would be round about a quarter to four – not later; I am sure I could not say exactly to the minute.'

'Who let him in?'

'The footman.'

'Did you see him then?'

'Yes; he was shown into the drawing-room, and I came down to him and brought him upstairs to her ladyship's bedroom.'

'Miss Dorland did not see him then?'

'No; she was sitting with her ladyship. She sent her excuses by me, and begged General Fentiman to come up.'

'Did the General seem quite well when you saw him?'

'So far as I could say he seemed well – always bearing in mind that he was a very old gentleman and he had heard bad news.'

'He was not bluish about the lips, or breathing very heavily, or anything of that kind?'

'Well, going up the stairs tired him rather.'

'Yes, of course it would.'

'He stood still on the landing for a few minutes to get his breath. I asked him whether he would like to take something, but he said no, he was all right.'

'Ah! I dare say it would have been a good thing if he had accepted your very wise suggestion, Mrs Mitcham.'

'No doubt he knew best,' replied the housekeeper primly. She considered that in making observations the policeman was stepping out of his sphere.

'And then you showed him in. Did you witness the meeting between himself and Lady Dormer?'

'I did not' (emphatically). 'Miss Dorland got up and said, "How do you do, General Fentiman?" and shook hands with him, and then I left the room, as it was my place to do.'

'Just so. Was Miss Dorland alone with Lady Dormer when General Fentiman was announced?'

'Oh, no – the nurse was there.'

'The nurse – yes, of course. Did Miss Dorland and the nurse stay in the room all the time that the General was there?'

'No. Miss Dorland came out again in about five minutes and came downstairs. She came to me in the housekeeper's room, and she looked rather sad. She said "Poor old dears" – just like that.'

'Did she say any more?'

'She said: "They quarrelled, Mrs Mitcham, ages and ages ago, when they were quite young, and they've never seen each other since." Of course, I was aware of that, having been with her ladyship all these years, and so was Miss Dorland.'

'I expect it would seem very pitiful to a young lady like Miss Dorland?'

'No doubt; she is a young lady with feelings; not like some of those you see nowadays.'

Parker wagged his head sympathetically.

'And then?'

'Then Miss Dorland went away again, after a little talk with me, and presently Nellie came in – that's the housemaid.'

'How long after was that?'

'Oh, some time. I had just finished my cup of tea which I have at four o'clock. It would be about half-past. She came to ask for some brandy for the General, as he was feeling badly. The spirits are kept in my room, you see, and I have the key.'

Parker showed nothing of his special interest in this piece of news.

'Did you see the General when you took the brandy?'

'I did not take it.' Mrs Mitcham's tone implied that fetching and carrying was not part of her duty. 'I sent it by Nellie.'

'I see. So you did not see the General again before he left?'

'No. Miss Dorland informed me later that he had had a heart attack.'

'I am very much obliged to you, Mrs Mitcham. Now I should like to ask Nellie a few questions.'

Mrs Mitcham touched a bell. A fresh-faced, pleasant-looking girl appeared in answer.

'Nellie, this police officer wants you to give him some information about that time General Fentiman came here. You must tell him what he wants to know, but remember he is busy and don't start your chattering. You can speak to Nellie here, officer.'

And she sailed out.

'A bit stiff, isn't she?' murmured Parker in an awe-struck whisper.

'She's one of the old-fashioned sort, I don't mind saying,' agreed Nellie with a laugh.

'She put the wind up me. Now, Nellie' – he took up the old formula – 'I hear you were sent to get some brandy for the old gentleman. Who told you about it?'

'Why, it was like this. After the General had been with Lady Dormer getting on for an hour, the bell rang in her ladyship's room. It was my business to answer that, so I went up, and Nurse Armstrong put her head out and said, "Get me a drop of brandy, Nellie, quick, and ask Miss Dorland to come here. General Fentiman's rather unwell." So I went for the brandy to Mrs Mitcham, and on the way up with it, I knocked at the studio door where Miss Dorland was.'

'Where's that, Nellie?'

'It's a big room on the first floor – built over the kitchen. It used to be a billiard-room in the old days, with a glass roof. That's where Miss Dorland does her paint-ing and messing about with bottles and things, and she uses it as a sitting-room, too.'

'Messing about with bottles?'

'Well, chemists' stuff and things. Ladies have to have their hobbies, you know, not having any work to do. It makes a lot to clear up.'

'I'm sure it does. Well, go on, Nellie – I didn't mean to interrupt.'

'Well, I gave Nurse Armstrong's message, and Miss Dorland said, "Oh, dear, Nellie," she said, "poor old gentleman. It's been too much for him. Give me the brandy; I'll take it along. And run along and get Dr Penberthy on the telephone." So I gave her the brandy and she took it upstairs.'

'Half a moment. Did you see her take it upstairs?'

'Well, no, I don't think I actually saw her go up – but I thought she did. But I was going down to the telephone, so I didn't exactly notice.'

'No – why should you?'

'I had to look Dr Penberthy's number up in the book, of course. There was two numbers, and when I got his private house they told me he was in Harley Street. While I was trying to get the second number, Miss Dorland called over the stairs to me. She said, "Have you got the doctor, Nellie?" and I said, "No, miss, not yet. The doctor's round in Harley Street." And she said, "Oh! well, when you get him, say General Fentiman's had a bad turn and he's coming round to see him at once." So I said, "Isn't the doctor to come here, miss?" And she said, "No; the General's better now, and he says he would rather go round there. Tell William to get a taxi." So she went back, and just then I got through to the surgery and said to Dr Penberthy's man to expect General Fentiman at once. And then he came downstairs with Miss Dorland and Nurse Armstrong holding on to him, and he looked mortal bad, poor old gentleman. William – the footman, you know – came in then and said he'd got the taxi, and he put General Fentiman into it, and then Miss Dorland and nurse went upstairs again, and that was the end of it.'

'I see. How long have you been here, Nellie?'

'Three years – sir.' The 'sir' was a concession to Parker's nice manners and educated way of speech. 'Quite the gentleman,' as Nellie remarked afterwards to Mrs Mitcham, who replied, 'No, Nellie – gentleman-like I will not deny, but a policeman is a person, and I will trouble you to remember it.'

'Three years? That's a long time as things go nowadays. Is it a comfortable place?'

'Not bad. There's Mrs Mitcham, of course, but I know how to keep the right side of her. And the old lady – well, she was a real lady in every way.'

'And Miss Dorland?'

'Oh, she gives no trouble, except clearing up after her. But she always speaks nicely and says please and thank you. I haven't any complaints.'

'Modified rapture,' thought Parker. Apparently Ann Dorland had not the knack of inspiring passionate devotion. 'Not a very lively house is it, for a young girl like yourself?'

'Dull as ditchwater,' agreed Nellie frankly, 'Miss Dorland would have what they called studio parties sometimes, but not at all smart and nearly all young ladies – artists and such-like.'

'And naturally it's been quieter still since Lady Dormer died. Was Miss Dorland very much distressed at her death?'

Nellie hesitated.

'She was very sorry, of course; her ladyship was the only one she had in the world. And then she was worried with all this lawyer's business – something about the will; I expect you know, sir?'

'Yes, I know about that. Worried, was she?'

'Yes, and that angry – you wouldn't believe. There was one day Mr Pritchard came, I remember particular, because I happened to be dusting the hall at the time, you see, and she was speaking that quick and loud I couldn't help hearing. "I'll fight it for all I'm worth," that was what she said, and "a . . . something – to defraud." What would that be, now?'

'Plot?' suggested Parker.

'No – a – a conspiracy, that's it. A conspiracy to defraud. And then I didn't hear any more till Mr Pritchard came out, and he said to her, "Very well, Miss Dorland, we will make an independent inquiry." And Miss Dorland looked so eager and angry, I was surprised. But it all seemed to wear off, like. She hasn't been the same person the last week or so.'

'How do you mean?'

'Well, don't you notice it yourself, sir? She seems so quiet and almost frightened-like. As if she'd had a shock. And she cried a dreadful lot. She didn't do that at first.'

'How long has she been so upset?'

'Well, I think it was when all this dreadful business came out about the poor old gentleman being murdered. It is awful, sir, isn't it? Do you think you'll catch the one as did it?'

'Oh, I expect so,' said Parker cheerfully. 'That came as a shock to Miss Dorland, did it?'

'Well, I should say so. There was a little bit in the paper, you know, sir, about Sir James Lubbock having found out about the poisoning, and when I called Miss Dorland in the morning I took leave to point it out. I said, "That's a funny thing, miss, isn't it, about General Fentiman being poisoned." – just like that, I said. And she said, "Poisoned, Nellie? You must be mistaken." So I showed her the bit in the paper and she looked just dreadful.'

'Well, well,' said Parker, 'it's a very horrid thing to hear about a person one knows. Anybody would be upset.'

'Yes, sir; me and Mrs Mitcham was quite overcome. "Poor old gentleman!" I said; "whatever should anybody want to do him in for? He must have gone off his head and made away with himself," I said. Do you think that was it, sir?'

'It's quite possible, of course,' said Parker genially.

'Cut up about his sister dying like that, don't you think? That's what I said to Mrs Mitcham. But she said a gentleman like General Fentiman wouldn't make away with himself and leave his affairs in confusion like he did. So I said, "Was his affairs in confusion, then?" and she said, "They're not your affairs, Nellie, so you needn't be discussing them." What do you think yourself, sir?'

'I don't think anything yet,' said Parker; 'but you have been very helpful. Now, would you kindly run and ask Miss Dorland if she could spare me a few minutes?'

Ann Dorland received him in the back drawing-room. He thought what an unattractive girl she was, with her sullen manner and gracelessness of form and movement. She sat huddled on one end of the sofa, in a black dress which made the worst of her sallow, blotched complexion. She had certainly been crying, Parker thought, and when she spoke to him it was curtly, in a voice roughened and hoarse and curiously lifeless.

'I am sorry to trouble you again,' said Parker politely.

'You can't help yourself, I suppose.' She avoided his eye, and lit a fresh cigarette from the stump of the last.

'I just want to have any details you can give me about General Fentiman's visit to his sister. Mrs Mitcham brought him up to her bedroom, I understand.'

She gave a sulky nod.

'You were there?'

She made no answer.

'Were you with Lady Dormer?' he insisted, rather more sharply.

'Yes.'

'And the nurse was there too?'

'Yes.'

She would not help him at all.

'What happened?'

'Nothing happened. I took him up to the bed and said, "Auntie, here's General Fentiman."'

'Lady Dormer was conscious, then?'

'Yes.'

'Very weak, of course?'

'Yes.'

'Did she say anything?'

'She said, "Arthur!" – that's all. And he said, "Felicity!" And I said, "You'd like to be alone," and went out.'

'Leaving the nurse there?'

'I couldn't dictate to the nurse. She had to look after her patient.'

'Quite so. Did she stay there throughout the interview?'

'I haven't the least idea.'

'Well,' said Parker patiently, 'you can tell me this. When you went in with the brandy, the nurse was in the bedroom then?'

'Yes, she was.'

'Now, about the brandy. Nellie brought that up to you in the studio, she tells me.'

'Yes.'

'Did she come into the studio?'

'I don't understand.'

'Did she come right into the room, or did she knock at the door and did you come out to her on the landing?'

This roused the girl a little.

'Decent servants don't knock at doors,' she said, with a contemptuous rudeness. 'She came in, of course.'

'I beg your pardon,' retorted Parker, stung. 'I thought she might have knocked at the door of your private room.'

'No.'

'What did she say to you?'

'Can't you ask *her* all these questions?'

'I have done so. But servants are not always accurate; I should like your corroboration.' Parker had himself in hand again now, and spoke pleasantly.

'She said that Nurse Armstrong had sent her for some brandy, because General Fentiman was feeling faint, and told her to call me. So I said she had better go and telephone Dr Penberthy while I took the brandy.'

All this was muttered hurriedly, and in such a low tone that the detective could hardly catch the words.

'And then did you take the brandy straight upstairs?'

'Yes, of course.'

'Taking it straight out of Nellie's hands? Or did she put it down on the table or anywhere?'

'How the hell should I remember?'

Parker disliked a swearing woman, but he tried hard not to let this prejudice him.

'You can't remember – at any rate, you know you went straight on up with it? You didn't wait to do anything else?'

She seemed to pull herself together and make an effort to remember.

'If it's so important as that, I think I stopped to turn down something that was boiling.'

'Boiling? On the fire?'

'On the gas ring,' she said impatiently.

'What sort of thing?'

'Oh, nothing – some stuff.'

'Tea, or cocoa, or something like that, do you mean?'

'No – some chemical things,' she said, letting the words go reluctantly.

'Were you making chemical experiments?'

189

'Yes – I did a bit – just for fun – a hobby, you know. I don't do anything at it now. I took up the brandy—'

Her anxiety to shelve the subject of chemistry seemed to be conquering her reluctance to get on with the story.

'You were making chemical experiments – although Lady Dormer was so ill?' said Parker severely.

'It was just to occupy my mind,' she muttered.

'What was the experiment?'

'I don't remember.'

'You can't remember at all?'

'NO!' she almost shouted at him.

'Never mind. You took the brandy upstairs?'

'Yes – at least, it isn't really upstairs. It's all on the same landing, only there are six steps up to Auntie's room. Nurse Armstrong met me at the door, and said, "He's better now," and I went in and saw General Fentiman sitting in a chair, looking very queer and grey. He was behind a screen where Auntie couldn't see him, or it would have been a great shock to her. Nurse said, "I've given him his drops and I think a little brandy will put him right again." So we gave him the brandy – only a small dose – and after a bit he got less deathly-looking and seemed to be breathing better. I told him we were sending for the doctor, and he said he'd rather go round to Harley Street. I thought it was rash, but Nurse Armstrong said he seemed really better, and it would be a mistake to worry him into doing what he didn't want. So I told Nellie to warn the doctor and send William for a taxi. General Fentiman seemed stronger then, so we helped him downstairs and he went off in the taxi.'

Out of this spate of words Parker fixed on the one thing he had not heard before.

'What drops were those the nurse gave him?'

'His own. He had them in his pocket.'

'Do you think she could possibly have given him too much? Was the quantity marked on the bottle?'

'I haven't the remotest. You'd better ask her.'

'Yes, I shall want to see her, if you will kindly tell me where to find her.'

'I've got the address upstairs. Is that all you want?'

'I should just like, if I may, to see Lady Dormer's room and the studio.'

'What for?'

'It's just a matter of routine. We are under orders to see everything there is to see,' replied Parker reassuringly.

They went upstairs. A door on the first-floor landing immediately opposite the head of the staircase led into a pleasant, lofty room, with old-fashioned bedroom furniture in it.

'This is my aunt's room. She wasn't really my aunt, of course, but I called her so.'

'Quite. Where does that second door lead to?'

'That's the dressing-room. Nurse Armstrong slept there while Auntie was ill.'

Parker glanced into the dressing-room, took in the arrangement of the bedroom and expressed himself satisfied.

She walked past him without acknowledgement while he held the door open. She was a sturdily-built girl, but moved with a languor distressing to watch – slouching, almost aggressively unalluring.

'You want to see the studio?'

'Please.'

She led the way down the six steps and along a short passage to the room which, as Parker already knew, was built out the back over the kitchen premises. He mentally calculated the distance as he went.

The studio was large and well-lit by its glass roof. One end was furnished like a sitting-room; the other was left bare, and devoted to what Nellie called 'mess'. A very ugly picture (in Parker's opinion) stood on an easel. Other canvases were stacked round the walls. In one corner was a table covered with American cloth, on which stood a gas ring, protected by a tin plate, and a Bunsen burner.

'I'll look up that address,' said Miss Dorland indifferently; 'I've got it here somewhere.'

She began to rummage in an untidy desk. Parker strolled up to the business end of the room and explored it with eyes, nose and fingers.

The ugly picture on the easel was newly painted; the smell told him that, and the dabs of paint on the palette were still soft and sticky. Work had been done there within the last two days, he was sure. The brushes had been stuck at random into a small pot of turpentine. He lifted them out; they were still clogged with paint. The picture itself was a landscape, he thought, roughly drawn and hot and restless in colour. Parker was no judge of art; he would have liked to get Wimsey's opinion. He explored further. The table with the Bunsen burner was bare, but in a cupboard close by he discovered a quantity of chemical apparatus of the kind he remembered using at school. Everything had been tidily washed and stacked away. Nellie's job, he imagined. There were a number of simple and familiar chemical substances in jars and packages occupying a couple of shelves. They would probably have to be analysed, he thought, to see if they were all they seemed. And what useless nonsense it all was, he thought to himself; anything suspicious would obviously have been destroyed weeks before. Still, there it was. A book in several volumes on the top shelf caught his attention; it was Quain's *Dictionary of Medicine*. He took down a volume in which he noticed a paper mark. Opening it at the marked place, his eye fell upon the words: '*Rigor mortis*', and a little later on, 'action of certain poisons'. He was about to read more, when he heard Miss Dorland's voice just behind him.

'That's all nothing,' she said. 'I don't do any of that muck now. It was just a passing craze. I paint, really. What do you think of this?' She indicated the unpleasant landscape.

Parker said it was very good.

'Aren't these your work, too?' he asked, indicating the other canvases.

'Yes,' she said.

He turned a few of them to the light, noticing at the same time how dusty they were. Nellie had scamped this bit of the work – or perhaps had been told not to touch. Miss Dorland showed a trifle more animation than she had done hitherto while displaying her works. Landscape seemed to be rather a new departure; most of the canvases were figure studies. Mr Parker thought that, on the whole, the artist had done wisely to turn to landscape. He was not well acquainted with the modern school of thought in painting, and had difficulty in expressing his opinion of these curious figures, with their faces like eggs and their limbs like rubber.

'That is the "Judgement of Paris",' said Miss Dorland.

'Oh, yes,' said Parker. 'And this?'

'Oh, just a study of a woman dressing. It's not very good. I think this portrait of Mrs Mitcham is rather decent, though.'

Parker stared aghast; it might possibly be a symbolic representation of Mrs Mitcham's character, for it was very hard and spiky; but it looked more like a Dutch doll, with its triangular nose, like a sharp-edged block of wood, and its eyes mere dots in an expanse of liver-coloured cheek.

'It's not very like her,' he said doubtfully.

'It's not meant to be.'

'This seems better – I mean, I like this better,' said Parker, turning the next picture up hurriedly.

'Oh, that's nothing – just a fancy head.'

Evidently this picture – the head of a rather cadaverous man, with a sinister smile and a slight cast in the eye – was despised, a Philistine back-sliding, almost like a human being. It was put away, and Parker tried to concentrate his attention on a 'Madonna and Child' which, to Parker's simple evangelical mind, seemed an abominable blasphemy.

Happily, Miss Dorland soon wearied, even of her paintings, and flung them all back into the corner.

'D'you want anything else?' she demanded abruptly. 'Here's that address.'

Parker took it.

'Just one more question,' he said, looking her hard in the eyes. 'Before Lady Dormer died – before General Fentiman came to see her – did you know what provision she had made for him in her will?'

The girl stared back at him, and he saw panic come into her eyes. It seemed to flow all over her like a wave. She clenched her hands at her sides, and her miserable eyes dropped beneath his gaze, shifting as though looking for a way out.

'Well?' said Parker.

'No!' she said. 'No! of course not. Why should I?'

Then, surprisingly, a dull crimson flush flooded her sallow cheeks and ebbed away, leaving her looking like death.

'Go away,' she said furiously; 'you make me sick!'

18

PICTURE-CARDS

'So I've put a man in and had all the things in that cupboard taken away for examination,' said Parker.

Lord Peter shook his head.

'I wish I had been there,' he said; 'I should have liked to see those paintings. However—'

'They might have conveyed something to you,' said Parker; 'you're artistic. You can come along and look at them any time, of course. But it's the time factor that's worrying me, you know. Supposing she gave the old boy digitalin in his B. and S., why should it wait all that time before working? According to the books, it ought to have pooped off in about an hour's time. It was a biggish dose, according to Lubbock.'

'I know. I think you're up against a snag there. That's why I should have liked to see the pictures.'

Parker considered this apparent *non sequitur* for a few moments, and gave it up.

'George Fentiman—' he began.

'Yes,' said Wimsey, 'George Fentiman. I must be getting emotional in my old age, Charles, for I have an unconquerable dislike to examining the question of George Fentiman's opportunities.'

'Bar Robert,' pursued Parker ruthlessly, 'he was the last interested person to see General Fentiman.'

'Yes – by the way, we have only Robert's unsupported word for what happened in that last interview between him and the old man.'

'Come, Wimsey – you're not going to pretend that Robert had any interest in his grandfather's dying before Lady Dormer. On the contrary.'

'No – but he might have had some interest in his dying before he made a will. Those notes on that bit of paper. The larger share was to go to George. That doesn't entirely agree with what Robert said. And if there was no will, Robert stood to get everything.'

'So he did. But by killing the General then, he made sure of getting nothing at all.'

'That's the awkwardness. Unless he thought Lady Dormer was already dead. But I don't see how he could have thought that. Or unless—'

'Well?'

'Unless he gave his grandfather a pill or something to be taken at some future time, and the old boy took it too soon by mistake.'

'That idea of a delayed-action pill is the most tiresome thing about this case. It makes almost anything possible.'

'Including, of course, the theory of its being given to him by Miss Dorland.'

'That's what I'm going to interview the nurse about, the minute I can get hold of her. But we've got away from George.'

'You're right. Let's face George. I don't want to, though. Like the lady in Maeterlinck who's running round the table while her husband tries to polish her off with a hatchet, I am not gay. George is the nearest in point of time. In fact he fits very well in point of time. He parted from General Fentiman at about half-past six, and Robert found Fentiman dead at about eight o'clock. So, allowing that the stuff was given in a pill—'

'Which it would have to be, in a taxi,' interjected Parker.

'As you say – in a pill, which would take a bit longer to get working than the same stuff taken in solution – why, then the General might quite well have been able to get to the Bellona and see Robert before collapsing.'

'Very nice. But how did George get the drug?'

'I know, that's the first difficulty.'

'And how did he happen to have it on him just at that time? He couldn't possibly have known that General Fentiman would run across him just at that moment. Even if he'd known of his being at Lady Dormer's, he could be expecting him to go from there to Harley Street.'

'He might have been carrying the stuff about with him, waiting for a good opportunity to use it. And when the old man called him up and started jawing him about his conduct and all that, he thought he'd better do the job quick, before he was cut out of the will.'

'Um! – but why should George be such a fool, then, as to admit he'd never heard about Lady Dormer's will? If he had heard of it, we couldn't possibly suspect him. He'd only to say the General told him about it in the taxi.'

'I suppose it hadn't struck him in that light.'

'Then George is a bigger ass than I took him for.'

'Possibly he is,' said Parker dryly. 'At any rate, I have put a man on to make inquiries at his home.'

'Oh, have you? I say, do you know, I wish I'd left this case alone. What the deuce did it matter if old Fentiman was pushed painlessly off a bit before his time? He was simply indecently ancient.'

'We'll see if you say that in sixty years' time,' said Parker.

'By that time we shall, I hope, be moving in different circles. I shall be in the one devoted to murderers, and you in the much lower and hotter one devoted to those who tempt others to murder them. I wash my hands of this case, Charles. There's nothing for me to do now you have come into it. It bores and annoys me. Let's talk about something else.'

Wimsey might wash his hands, but, like Pontius Pilate, he found society irrationally determined to connect him with an irritating and unsatisfactory case.

At midnight the telephone bell rang.

He had just gone to bed, and cursed it.

'Tell them I'm out,' he shouted to Bunter, and cursed again on hearing the man assure the unknown caller that he would see whether his lordship had returned. Disobedience in Bunter spelt urgent necessity.

'Well?'

'It is Mrs George Fentiman, my lord; she appears to be in great distress. If your lordship wasn't in I was to beg you to communicate with her as soon as you arrived.'

'Punk! they're not on the phone.'

'No, my lord.'

'Did she say what the matter was?'

'She began by asking if Mr George Fentiman was here, my lord.'

'Oh, Hades!'

Bunter advanced gently with his master's dressing-gown and slippers. Wimsey thrust himself into them savagely and padded away to the telephone.

'Hallo!'

'Is that Lord Peter? Oh, *good*!' The line sighed with relief – a harsh sound, like a death-rattle. 'Do you know where George is?'

'No idea. Hasn't he come home?'

'No – and I'm – frightened. Some people were here this morning . . .'

'The police.'

'Yes . . . George . . . they found something . . . I can't say it all over the phone . . . but George went off to Walmisley-Hubbard's with the car . . . and they say he never came back there . . . and . . . you remember that time he was so funny before . . . and got lost . . .'

'Your six minutes are up,' boomed the voice of the Exchange; 'will you have another call?'

'Yes, please . . . oh, don't cut us off . . . wait . . . oh! I haven't any more pennies . . . Lord Peter . . .'

'I'll come round at once,' said Wimsey, with a groan.

'Oh, thank you – thank you so much!'

'I say – where's Robert?'

'Your six minutes are up,' said the voice finally, and the line went dead with a metallic crash.

'Get me my clothes,' said Wimsey bitterly; 'give me those loathsome and despicable rags which I hoped to have put off for ever. Get me a taxi. Get me a drink. Macbeth has murdered sleep. Oh! and get me Robert Fentiman, first.'

Major Fentiman was not in town, said Woodward. He had gone back to Richmond again. Wimsey tried to get through to Richmond. After a long time, a female voice, choked with sleep and fury, replied. Major Fentiman had not come home. Major Fentiman kept very late hours. Would she give Major Fentiman a message when he did come in? Indeed she would not. She had other things to do than to stay up all night answering telephone calls and giving messages to Major Fentiman. This was the second time that night, and she had told the other party that she could not be responsible for telling Major Fentiman this, that and the other. Would she leave a note for Major Fentiman, asking him to go round to his brother's house at once? Well, now, was it reasonable to expect her to sit up on a bitter cold night writing letters? Of course not; but this was a case of urgent illness. It would be a very great kindness. Just that – to go round to his brother's house and say the call came from Lord Peter Wimsey.

'Who?'

'Lord Peter Wimsey.'

'Very well, sir. I beg your pardon if I was a bit short, but really—'

'You weren't, you snobby old cat, you were infernally long,' breathed his lordship inaudibly. He thanked her, and rang off.

Sheila Fentiman was anxiously waiting for him on the doorstep, so that he was saved the embarrassment of trying to remember which was the right number of rings to give. She clasped his hand eagerly as she drew him in.

'Oh, it is good of you! I'm so worried. I say, don't make a noise, will you? They complain, you know.' She spoke in a harassed whisper.

'Blast them, let them complain,' said Wimsey cheerfully. 'Why shouldn't you make a row when George is upset? Besides, if we whisper, they'll think we're no better than we ought to be. Now, my child, what's all this? You're as cold as a *pêche Melba*. That won't do. Fire half out – where's the whisky?'

'Hush! I'm all right, really. George—'

'You're not all right. Nor am I. As George Robey says, this getting up from my warm bed and going into the cold night air doesn't suit me.' He flung a generous shovelful of coals on the fire and thrust the poker between the bars. 'And you've had no grub. No wonder you're feeling awful.'

Two places were set at the table – untouched – waiting for George. Wimsey plunged into the kitchen premises, followed by Sheila uttering agitated remonstrances. He found some disagreeable remnants – a watery stew, cold and sodden; a basin half-full of some kind of tinned soup; a chill suet pudding put away on a shelf.

'Does your woman cook for you? I suppose she does, as you're both out all day. Well, she can't cook, my child. No matter, here's some Bovril – she can't have hurt that. You go and sit down and I'll make you some.'

'Mrs Munns—'

'Blow Mrs Munns!'

'But I must tell you about George.'

He looked at her, and decided that she really must tell him about George.

'I'm sorry. I didn't mean to bully. One has an ancestral idea that women must be treated like imbeciles in a crisis. Centuries of the "women-and-children-first" idea, I suppose. Poor devils!'

'Who – the women?'

'Yes. No wonder they sometimes lose their heads. Pushed into corners, told nothing of what's happening, and made to sit quiet and do nothing. Strong men would go dotty in the circs. I suppose that's why we've always grabbed the privilege of rushing about and doing the heroic bits.'

'That's quite true. Give me the kettle.'

'No, no, I'll do that. You sit down and – I mean, sorry, *take* the kettle. Fill it, light the gas, put it on. And tell me about George.'

The trouble, it seemed, had begun at breakfast. Ever since the story of the murder had come out, George had been very nervy and jumpy, and, to Shella's horror, had 'started muttering again.' 'Muttering', Wimsey remembered, had formerly been the prelude to one of George's 'queer fits'. These had been a form of shell-shock, and they had generally ended in his going off and wandering about in a distraught manner for several days, sometimes with partial and occasionally with complete temporary loss of memory. There was the time when he had been found dancing naked in a field among a flock of sheep, and singing to them. It had been the more ludicrously painful in that George was altogether tone-deaf, so that his singing, though loud, was like a hoarse and rumbling wind in the chimney. Then there was a dreadful time when George had deliberately walked into a bonfire. That was when they had been staying down in the country. George had been badly burnt, and the shock of the pain had brought him round. He never remembered afterwards why he had tried to do these things, and had only the faintest recollection of having done them at all. The next vagary might be even more disconcerting.

At any rate, George had been 'muttering'.

They were at breakfast that morning, when they saw two men coming up the path. Sheila, who sat opposite the window, saw them first, and said carelessly: 'Hallo! who are these? They look like plain-clothes policemen.' George took one look, jumped up and rushed out of the room. She called to him to know what was the matter, but he did not answer, and she heard him 'rummaging' in the back room, which was the bedroom. She was going to him, when she heard Mr Munns open the door to the policemen and then heard them inquiring for George. Mr Munns ushered them into the front room with a grim face on which 'police' seemed written in capital letters. George—

At this point the kettle boiled. Sheila was taking it off the stove to make the Bovril, when Wimsey became aware of a hand on his coat-collar. He looked round into the face of a gentleman who appeared not to have shaved for several days.

'Now then,' said this apparition, 'what's the meaning of this?'

'Which,' added an indignant voice from the door, 'I thought as there was something behind all this talk of the Captain being missing. You didn't expect him to be missing, I suppose, ma'am. Oh, dear no! Nor your gentleman friend, neither, sneaking up in a taxi and you waiting at the door so's Munns and me shouldn't hear. But I'll have you know this is a respectable house, Lord Knows Who or whatever you call yourself – more likely one of these low-down confidence fellers, I expect, if the truth was known. With a monocle, too, like that man we was reading about in the *News of the World*. And in my kitchen, too, and drinking my Bovril in the middle of the night – the impudence! Not to speak of the goings-in-and-out all day, banging the front door, and that the police come here this morning – you think I didn't know? Up to something, that's what they've been, the pair of them, and the Captain as he says he is – but that's as may be. I dare say he had his reasons for clearing off, and the sooner you goes after him, my fine madam, the better I'll be pleased, I can tell you.'

'That's right,' said Mr Munns – 'Ow!'

Lord Peter had removed the intrusive hand from his collar with a sharp jerk which happened to cause anguish out of all proportion to the force used.

'I'm glad you've come along,' he said. 'In fact, I was just going to give you a call. Have you anything to drink in the house, by the way?'

'Drink?' cried Mrs Munns on a high note; 'the impudence! And if I see you, Joe, giving drinks to thieves and worse in the middle of the night in my kitchen, you'll get a piece of my mind. Coming in here as bold as brass, and the Captain run away, and asking for drink—'

'Because,' said Wimsey, fingering his note-case, 'the public-houses in this law-abiding neighbourhood are, of course, closed. Otherwise a bottle of Scotch—'

Mr Munns appeared to hesitate.

'Call yourself a man!' said Mrs Munns.

'Of course,' said Mr Munns, 'if I was to go in a friendly manner to Jimmy Rowe at the "Dragon", and ask him to give me a bottle of Johnnie Walker as a friend to a friend, and provided no money was to pass between him and me, that is—'

'A good idea,' said Wimsey cordially.

Mrs Munns gave a loud shriek.

'The ladies,' said Mr Munns, 'gets nervous at times.' He shrugged his shoulders.

'I dare say a drop of Scotch wouldn't do Mrs Munns's nerves any harm,' said Wimsey.

'If you dare, Joe Munns,' said the landlady, 'if you dare go out at this time of night, hob-nobbing with Jimmy Rowe and making a fool yourself with burglars and such—'

Mr Munns executed a sudden *volte-face*.

'You shut up!' he shouted. 'Always sticking your face in where you aren't wanted.'

'Are you speaking to me?'

'Yes. Shut up!'

Mrs Munns sat down suddenly on a kitchen chair and began to sniff.

'I'll just hop round to the "Dragon" now, sir,' said Mr Munns, 'before old Jimmy goes to bed. And then we'll go into this here.'

He departed. Possibly he forgot what he had said about no money passing, for he certainly took the note which Wimsey absent-mindedly held out to him.

'Your drink's getting cold,' said Wimsey to Sheila.

She came across to him.

'Can't we get rid of these people?'

'In half a jiff. It's no good having a row with them. I'd do it like a shot, only, you see, you've got to stay on here for a bit, in case George comes back.'

'Of course. I'm sorry for all this upset, Mrs Munns,' she added, a little stiffly, 'but I'm so worried about my husband.'

'Husband?' snorted Mrs Munns. 'A lot husbands are to worry about. Look at that Joe. Off he goes to the "Dragon", never mind what I say to him. They're dirt, that's what husbands are, the whole pack of them. And I don't care what anybody says.'

'Are they?' said Wimsey. 'Well, I'm not one – yet – so you needn't mind what you say to me.'

'It's the same thing,' said the lady viciously; 'husbands and parricides, there's not a halfpenny to choose between them. Only parricides aren't respectable – but then, they're easier got rid of.'

'Oh!' replied Wimsey, 'but I'm not a parricide either – not Mrs Fentiman's parricide, at any rate, I assure you. Hallo! here's Joe. Did you get the doings, old man? You did? Good work. Now, Mrs Munns, have just a spot with us. You'll feel all the better for it. And why shouldn't we go into the sitting-room where it's warmer?'

Mrs Munns complied. 'Oh, well,' she said, 'here's friends all round. But you'll allow it all looked a bit queer, now, didn't it? And the police this morning, asking all those questions, and emptying the dustbin all over the backyard.'

'Whatever did they want with the dustbin?'

'Lord knows; and that Cummins woman looking on all the time over the wall. I can tell you, I was vexed.

"Why, Mrs Munns," she said, "have you been poisoning people?" she said. "I always told you," she said, "your cooking 'ud do for somebody one of these days." The nasty cat.'

'What a rotten thing to say,' said Wimsey sympathetically. 'Just jealousy, I expect. But what did the police find in the dustbin?'

'Find? Them find anything? I should like to see them finding things in my dustbin. The less I see of their interfering ways the better I'm pleased. I told them so. I said, "If you want to come upsetting my dustbin," I said, "you'll have to come with a search-warrant," I said. That's the law, and they couldn't deny it. They said Mrs Fentiman had given them leave to look, so I told them Mrs Fentiman had no leave to give them. It was my dustbin, I told them, not hers. So they went off with a flea in their ear.'

'That's the stuff to give 'em, Mrs Munns.'

'Not but what I'm respectable. If the police come to me in a right and lawful manner, I'll gladly give them any help they want. I don't want to get into trouble, not for any number of captains. But interference with a free-born woman and no search-warrant I will *not* stand. And they can either come to me in a fitting way, or they can go and whistle for their bottle.'

'What bottle?' asked Wimsey quickly.

'The bottle they were looking for in my dustbin, what the Captain put there after breakfast.'

Sheila gave a faint cry.

'What bottle was that, Mrs Munns?'

'One of them little tablet bottles,' said Mrs Munns, 'same as you have standing on the wash-hand stand, Mrs Fentiman. When I saw the Captain smashing it up in the yard with a poker—'

'There now, Primrose,' said Mr Munns, 'can't you see as Mrs Fentiman ain't well?'

'I'm quite all right,' said Sheila hastily, pushing away the hair which clung damply to her forehead. 'What was my husband doing?'

'I saw him,' said Mrs Munns, 'run out into the backyard – just after your breakfast it was, because I recollect Munns was letting the officers into the house at the time. Not that I knew then who it was, for, if you'll excuse me mentioning of it, I was in the outside lavatory, and that was how I come to see the Captain. Which ordinarily, you can't see the dustbin from the house – my lord I should say, I suppose, if you really are one, but you meet so many bad characters nowadays that one can't be too careful – on account of the lavatory standing out as you may say and hiding it.'

'Just so,' said Wimsey.

'So when I saw the Captain breaking the bottle as I said, and throwing the bits into the dustbin, 'Hallo!' I said, 'that's funny' and I went to see what it was and I put it in an envelope, thinking, you see, as it might be something poisonous, and the cat such a dreadful thief as he is, I never can keep him out of that dustbin. And when I came in, I found the police here. So after a bit, I found them poking about in the yard and I asked them what they were doing there. Such a mess as they'd made, you never would believe. So they showed me a little cap they'd found, same as it might be off that tablet bottle. "Did I know where the rest of it was?" they said. And I said, what business had they got with the dustbin at all. So they said—'

'Yes, I know,' said Wimsey. 'I think you acted very sensibly, Mrs Munns. And what did you do with the envelope and things?'

'I kept it,' replied Mrs Munns, nodding her head. 'I kept it. Because, you see, if they *did* return *with* a warrant and I'd destroyed that bottle, where should *I* be?'

'Quite right,' said Wimsey, with his eye on Sheila.

'Always keep on the right side of the law,' agreed Mr Munns, 'and nobody can't interfere with you. That's what I say. I'm a Conservative, I am. I don't hold with these Socialist games. Have another.'

'Not just now,' said Wimsey. 'And we really must not keep you and Mrs Munns up any longer. But, look here! You see, Captain Fentiman had shell-shock after the War, and he is liable to do these little odd things at times – break things up, I mean, and lose his memory and go wandering about. So Mrs Fentiman is naturally anxious about his not having turned up this evening.'

'Aye,' said Mr Munns, with relish, 'I knew a fellow like that. Went clean off his rocker he did one night. Smashed up his family with a beetle – a paviour he was by profession, and that's how he came to have a beetle in the house – pounded 'em to a jelly, he did, his wife and five little children, and went off and drownded himself in the Regent's Canal. And, what's more, when they got him out, he didn't remember a word about it, not one word. So they sent him to – what's that place? Dartmoor? no, Broadmoor, that's it, where Ronnie True went to with his little toys and all.'

'Shut up, you fool,' said Wimsey savagely.

'Haven't you got feelings?' demanded his wife.

Sheila got up, and made a blind effort in the direction of the door.

'Come and lie down,' said Wimsey, 'you're worn out. Hallo! there's Robert, I expect. I left a message for him to come round as soon as he got home.'

Mr Munns went to answer the bell.

'We'd better get her to bed as quickly as possible,' said Wimsey to the landlady. 'Have you got such a thing as a hot-water bottle?'

Mrs Munns departed to fetch one, and Sheila caught Wimsey's hand.

'Can't you get hold of that bottle? Make her give it to you. You can. You can do anything. Make her.'

'Better not,' said Wimsey. 'Look suspicious. Look here, Sheila, what *is* the bottle?'

'My heart medicine. I missed it. It's something to do with digitalin.'

'Oh, lord,' said Wimsey, as Robert came in.

'It's all pretty damnable' said Robert.

He thumped the fire gloomily; it was burning badly, the lower bars were choked with the ashes of a day and night.

'I've been having a talk with Frobisher,' he added. 'All this talk in the Club – and the papers – naturally he couldn't overlook it.'

'Was he decent?'

'Very decent. But of course I couldn't explain the thing. I'm sending in my papers.'

Wimsey nodded. Colonel Frobisher could scarcely overlook an attempted fraud – not after things had been said in the papers.

'If I'd only let the old man alone. Too late now. He'd have been buried. Nobody would have asked questions.'

'I didn't *want* to interfere,' said Wimsey, defending himself against the unspoken reproach.

'Oh, I know. I'm not blaming you. People . . . money oughtn't to depend on people's deaths . . . old people, with no use for their lives . . . it's a devil of a temptation.

Look here, Wimsey, what are we to do about this woman?'

'The Munns female?'

'Yes. It's the devil and all she should have got hold of the stuff. If they find out what it's supposed to be, we shall be blackmailed for the rest of our lives.'

'No,' said Wimsey, 'I'm sorry, old man, but the police have got to know about it.'

Robert sprang to his feet.

'My God! – you wouldn't—'

'Sit down, Fentiman. Yes, I must. Don't you see I must? We can't suppress things. It always means trouble. It's not even as though they hadn't got their eye on us already. They're suspicious—'

'Yes, and why?' burst out Robert violently. 'Who put it into their heads? . . . For God's sake don't start talking about law and justice! Law and justice! You'd sell your best friend for the sake of making a sensational appearance in the witness-box, you infernal little police spy!'

'Chuck that, Fentiman!'

'I'll not chuck it! You'd go and give away a man to the police – when you know perfectly well he isn't responsible – just because you can't afford to be mixed up in anything unpleasant. I know you. Nothing's too dirty for you to meddle in, provided you can pose as the pious little friend of justice. You make me sick!'

'I tried to keep out of this—'

'You tried! – don't be a blasted hypocrite! You get out of it now, and stay out – do you hear?'

'Yes, but listen a moment—'

'Get out!' said Robert.

Wimsey stood up.

'I know how you feel, Fentiman—'

'Don't stand there being righteous and forbearing, you

sickening prig. For the last time – are you going to shut up, or are you going to trot round to your policeman friend and earn the thanks of a grateful country for splitting on George? Get on! Which is it to be?'

'You won't do George any good—'

'Never mind that. Are you going to hold your tongue?'

'Be reasonable, Fentiman.'

'Reasonable be damned. Are you going to the police? No shuffling. Yes or no?'

'Yes.'

'You dirty little squirt,' said Robert, striking out passionately. Wimsey's return blow caught him neatly, on the chin and landed him in the waste-paper basket.

'And now, look here,' said Wimsey, standing over him, hat and stick in hand. 'It's no odds to me what you do or say. You think your brother murdered your grandfather. I don't know whether he did or not. But the worst thing you can do for him is to try and destroy evidence. And the worst thing you can possibly do for his wife is to make her a party to anything of this sort. And next time you try to smash anybody's face in, remember to cover up your chin. That's all, I can let myself out. Good-bye.'

He went round to 12, Great Ormond Street and routed Parker out of bed.

Parker listened thoughtfully to what he had to say.

'I wish we'd stopped Fentiman before he bolted,' he said.

'Yes; why didn't you?'

'Well, Dykes seems to have muffed it rather. I wasn't there myself. But everything seemed all right. Fentiman looked a bit nervy, but many people do when they're interviewed by the police – think of their hideous pasts, I suppose, and wonder what's coming next. Or else it's just

212

stagefright. He stuck to the same tale he told you – said he was quite sure the old General hadn't taken any pills or anything in the taxi – didn't attempt to pretend he knew anything about Lady Dormer's will. There was nothing to detain him for. He said he had to get to his job in Great Portland Street. So they let him go. Dykes sent a man to follow him up, and he went along to Walmisley-Hubbard's all right. Dykes said, might he just have a look round the place before he went, and Mrs Fentiman said certainly. He didn't expect to find anything, really. Just happened to step into the backyard, and saw a bit of broken glass. He then had a look round, and there was the cap of the tablet-bottle in the dustbin. Well, then, of course, he started to get interested, and was just having a hunt through the rest of it, when old mother Munns appeared and said the dustbin was her property. So they had to clear out. But Dykes oughtn't to have let Fentiman go till they'd finished going over the place. He phoned through to Walmisley-Hubbard's at once, and heard that Fentiman had arrived and immediately gone out with the car, to visit a prospective customer in Herts. The fellow who was supposed to be trailing Fentiman got carburettor trouble just beyond St Albans, and by the time he was fixed, he'd lost Fentiman.'

'Did Fentiman go to the customer's house?'

'Not he. Disappeared completely. We shall find the car, of course – it's only a matter of time.'

'Yes,' said Wimsey. His voice sounded tired and constrained.

'This alters the look of things a bit,' said Parker, 'doesn't it?'

'Yes.'

'What have you done to your face, old man?'

Wimsey glanced at the looking-glass, and saw that an angry red flush had come up on the cheek-bone.

'Had a bit of a dust-up with Robert,' he said.

'Oh!'

Parker was aware of a thin veil of hostility, drawn between himself and the friend he valued. He knew that for the first time, Wimsey was seeing him as the police. Wimsey was ashamed and his shame made Parker ashamed too.

'You'd better have some breakfast,' said Parker. His voice sounded awkward to himself.

'No – no thanks, old man. I'll go home and get a bath and shave.'

'Oh, right-oh!'

There was a pause.

'Well, I'd better be going,' said Wimsey.

'Oh, yes,' said Parker again. 'Right-oh!'

'Er – cheerio!' said Wimsey at the door.

'Cheerio!' said Parker.

The bedroom-door shut. The flat-door shut. The front-door shut.

Parker pulled the telephone towards him and called up Scotland Yard.

The atmosphere of his own office was bracing to Parker when he got down there. For one thing, he was taken aside by a friend and congratulated in conspiratorial whispers.

'Your promotion's gone through,' said the friend. 'Dead certainty. The Chief's no end pleased. Between you and me, of course. But you've got your Chief-Inspectorship all right. Damn good.'

Then, at 10 o'clock, the news came through that the missing Walmisley-Hubbard had turned up. It had been abandoned in a remote Hertfordshire lane. It was in perfectly good order, the gear-lever in neutral and the tank full of petrol. Evidently, Fentiman had left it and wandered away somewhere, but he could not be far off. Parker made the necessary arrangements for combing out the neighbourhood. The bustle and occupation soothed his mind. Guilty or insane or both, George Fentiman had to be found; it was just a job to be done.

The man who had been sent to interview Mrs Munns (armed this time with a warrant) returned with the fragments of the bottle and tablets. Parker duly passed these along to the police analyst. One of the detectives who was shadowing Miss Dorland rang up to announce that a young woman had come to see her, and that the two had then come out carrying a suit-case and driven away in a taxi. Maddison, the other detective, was following them. Parker said, 'All right; stay where you are for the present,' and considered this new development. The telephone rang again. He thought it would be Maddison, but it was Wimsey – a determinedly brisk and cheerful Wimsey this time.

'I say, Charles, I want something.'

'What?'

'I want to go and see Miss Dorland.'

'You can't. She's gone off somewhere. My man hasn't reported yet.'

'Oh! Well, never mind her. What I really want to see is her studio.'

'Yes? Well, there's no reason why you shouldn't.'

'Will they let me in?'

'Probably not. I'll meet you there and take you in with me. I was going out anyway. I've got to interview the nurse. We've just got hold of her.'

'Thanks awfully. Sure you can spare the time?'

'Yes. I'd like your opinion.'

'I'm glad somebody wants it. I'm beginning to feel like a pelican in the wilderness.'

'Rot! I'll be round in ten minutes.'

'Of course,' explained Parker, as he ushered Wimsey into the studio, 'we've taken away all the chemicals and things. There's not much to look at, really.'

'Well, you can deal best with all that. It's the books and paintings I want to look at. H'm! Books, you know, Charles, are like lobster-shells. We surround ourselves with 'em, and then we grow out of 'em and leave 'em behind, as evidences of our earlier stages of development.'

'That's a fact,' said Parker. 'I've got rows of schoolboy stuff at home – never touch it now, of course. And W.J. Locke – read everything he wrote, once upon a time. And Le Queux, and Conan Doyle, and all that stuff.'

'And now you read theology. And what else?'

'Well, I read Hardy a good bit. And when I'm not too tired I have a go at Henry James.'

'The refined self-examinations of the infinitely-sophisticated. 'M-m. Well now. Let's start with the shelves by the fireplace. Dorothy Richardson – Virginia Woolf – E. B. C. Jones – May Sinclair – Katherine Mansfield – the modern female writers are well represented, aren't they? Galsworthy. Yes. No J. D. Beresford – no Wells – no Bennett. Dear me, quite a row of D. H. Lawrence. I wonder if she reads him very often?'

He pulled down *Women in Love* at random, and slapped the pages open and shut.

'Not kept very well dusted, are they? But they have been read. Compton Mackenzie – Storm Jameson – yes – I see.'

'The medical stuff is over here.'

'Oh! – a few textbooks – first steps in chemistry. What's that tumbled down at the back of the book-case. Louis Berman, eh? *The Personal Equation.* And here's *Why We Behave Like Human Beings.* And Julian Huxley's essays. A determined effort at self-education, what?'

'Girls seem to go in for that sort of thing nowadays.'

'Yes – hardly nice, is it? Hallo!'

'What?'

'Over here by the couch. This represents the latest of our lobster-shells, I fancy. Austin Freeman, Austin Freeman, Austin Freeman – bless me! she must have ordered him in wholesale. *Through the Wall* – that's a good 'tec story, Charles – all about the third degree – Isabel Ostrander – three Edgar Wallaces – the girl's been indulging in an orgy of crime!'

'I shouldn't wonder,' said Parker, with emphasis. 'That fellow Freeman is full of plots about poisonings and wills and survivorship, isn't he?'

'Yes.' Wimsey balanced *A Silent Witness* gently in his hand, and laid it down again. 'This one, for instance, is all about a bloke who murdered somebody and kept him in cold storage till he was ready to dispose of him. It would suit Robert Fentiman.'

Parker grinned.

'A bit elaborate for the ordinary criminal. But I dare say people do get ideas out of these books. Like to look at the pictures? They're pretty awful.'

'Don't try to break it gently. Show us the worst at once . . . Oh, lord!'

'Well, it gives *me* a pain,' said Parker. But I thought perhaps that was my lack of artistic education.'

'It was your natural good taste. What vile colour, and viler drawing.'

'But nobody cares about drawing nowadays, do they?'

'Ah! but there's a difference between the man who can draw and won't draw, and the man who can't draw at all. Go on. Let's see the rest.'

Parker produced them, one after the other. Wimsey glanced quickly at each. He had picked up the brush and palette and was fingering them as he talked.

'These,' he said, 'are the paintings of a completely untalented person, who is, moreover, trying to copy the mannerisms of a very advanced school. By the way, you have noticed, of course, that she has been painting within the last few days, but chucked it in sudden disgust. She has left the paints on the palette, and the brushes are still stuck in the turps, turning their ends up and generally ruining themselves. Suggestive, I fancy. The – stop a minute! Let's look at that again.'

Parker had brought forward the head of the sallow, squinting man which he had mentioned to Wimsey before.

'Put that up on the easel. That's very interesting. The others, you see, are all an effort to imitate other people's art, but this – this is an effort to imitate nature. Why? It's very bad, but it's meant for somebody. And it's been worked on a lot. Now what was it made her do that?'

'Well, it wasn't for his beauty, I should think.'

'No? But there must have been a reason. Dante, you may remember, once painted an angel. Do you know the limerick about the old man of Khartum?'

'What did he do?'

'He kept two black sheep in his room. They remind me (he said) Of two friends who are dead, But I cannot remember of whom.'

'If that reminds you of anyone you know, I don't care much for your friends. I never saw an uglier mug.'

'He's not beautiful. But I think the sinister squint is

chiefly due to bad drawing. It's very difficult to get eyes looking the same way, when you can't draw. Cover up one eye, Charles – not yours, the portrait's.'

Parker did so.

Wimsey looked again, and shook his head.

'It escapes me for the moment,' he said. 'Probably it's nobody I know after all. But, whoever it is, surely this room tells you something.'

'It suggests to me,' said Parker, 'that the girl's been taking more interest in crimes and chemistry stuff than is altogether healthy in the circumstances.'

Wimsey looked at him for a moment.

'I wish I could think as you do.'

'What *do* you think?' demanded Parker impatiently.

'No,' said Wimsey. 'I told you about that George business this morning, because glass bottles are facts, and one mustn't conceal facts. But I'm not obliged to tell you what I think.'

'You don't think, then, that Ann Dorland did the murder?'

'I don't know about that, Charles. I came here hoping that this room could tell me the same thing that it told you. But it hasn't. It's told me different. It's told me what I thought all along.'

'A penny for your thoughts, then,' said Parker, trying desperately to keep the conversation on a jocular footing.

'Not even thirty pieces of silver,' replied Wimsey mournfully.

Parker stacked the canvases away without another word.

'Do you want to come with me to the Armstrong woman?'

'May as well,' said Wimsey; 'you never know.'

Nurse Armstrong belonged to an expensive nursing-home in Great Wimpole Street. She had not been interviewed before, having only returned the previous evening from escorting an invalid lady to Italy. She was a large, good-looking, imperturbable woman, rather like the Venus of Milo, and she answered Parker's questions in a cheerful, matter-of-fact tone, as though they had been about bandages or temperatures.

'Oh, yes, constable; I remember the poor old gentleman being brought in, perfectly.'

Parker had a natural dislike to being called constable. However, a detective must not let little things like that irritate him.

'Was Miss Dorland present at the interview between your patient and her brother?'

'Only for a few moments. She said good afternoon to the old gentleman and led him up to the bed, and then, when she saw them comfortable together, she went out.'

'How do you mean, comfortable together?'

'Well, the patient called the old gentleman by his name, and he answered, and then he took her hand and said, "I'm sorry, Felicity; forgive me," or something of that sort, and she said, "There's nothing to forgive;

don't distress yourself, Arthur" – crying, he was, the poor old man. So he sat down on the chair by the bed, and Miss Dorland went out.'

'Nothing was said about the will?'

'Not while Miss Dorland was in the room, if that's what you mean.'

'Suppose anybody had listened at the door afterwards – could they have heard what was said?'

'Oh, no! the patient was very weak and spoke very low. I couldn't hear myself half she said.'

'Where were you?'

'Well, I went away, because I thought they'd like to be alone. But I was in my own room with the door open between, and I was looking in most of the time. She was so ill, you see, and the old gentleman looked so frail, I didn't like to go out of earshot. In our work, you see, we often have to see and hear a lot that we don't say anything about.'

'Of course, nurse – I am sure you did quite right. Now, when Miss Dorland brought the brandy up – the General was feeling very ill?'

'Yes – he had a nasty turn. I put him in the big chair and bent him over till the spasm went off. He asked for his own medicine, and I gave it to him – no, it wasn't drops – it was amyl nitrate; you inhale it. Then I rang the bell and sent the girl for the brandy.'

'Amyl nitrate – you're sure that's all he had?'

'Positive; there wasn't anything else. Lady Dormer had been having strychnine injections to keep her heart going, of course, and we'd tried oxygen; but we shouldn't give him those, you know.'

She smiled, competently, condescendingly.

'Now, you say Lady Dormer had been having this, that and the other. Were there any medicines lying about that

General Fentiman might have accidentally taken up and swallowed?'

'Oh, dear no.'

'No drops or tabloids or anything of that kind?'

'Certainly not; the medicines were kept in my room.'

'Nothing on the bedside table or the mantelpiece?'

'There was a cup of diluted Listerine by the bed, for washing out the patient's mouth from time to time, that was all.'

'And there's no digitalin in Listerine – no, of course not. Well, now, who brought up the brandy-and-water?'

'The housemaid went to Mrs Mitcham for it. I should have had some upstairs, as a matter of fact, but the patient couldn't keep it down. Some of them can't, you know.'

'Did the girl bring it straight up to you?'

'No – she stopped to call Miss Dorland on the way. Of course, she ought to have brought the brandy at once and gone to Miss Dorland afterwards – but it's anything to save trouble with these girls, as I dare say you know.'

'Did Miss Dorland bring it straight up –' began Parker. Nurse Armstrong broke in upon him.

'If you're thinking, did she put the digitalin into the brandy, you can dismiss that from your mind, constable. If he'd had as big a dose as that in solution at half-past four, he'd have been taken ill ever so much earlier than he was.'

'You seem to be well up in the case, nurse.'

'Oh, I am. Naturally I was interested, Lady Dormer being my patient and all.'

'Of course. But all the same, *did* Miss Dorland bring the brandy straight along to you?'

'I think so. I heard Nellie go along the passage on the half landing, and looked out to call to her, but by the time I'd got the door open I saw Miss Dorland coming out of the studio with the brandy in her hand.'

'And where was Nellie then?'

'Just got back to the end of the passage and starting downstairs to the telephone.'

'At that rate, Miss Dorland couldn't have been more than ten seconds alone with the brandy,' said Peter thoughtfully. 'And who gave it to General Fentiman?'

'I did. I took it out of Miss Dorland's hand at the door and gave it to him at once. He seemed better then, and only took a little of it.'

'Did you leave him again?'

'I did not. Miss Dorland went out on to the landing presently to see if the taxi was coming.'

'She was never alone with him?'

'Not for a moment.'

'Did you like Miss Dorland, nurse? Is she a nice girl, I mean?' Wimsey had not spoken for so long that Parker quite started.

'She was always very pleasant to me,' said Nurse Armstrong. 'I shouldn't call her an attractive girl, not to my mind.'

'Did she ever mention Lady Dormer's testamentary arrangements in your hearing?' asked Parker, picking up what he conceived to be Wimsey's train of thought.

'Well – not exactly. But I remember her once talking about her painting, and saying she did it for a hobby, as her aunt would see she always had enough to live on.'

'That's true enough,' said Parker. 'At the worst, she would get fifteen thousand pounds, which, carefully invested, might mean six or seven hundred a year. She didn't say she expected to be very rich?'

'No.'

'Nor anything about the General?'

'Not a word.'

'Was she happy?' asked Wimsey.

'She was upset, naturally, with her aunt being so ill.'

'I don't mean that. You are the sort of person who observes a lot – nurses are awfully quick about that kind of thing, I've noticed. Did she strike you as a person who – who felt right with life, as you might say?'

'She was one of the quiet ones. But – yes – I should say she was satisfied with things all right.'

'Did she sleep well?'

'Oh, she was a very sound sleeper. It was a job to wake her if anything was wanted in the night.'

'Did she cry much?'

'She cried over the old lady's death; she had very nice feelings.'

'Some natural tears she shed, and all that. She didn't lie about and have awful howling fits or anything like that?'

'Good gracious, no!'

'How did she walk?'

'Walk?'

'Yes, walk. Was she what you'd call droopy?'

'Oh, no – quick and brisk.'

'What was her voice like?'

'Well, now, that was one of the nice things about her. Rather deep for a woman, but with what I might call a tune in it. Melodious,' said Nurse Armstrong, with a faint giggle, 'that's what they call it in novels.'

Parker opened his mouth and shut it again.

'How long did you stay on at the house after Lady Dormer died?' pursued Wimsey.

'I waited on till after the funeral, just in case Miss Dorland should need anybody.'

'Before you left, did you hear anything of this trouble about the lawyers and the wills?'

'They were talking about it downstairs. Miss Dorland said nothing to me herself.'

'Did she seem worried?'

'Not to notice.'

'Had she any friends with her at the time?'

'Not staying in the house. She went out to see some friends one evening. I think – the evening before I left. She didn't say who they were.'

'I see. Thank you, nurse.'

Parker had no more questions to put, and they took their leave.

'Well,' said Parker, 'how anybody could admire that girl's voice—'

'You noticed that! My theory is coming out right, Charles. I wish it wasn't. I'd *rather* be wrong. I should like to have you look pitifully at me and say, "I told you so." I can't speak more strongly than that.'

'Hang your theories!' said Parker. 'It looks to me as if we shall have to wash out the idea that General Fentiman got his dose in Portman Square. By the way, didn't you say you'd met the Dorland girl at the Rushworths?'

'No. I said I went hoping to meet her, but she wasn't there.'

'Oh, I see. Well, that'll do for the moment. How about a spot of lunch?'

At which point they turned the corner and ran slap into Salcombe Hardy, emerging from Harley Street. Wimsey clutched Parker's arm suddenly. 'I've remembered,' he said.

'What?'

'Who that portrait reminds me of. Tell you later.'

Sally, it appeared, was also thinking of grub. He was, in fact, due to meet Waffles Newton at the Falstaff. It ended in their all going to the Falstaff.

'And how's it all going?' demanded Sally, ordering boiled beef and carrots.

He looked limpidly at Parker, who shook his head.

'Discreet man, your friend,' said Sally to Peter. 'I suppose the police are engaged in following up a clue – or have we reached the point when they are completely baffled? Or do we say that an arrest is imminent, eh?'

'Tell us your own version, Sally. Your opinion's as good as anybody's.'

'Oh, mine! Same as yours – same as everybody's. The girl was in league with the doctor, of course. Pretty obvious, isn't it?'

'Maybe,' said Parker cautiously. 'But that's a hard thing to prove. We know, of course, that they both sometimes went to Mrs Rushworth's house, but there's no evidence that they knew each other well.'

'But, you ass, she –' Wimsey blurted out. He shut his mouth again with a snap. 'No, I won't. Fish it out for yourselves.'

Illumination was flooding in on him in great waves. Each point of light touched off a myriad others. Now a date was lit up, and now a sentence. The relief in his mind would have been overwhelming, had it not been for that nagging central uncertainty. It was the portrait that worried him most. Painted as a record, painted to recall beloved features – thrust face to the wall and covered with dust.

Sally and Parker were talking.

'. . . moral certainty is not the same thing as proof.'

'Unless we can show that she knew the terms of the will . . .'

'. . . why wait till the last minute? It could have been done safely any time . . .'

'They probably thought it wasn't necessary. The old lady looked like seeing him into his grave easily. If it hadn't been for the pneumonia . . .'

'Even so, they had five days.'

'Yes – well, say she didn't know till the very day of Lady Dormer's death . . .'

'She might have told her then. Explained . . . seeing the thing had become a probability . . .'

'And the Dorland girl arranged for the visit to Harley Street . . .'

'. . . plain as the nose on your face.'

Hardy chuckled.

'They must have got a thundering shock when the body turned up the next morning at the Bellona. I suppose you gave Penberthy a good gruelling about that *rigor*?'

'Pretty fair. He fell back on professional caution, naturally.'

'It's coming to him in the witness-box. Does he admit knowing the girl?'

'He says he just knows her to speak to. But one's got to find somebody who has seen them together. You remember the Thompson case. It was the interview in the teashop that clinched it.'

'What I want to know,' said Wimsey 'is why—'

'Why what?'

'Why didn't they compromise?' It was not what he had been going to say, but he felt defeated, and those words would end the sentence as well as any others.

'What's that?' asked Hardy quickly.

Peter explained.

'When the question of survivorship came up, the Fentiman's were ready to compromise and split the money. Why didn't Miss Dorland agree? If your idea's the right one, it was much the safest way. But it was she who insisted on an inquiry.'

'I didn't know that,' said Hardy. He was annoyed. All kinds of 'stories' were coming his way today, and tomorrow there would probably be an arrest, and he wouldn't be able to use them.

'They *did* agree to compromise in the end,' said Parker. 'When was that?'

'After I told Penberthy there was going to be an exhumation,' said Wimsey, as though in spite of himself.

'There you are! They saw it was getting too dangerous.'

'Do you remember how nervous Penberthy was at the exhumation?' said Parker. 'That man – what's his name? – his joke about Palmer, and knocking over the jar?'

'What was that?' demanded Hardy again. Parker told him, and he listened, grinding his teeth. Another good story gone west. But it would all come out at the trial, and would be worth a headline.

'Robert Fentiman ought to be given a medal,' said Hardy. 'If he hadn't gone butting in—'

'Robert Fentiman?' inquired Parker distantly.

Hardy grinned.

'If he didn't fix up the old boy's body, who did? Give us credit for a little intelligence.'

'One admits nothing,' said Parker, 'but—'

'But everybody says he did it. Leave it at that. Somebody did it. If Somebody hadn't butted in, it would have been jam for the Dorland.'

'Well, yes. Old Fentiman would just have gone home and pegged out quietly – and Penberthy would have given the certificate.'

'I'd like to know how many inconvenient people are polished off that way. Damn it – it's so easy.'

'I wonder how Penberthy's share of the boodle was to be transferred to him.'

'I don't,' said Hardy. 'Look here – here's this girl. Calls herself an artist. Paints bad pictures. Right. Then she meets this doctor fellow. He's mad on glands. Shrewd man – knows there's money in glands. *She* starts taking up glands. Why?'

'That was a year ago.'

'Precisely. Penberthy isn't a rich man. Retired Army Surgeon, with a brass plate and a consulting-room in Harley Street – shares the house with two other hard-up brass-platers. Lives on a few old dodderers down at the Bellona. Has an idea, if only he could start one of these clinics for rejuvenating people, he could be a millionaire. All these giddy old goats who want their gay time over again – why, they're a perfect fortune to the man with a bit of capital and a hell of a lot of cheek. Then this girl comes along – rich old woman's heiress – and he goes after her. It's all fixed up. He's to accommodate her by removing the obstacle to the fortune, and she obligingly responds by putting the money into his clinic. In order not to make it too obvious, she has to pretend to get a dickens of an interest in glands. So she drops painting and takes to medicine. What could be clearer?'

'But that means,' put in Wimsey, 'that she must have known all about the will at least a year ago.'

'Why not?'

'Well, that brings us back to the old question: why the delay?'

'And it gives us the answer,' said Parker. 'They wait till the interest in the glands and things was so firmly established and recognised by everybody that nobody would connect it with the General's death.'

'Of course,' said Wimsey. He felt that matters were

rushing past him at a bewildering rate. But George was safe, anyhow.

'How soon do you think you'll be able to take action?' asked Hardy. 'I suppose you'll want a bit more solid proof before you actually arrest him?'

'I'd have to be certain that they don't wriggle out of it,' said Parker slowly. 'It's not enough to prove that they were acquainted. There may be letters, of course, when we go over the girl's things. Or Penberthy's – though he's hardly the man to leave compromising documents lying about.'

'You haven't detained Miss Dorland?'

'No; we've let her loose – on a string. I don't mind telling you one thing. There's been no communication of any kind with Penberthy.'

'Of course there hasn't,' said Wimsey. 'They've quarrelled.'

The others stared at him.

'How do you know that?' demanded Parker annoyed.

'Oh, well – it doesn't matter – I *think* so, that's all. And anyway, they would take jolly good care not to communicate, once the alarm was given.'

'Hallo!' broke in Hardy, 'here's Waffles. Late again, Waffles! – what *have* you been doing, old boy?'

'Interviewing the Rushworths,' said Waffles, edging his way into a chair by Hardy. He was a thin, sandy person, with a tired manner. Hardy introduced him to Wimsey and Parker.

'Got your story in?'

'Oh, yes. Awful lot of cats the women are. Ma Rushworth – she's the sloppy sort of woman with her head in the clouds all the time, who never sees anything till it's stuck right under her nose – she pretends, of course, that she always thought Ann Dor-

230

land was an unwholesome kind of girl. I nearly asked why, in that case, she had her about the house; but I didn't. Anyway, Mrs Rushworth said, they didn't know her very intimately. They wouldn't, of course. Wonderful how these soulful people sheer off at the least suggestion of unpleasantness.'

'Did you get anything about Penberthy?'

'Oh, yes – I got something.'

'Good?'

'Oh, yes.'

Hardy, with Fleet Street's delicate reticence towards the man with an exclusive story, did not press the question. The talk turned back and went over the old ground. Waffles Newton agreed with Salcombe Hardy's theory.

'The Rushworths must surely know something. Not the mother, perhaps – but the girl. If she's engaged to Penberthy, she'll have noticed any other woman who seemed to have an understanding with him. Women see these things.'

'You don't suppose that they're going to confess that dear Dr Penberthy ever had an understanding with anybody but dear Naomi,' retorted Newton. 'Besides, they aren't such fools as not to know that Penberthy's connection with the Dorland girl must be smothered up at all costs. They know she did it, all right, but they aren't going to compromise him.'

'Of course not,' said Parker, rather shortly. 'The mother probably knows nothing, anyway. It's a different matter if we get the girl in the witness-box—'

'You won't,' said Waffles Newton. 'At least, you'll have to be jolly quick.'

'Why?'

Newton waved an apologetic hand.

'They're being married tomorrow,' he said – 'special licence. I say, that's not to go further, Sally.'

'That's all right, old man.'

'Married?' said Parker. 'Good lord! that forces our hand a bit. Perhaps I'd better poop off. So long – and thanks very much for the tip, old man.'

Wimsey followed him into the street.

'We'll have to have put the stopper on this marriage business, quick,' said Parker, madly waving to a taxi, which swooped past and ignored him. 'I didn't want to move just at present, because I wasn't ready, but it'll be the devil and all if the Rushworth girl gets hitched up to Penberthy and we can't take her evidence. Devil of it is, if she's determined to go on with it, we can't stop it without arresting Penberthy. Very dangerous, when there's no real proof. I think we'd better have him down to the Yard for interrogation and detain him.'

'Yes,' said Wimsey. 'But – look here, Charles.'

A taxi drew up.

'What?' said Parker sharply, with his foot on the step. 'I can't wait, old man. What is it?'

'I – look here, Charles – this is all wrong,' pleaded Wimsey. 'You may have got the right solution, but the working of the sum's all wrong. Same as mine used to be at school, when I'd looked up the answer in the crib and had to fudge in the middle part. I've been a fool. I ought to have known about Penberthy. But I don't believe this story about bribing and corrupting him, and getting him to do the murder. It doesn't fit.'

'Doesn't fit what?'

'Doesn't fit the portrait. Or the books. Or the way Nurse Armstrong described Ann Dorland. Or your description of her. It's a mechanically perfect explanation, but I swear it's all wrong.'

232

'If it's mechanically perfect,' said Parker, 'that's good enough. It's far more than most explanations are. You've got that portrait on the brain. It's because you're artistic, I suppose.'

For some reason, the word 'artistic' produces the most alarming reactions in people who know anything about art.

'Artistic be damned!' said Wimsey, spluttering with fury. 'It's because I'm an ordinary person, and have met women, and talked to them like ordinary human beings—'

'You and your women,' said Parker rudely.

'Well – I and my women, what about it? One learns something. You're on the wrong track about this girl.'

'I've met her and you haven't,' objected Parker. 'Unless you're suppressing something. You keep on hinting things. Anyhow, I've met the girl, and she impressed me as being guilty.'

'And I haven't met her, and I'll swear she isn't guilty.'

'You must know, of course.'

'I do happen to know about this.'

'I'm afraid your unsupported opinion will hardly be sufficient to refute the weight of evidence.'

'You haven't any real evidence, if it comes to that. You don't know that they were ever alone together; you don't know that Ann Dorland knew about the will; you can't prove that Penberthy administered the poison—'

'I don't despair of getting all the evidence necessary,' said Parker coldly, 'provided you don't keep me here *all* day.' He slammed the taxi door.

'What a beast of a case this is,' thought Wimsey. 'That makes two silly, sordid rows today. Well, what next?' He considered a moment.

'My spirit needs soothing,' he decided. 'Feminine society is indicated. Virtuous feminine society. No emotions. I'll go and have tea with Marjorie Phelps.'

20

ANN DORLAND GOES MISERE

THE studio door was opened by a girl he did not know. She was not tall, but compactly and generously built. He noticed the wide shoulders and the strong swing of the thighs before he had taken in her face. The uncurtained window behind her threw her features into shadow; he was only aware of thick black hair, cut in a square bob, with a bang across the forehead.

'Miss Phelps is out.'

'Oh! – will she be long?'

'Don't know. She'll be in to supper.'

'Do you think I might come in and wait?'

'I expect so, if you're a friend of hers.'

The girl fell back from the doorway and let him pass. He laid his hat and stick on the table and turned to her. She took no notice of him, but walked over to the fireplace and stood with one hand on the mantelpiece. Unable to sit down, since she was still standing, Wimsey moved to the modelling-board, and raised the wet cloth that covered the little mound of clay.

He was gazing with an assumption of great interest at the half-modelled figure of an old flower-seller, when the girl said:

'I say!'

She had taken up Marjorie Phelps's figurine of himself, and was twisting it over in her fingers.

'Is this you?'

'Yes – rather good of me, don't you think?'

'What do you want?'

'Want?'

'You've come here to have a look at me, haven't you?'

'I came to see Miss Phelps.'

'I suppose the policeman at the corner comes to see Miss Phelps too.'

Wimsey glanced out at the window. There *was* a man at the corner – an elaborately indifferent lounger.

'I am sorry,' said Wimsey with sudden enlightenment. 'I'm really awfully sorry to seem so stupid, and so intrusive. But honestly, I had no idea who you were till this moment.'

'Hadn't you? Oh, well, it doesn't matter.'

'Shall I go?'

'You can please yourself.'

'If you really mean that, Miss Dorland, I should like to stay. I've been wanting to meet you, you know.'

'That was nice of you,' she mocked. 'First you wanted to defraud me, and now you're trying to—'

'To what?'

She shrugged her wide shoulders.

'Yours is not a pleasant hobby, Lord Peter Wimsey.'

'Will you believe me,' said Wimsey, 'when I assure you that I was never a party to the fraud. In fact, I showed it up. I did really.'

'Oh, well. It doesn't matter now.'

'But do, please, believe that.'

'Very well. If you say so, I must believe it.'

She threw herself on the couch near the fire.

'That's better,' said Wimsey. 'Napoleon or somebody said that you could always turn a tragedy into a comedy by sittin' down. Perfectly true, isn't it? Let's talk about something ordinary till Miss Phelps comes in. Shall we?'

'What do you want to talk about?'

'Oh, well – that's rather embarrassin'. Books.' He waved a vague hand. 'What have you been readin' lately?'

'Nothing much.'

'Don't know what I should do without books. Fact, I always wonder what people did in the old days. Just think of it. All sorts of bothers goin' on – matrimonial rows and love-affairs – prodigal sons and servants and worries – and no books to turn to.'

'People worked with their hands instead.'

'Yes – that's frightfully jolly for the people who can do it. I envy them myself. You paint, don't you?'

'I try to.'

'Portraits?'

'Oh, no – figure and landscape chiefly.'

'Oh! . . . A friend of mine – well, it's no use disguising it – he's a detective – you've met him, I think.'

'That man? Oh, yes. Quite a polite sort of detective.'

'He told me he's seen some stuff of yours. It rather surprised him, I think. He's not exactly a modernist. He seemed to think your portraits were your best work.'

'There weren't many portraits. A few figure-studies . . .'

'They worried him a bit.' Wimsey laughed. 'The only thing he understood, he said, was a man's head in oils—'

'Oh, that! – just an experiment – a fancy thing. My best stuff is some sketches I did of the Wiltshire Downs a year or two ago. Direct painting, without any preliminary sketch.'

She described a number of these works.

'They sound ever so jolly,' said Wimsey. 'Great stuff. I wish I could do something of that kind. As I say, I have to fall back on books for my escape. Reading *is* an escape to me. Is it to you?'

'How do you mean?'

'Well – it is to most people, I think. Servants and factory hands read about beautiful girls loved by dark, handsome men, all covered over with jewels and moving in scenes of gilded splendour. And passionate spinsters read Ethel M. Dell. And dull men in offices read detective stories. They wouldn't, if murder and police entered into their lives.'

'I don't know,' she said. 'When Crippen and Le Neve were taken on the steamer, they were reading Edgar Wallace.' Her voice was losing its dull harshness; she sounded almost interested.

'Le Neve was reading it,' said Wimsey, 'but I've never believed she knew about the murder. I think she was fighting desperately to know nothing about it – reading horrors, and persuading herself that nothing of that kind had happened, or could happen, to her. I think one might do that, don't you?'

'I don't know,' said Ann Dorland. 'Of course, a detective story keeps your brain occupied. Rather like chess. Do you play chess?'

'No good at it. I like it – but I keep on thinking about the history of the various pieces, and the picturesqueness of the moves. So I get beaten. I'm not a player.'

'Nor am I. I wish I were.'

'Yes – that would keep one's mind off things with a vengeance. Draughts or dominoes or patience would be even better. No connection with anything. I remember,' added Wimsey, 'one time when something perfectly grinding and hateful had happened to me. I played patience all day. I was in a nursing home – with shell-shock – and other things. I only played one game, the very simplest . . . the demon . . . a silly game with no ideas in it at all. I just went on laying it out and gathering it up . . . a hundred times in an evening . . . so as to stop thinking.'

'Then you, too . . .'

Wimsey waited; but she did not finish the sentence.

'It's a kind of drug, of course. That's an awfully trite thing to say, but it's quite true.'

'Yes, quite.'

'I read detective stories, too. They were about the only thing I could read. All the others had the War in them – or love . . . or some damn' thing I didn't want to think about.'

She moved restlessly.

'You've been through it, haven't you?' said Wimsey gently.

'Me? . . . Well . . . all this . . . it isn't pleasant, you know . . . the police . . . and . . . and everything.'

'You're not really worried about the police, are you?'

She had cause to be, if she only knew it, but he buried this knowledge at the bottom of his mind, defying it to show itself.

'Everything's pretty hateful, isn't it?'

'Something's hurt you . . . all right . . . don't talk about it if you don't want to . . . a man?'

'It usually is a man, isn't it?'

Her eyes were turned away from him, and she answered with a kind of shamefaced defiance.

'Practically always,' said Wimsey. 'Fortunately, one gets over it.'

'Depends what it is.'

'One gets over everything,' repeated Wimsey firmly. 'Particularly if one tells somebody about it.'

'One can't always tell things.'

'I can't imagine anything really untellable.'

'Some things are so beastly.'

'Oh, yes – quite a lot of things. Birth is beastly – and death – and digestion, if it comes to that. Sometimes when I think of what's happening inside me to a beautiful *suprème de sole*, with the caviare in boats, and the *croûtons* and the jolly little twists of potato and all the gadgets – I could cry. But there it is, don't you know?'

Ann Dorland suddenly laughed.

'That's better,' said Wimsey. 'Look here, you've been brooding over this and you're seeing it all out of proportion. Let's be practical and frightfully ordinary. Is it a baby?'

'Oh, no!'

'Well – that's rather a good thing, because babies, though no doubt excellent in their way, take a long time and come expensive. Is it blackmail?'

'Good heavens, no!'

'Good! Because blackmail is even longer and more expensive than babies. Is it Freudian, or sadistic, or any of those popular modern amusements?'

'I don't believe you'd turn a hair if it was.'

'Why should I? – I can't think of anything worse to suggest, except what Rose Macaulay refers to as "nameless orgies". Or disease, of course. It's not leprosy or anything?'

'What a mind you've got,' she said, beginning to laugh. 'No, it isn't leprosy.'

'Well, what *did* the blighter do?'

Ann Dorland smiled faintly. 'It's nothing, really.'

'If only Heaven prevents Marjorie Phelps from coming in,' thought Wimsey, 'I'm going to get it now . . . It must have been something, to upset you like this,' he pursued aloud; 'you're not the kind of woman to be upset about nothing.'

'You don't think I am?' She got up and faced him

squarely. 'He said . . . he said . . . I imagined things . . .
He said . . . he said I had a mania about sex. I suppose
you would call it Freudian, really,' she added hastily,
flushing an ugly crimson.

'Is that all?' said Wimsey. 'I know plenty of people
who would take that as a compliment . . . But obviously
you don't. What exact form of mania did he suggest . . .?'

'Oh! the gibbering sort that hangs round church doors
for curates,' she broke out fiercely. 'It's a lie. He did – he
did – pretend to – want me and all that. The beast! . . . I
can't tell you the things he said . . . and I'd made such a
fool of myself . . .'

She was back on the couch, crying, with large, ugly,
streaming tears, and snorting into the cushions. Wimsey
sat down beside her.

'Poor kid,' he said. This, then, was at the back of
Marjorie's mysterious hints, and those scratch-cat sneers
of Naomi Rushworth's. The girl had wanted love affairs,
that was certain; imagined them, perhaps. There had
been Ambrose Ledbury. Between the normal and the
abnormal, the gulf is deep, but so narrow that misrepre-
sentation is made easy.

'Look here.' He put a comforting arm round Ann's
heaving shoulders. 'This fellow – was it Penberthy, by the
way?'

'How did you know?'

'Oh! – the portrait, and lots of things. The things you
liked once, and then wanted to hide away and forget.
He's a rotter, anyway, for saying that kind of thing –
even if it was true, which it isn't. You got to know him at
the Rushworths', I take it – when?'

'Nearly two years ago.'

'Were you keen on him then?'

'No. I – well, I was keen on somebody else. Only that

was a mistake too. He – he was one of those people, you know.'

'They can't help themselves,' said Wimsey, soothingly. 'When did the change-over happen?'

'The other man went away. And later on Dr Penberthy – oh! I don't know! He walked home with me once or twice, and then he asked me to dine with him – in Soho.'

'Had you at that time told anyone about this comic will of Lady Dormer's?'

'Of course not. How could I? I never knew anything about it till after she died.'

Her surprise sounded genuine enough.

'What did you think? Did you think the money would come to you?'

'I knew that some of it would; Auntie told me she would see me provided for.'

'There were the grandsons, of course.'

'Yes; I thought she would leave most of it to them. It's a pity she didn't, poor dear. Then there wouldn't have been all this dreadful bother.'

'People so often seem to lose their heads when they make wills. So you were a sort of dark horse at that time. H'm. Did this precious Penberthy ask you to marry him?'

'I thought he did. But he says he didn't. We talked about founding his clinic; I was to help him.'

'And that was when you chucked painting for books about medicine and first-aid classes. Did your aunt know about the engagement?'

'He didn't want her told. It was to be our secret till he got a better position. He was afraid she might think he was after the money.'

'I dare say he was.'

'He made out he was fond of me,' she said miserably.

241

'Of course, my dear child; your case is not unique. Didn't you tell any of your friends?'

'No.' Wimsey reflected that the Ledbury episode had probably left a scar. Besides – did women tell things to other women? He had long doubted it.

'You were still engaged when Lady Dormer died, I take it?'

'As engaged as we ever were. Of course, he told me that there was something funny about the body. He said you and the Fentimans were trying to defraud me of the money. I shouldn't have minded for myself – it was more money than I should have known what to do with. But it would have meant the clinic, you see.'

'Yes, you could start a pretty decent clinic with half a million. So that was why you shot me out of the house.'

He grinned – and then reflected a few moments.

'Look here,' he said, 'I'm going to give you a bit of a shock, but it'll have to come sooner or later. Has it ever occurred to you that it was Penberthy who murdered General Fentiman?'

'I – wondered,' she said slowly. 'I couldn't think – who else. But you know they suspect *me*?'

'Oh, well – *cui bono*? and all that – they couldn't overlook you. They have to suspect every possible person, you know.'

'I don't blame them at all. But I didn't, you know.'

'Of course not. It was Penberthy. I look at it like this. Penberthy wanted money; he was sick of being poor, and he knew you would be certain to get *some* of Lady Dormer's money. He'd probably heard all about the family quarrel with the General, and expected it would be the lot. So he started to make your acquaintance. But he was careful. He asked you to keep it quiet – just in

242

case, you see. The money might be so tied up that you couldn't give it him, or you might lose it if you married, or it might only be quite a small annuity, in which case he'd want to look for somebody richer.'

'We considered those points when we talked over about the clinic.'

'Yes. Well, then, Lady Dormer fell ill. The General went round and heard about the legacy that was coming to him. And then he toddled along to Penberthy, feeling very groggy, and promptly told him all about it. You can imagine him saying, "You've got to patch me up long enough to get the money." That must have been a nasty jar for Penberthy.'

'It was. You see, he didn't even hear about my twelve thousand.'

'Oh?'

'No. Apparently what the General said was, "If only I last out poor Felicity, all the money comes to me. Otherwise it goes to the girl and my boys only get seven thousand apiece." That was why—'

'Just a moment. When did Penberthy tell you about that?'

'Why, later – when he said I was to compromise with the Fentimans.'

'That explains it. I wondered why you gave in so suddenly. I thought then, that you – Well, anyhow, Penberthy hears this, and gets the brilliant idea of putting General Fentiman out of the way. So he gives him a slow-working kind of pill—'

'Probably a powder in a very tough capsule that would take a long time to digest.'

'Good idea. Yes, very likely. And then the General, instead of heading straight for home, as he expected, goes off to the Club and dies there. And then Robert . . .'

He explained in detail what Robert had done, and resumed.

'Well, now – Penberthy was in a bad fix. If he drew attention at the time to the peculiar appearance of the corpse, he couldn't reasonably give a certificate. In which case there would be a post-mortem and an analysis, and the digitalin would be found. If he kept quiet, the money might be lost and all his trouble would be wasted. Maddenin' for him, wasn't it? So he did what he could. He put the time of the death as early as he dared, and hoped for the best.'

'He told me he thought there would be some attempt to make it seem later than it really was. I thought it was *you* who were trying to hush everything up. And I was so furious that, of course, I told Mr Pritchard to have a proper inquiry made and on no account to compromise.'

'Thank God you did,' said Wimsey.

'Why?'

'I'll tell you presently. But Penberthy now – I can't think why *he* didn't persuade you to compromise. That would have made him absolutely safe.'

'But he did! That's what started our first quarrel. As soon as he heard about it he said I was a fool not to compromise. I couldn't understand his saying that, since he himself had said there was something wrong. We had a fearful row. That was the time I mentioned the twelve thousand that was coming to me anyway.'

'What did he say?'

' "I didn't know that." Just like that. And then he apologised and said that the law was so uncertain, it would be best to agree to divide the money, anyhow. So I rang up Mr Pritchard and told him not to make any more fuss. And we were friends again.'

'Was it the day after that, that Penberthy – er – said things to you?'

'Yes.'

'Right. Then I can tell you one thing: he would never have been so brutal if he hadn't been in fear of his life. Do you know what had happened in between?'

She shook her head.

'I had been on the phone to him, and told him there was going to be an autopsy.'

'Oh!'

'Yes – listen – you needn't worry any more about it. He knew that the poison would be discovered, and that if he was known to be engaged to you he was absolutely bound to be suspected. So he hurried to cut the connection with you – purely in self-defence.'

'But why do it in that brutal way?'

'Because, my dear, he knew that that particular accusation would be the very last thing a girl of your sort would tell people about. He made it absolutely impossible for you to claim him publicly. And he bolstered it up by engaging himself to the Rushworth female.'

'He didn't care how I suffered.'

'He was in a beast of a hole,' said Wimsey apologetically. 'Mind you, it was a perfectly diabolical thing to do. I dare say he's feeling pretty rotten about it.'

Ann Dorland clenched her hands.

'I've been so horribly ashamed—'

'Well, you aren't any more, are you?'

'No – but –' A thought seemed to strike her. 'Lord Peter – I can't *prove* a word of this. Everybody will think I was in league with him. And they'll think that our quarrel and his getting engaged to Naomi was just a put-up job between us to get us both out of a difficulty.'

'You've got brains,' said Wimsey admiringly. '*Now* you see why I thanked God you'd been so keen on an inquiry at first. Pritchard can make it pretty certain that you weren't an accessory before the fact, anyhow.'

'Of course – so he can. Oh, I'm so glad! I *am* so glad.' She burst into excited sobs and clutched Wimsey's hand. 'I wrote him a letter – right at the beginning – saying I'd read about a case in which they'd proved the time of somebody's death by looking into his stomach, and asking if General Fentiman couldn't be dug up.'

'Did you? Splendid girl! You *have* got a head on your shoulders! . . . No, I observe that it's on my shoulders. Go on. Have a real good howl – I feel rather like howling myself. I've been quite worried about it all. But it's all right now, isn't it?'

'I am a fool . . . but I'm so thankful you came.'

'So am I. Here, have a hanky. Poor old dear! . . . Hallo! there's Marjorie.'

He released her and went out to meet Marjorie Phelps at the door.

'Lord Peter! Good lord!'

'Thank you, Marjorie,' said Wimsey gravely.

'No, but listen! Have you seen Ann? I took her away. She's frightfully queer – and there's a policeman outside. But whatever she's done, I couldn't leave her alone in that awful house. You haven't come to – to—'

'Marjorie!' said Wimsey, 'don't you ever talk to me again about feminine intuition. You've been thinking all this time that that girl was suffering from guilty conscience. Well, she wasn't. It was a man, my child – a MAN!'

'How do you know?'

'My experienced eye told me as much at the first glance. It's all right now. Sorrow and sighing have fled away. I am going to take your young friend out to dinner.'

'But why didn't she tell me what it was all about?'

'Because,' said Wimsey mincingly, 'it wasn't the kind of thing one woman tells another.'

21

LORD PETER CALLS A BLUFF

'IT is new to me,' said Lord Peter, glancing from the back window of the taxi at the other taxi which was following them, 'to be shadowed by the police, but it amuses them and doesn't hurt us.'

He was revolving ways and means of proof in his mind. Unhappily, all the evidence in favour of Ann Dorland was evidence against her as well – except, indeed, the letter to Pritchard. Damn Penberthy! The best that could be hoped for now was that the girl should escape from public inquiry with a verdict of 'Not proven'. Even if acquitted – even if never charged with the murder – she would always be suspect. The question was not one which could be conveniently settled by a brilliant flash of deductive logic, or the discovery of a blood-stained thumb-mark. It was a case for lawyers to argue – for a weighing of the emotional situation by twelve good and lawful persons. Presumably the association could be proved – the couple had met and dined together; probably the quarrel could be proved – but what next? Would a jury believe in the cause of the quarrel? Would they think it a prearranged blind, perhaps – or mistake it for the falling-out of rogues among themselves? What would they think of this plain, sulky, inarticulate girl, who had never had any real friends, and whose clumsy and tentative graspings after passion had been so obscure, so disastrous?

Penberthy, too – but Penberthy was easier to understand.

Penberthy, cynical and bored with poverty, found himself in contact with this girl, who might be so well off some day. And Penberthy, the physician, would not mistake the need for passion that made the girl such easy stuff to work on. So he carried on – bored with the girl, of course – keeping it all secret, till he saw which way the cat was going to jump. Then the old man – the truth about the will – the opportunity. And then, upsettingly Robert . . . Would the jury see it like that?

Wimsey leaned out of the cab window and told the driver to go to the Savoy. When they arrived, he handed the girl over to the cloakroom attendant. 'I am going up to change,' he added, and, turning, had the pleasure of seeing his sleuth arguing with the porter in the entrance hall.

Bunter, previously summoned by telephone, was already in attendance with his master's dress clothes. Having changed, Wimsey passed through the hall again. The sleuth was there, quietly waiting. Wimsey grinned at him and offered him a drink.

'I can't help it, my lord,' said the detective.

'Of course not; you've sent for a bloke in a boiled shirt to take your place, I suppose?'

'Yes, my lord.'

'More power to his elbow. So long.'

He rejoined his charge and they went into the dining-room. Dressed in a green which did not suit her, she was undoubtedly plain. But she had character; he was not ashamed of her. He offered her the menu.

'What shall it be?' he asked. 'Lobster and champagne?'

She laughed at him.

'Marjorie says you are an authority on food. I don't believe authorities on food ever take lobster and champagne. Anyway, I don't like lobster much. Surely there's something they do best here, isn't there? Let's have that.'

'You show the right spirit,' said Wimsey. 'I will compose a dinner for you.'

He called the head waiter, and went into the question scientifically.

'*Huîtres Musgrave* – I am opposed on principle to the cooking of oysters, but it is a dish so excellent that one may depart from the rules in its favour. Fried in their shells, Miss Dorland, with little strips of bacon. Shall we try it? The soup must be *tortue vraie*, of course. The fish – oh, just a *filet de sole*, the merest mouthful, a hyphen between the prologue and the main theme.'

'That all sounds delightful. And what is the main theme to be?'

'I think a *faisan rôti* with *pommes Byron*. And a salad to promote digestion. And, waiter, be sure the salad is dry and perfectly crisp. A *soufflé glacé* to finish up with. And bring me the wine list.'

They talked. When she was not on the defensive, the girl was pleasant enough in manner; a trifle downright and aggressive, perhaps, in her opinions, but needing only mellowing.

'What do you think of the Romanée Conti?' he asked suddenly.

'I don't know much about wine. It's good. Not sweet, like Sauterne. It's a little – well – harsh. But it's harsh without being thin – quite different from that horrid Chianti people always seem to drink at Chelsea parties.'

'You're right; it's rather unfinished, but it has plenty of body – it'll be a grand wine in ten years' time. It's 1915. Now, you see. Waiter, take this away and bring me a bottle of the 1908.'

He leaned towards his companion.

'Miss Dorland – may I be impertinent?'

'How? Why?'

'Not an artist, not a bohemian, and not a professional man; a man of the world.'

'What *do* you mean by those cryptic words?'

'For you. That is the kind of man who is going to like you very much. Look! that wine I've sent away – it's no good for the champagne-and-lobster sort of person, nor for very young people – it's too big and rough. But it's got the essential guts. So have you. It takes a fairly experienced palate to appreciate it. But you and it will come into your own one day. Get me?'

'Do you think so?'

'Yes. But your man won't be at all the sort of person you're expecting. You have always thought of being dominated by somebody, haven't you?'

'Well—'

'But you'll find that *yours* will be the leading brain of the two. He will take great pride in the fact. And you will find the man reliable and kind, and it will turn out quite well.'

'I didn't know you were a prophet.'

'I am, though.'

Wimsey took the bottle of 1908 from the waiter and glanced over the girl's head at the door. A man in a boiled shirt was making his way in, accompanied by the manager.

'I am a prophet,' said Wimsey. 'Listen. Something tiresome is going to happen – now, this minute. But don't worry. Drink your wine, and trust.'

The manager had brought the man to their table. It was Parker.

'Ah!' said Wimsey brightly. 'You'll forgive our starting without you, old man. Sit down. I think you know Miss Dorland.'

Parker bowed and sat down.

'Have you come to arrest me?' asked Ann.

'Just to ask you to come down to the Yard with me,' said Parker, smiling pleasantly and unfolding his napkin.

Ann looked palely at Wimsey, and took a gulp of the wine.

'Right,' said Wimsey. 'Miss Dorland has quite a lot to tell you. After dinner will suit us charmingly. What will you have?'

Parker, who was not imaginative, demanded a grilled steak.

'Shall we find any other friends at the Yard?' pursued Wimsey.

'Possibly,' said Parker.

'Well, cheer up! You put me off my food, looking so grim. Hullo! Yes, waiter, what is it?'

'Excuse me, my lord – is this gentleman Detective-Inspector Parker?'

'Yes, yes,' said Parker; 'what's the matter?'

'You're wanted on the phone, sir.'

Parker departed.

'It's all right,' said Wimsey to the girl. 'I know you're straight, and I'll damn' well see you through.'

'What am I to do?'

'Tell the truth.'

'It sounds so silly.'

'They've heard lots of very much sillier stories than that.'

'But – I don't want to – to be the one to—'

'You're still fond of him, then?'

'No! – but I'd rather it wasn't me.'

'I'll be frank with you. I think it's going to be between you and him that suspicion will lie.'

'In that case' – she set her teeth – 'he can have what's coming to him.'

'Thank the Lord! I thought you were going to be noble and self-sacrificing and tiresome. You know. Like the people whose noble motives are misunderstood in chapter one, and who get dozens of people tangled up in their miserable affairs till the family lawyer solves everything on the last page but two.'

Parker had come back from the telephone.

'Just a moment!' He spoke in Peter's ear.

'Hallo?'

'Look here; this is awkward. George Fentiman—'

'Yes?'

'He's been found in Clerkenwell.'

'Clerkenwell?'

'Yes; must have wandered back by bus or something. He's at the police station; in fact he's given himself up.'

'Good Lord!'

'For the murder of his grandfather.'

'The devil he has!'

'It's a nuisance; of course it must be looked into. I think perhaps I'd better put off interrogating Dorland and Penberthy. What are you doing with the girl, by the way?'

'I'll explain later. Look here – I'll take Miss Dorland back to Marjorie Phelps's place, and then come along and join you. The girl won't run away; I know that. And, anyhow, you've got a man looking after her.'

'Yes, I rather wish you would come with me; Fentiman is pretty queer, by all accounts. We've sent for his wife.'

'Right. You buzz off, and I'll join you in – say in three-quarters of an hour. What address? Oh, yes, righty-ho! Sorry you're missing your dinner.'

'It's all in the day's work,' growled Parker, and took his leave.

George Fentiman greeted them with a tired, white smile.

'Hush!' he said. 'I've told them all about it. *He*'s asleep; don't wake him.'

'Who's asleep, dearest?' said Sheila.

'I mustn't say the name,' said George cunningly. 'He'd hear it – even in his sleep – even if you whispered it. But he's tired; and he nodded off. So I ran in here and told them all about it while he snored.'

The police superintendent tapped his forehead significantly behind Sheila's back.

'Has he made any statement?' asked Parker.

'Yes; he insisted on writing it himself. Here it is. Of course . . .' The Superintendent shrugged his shoulders.

'That's all right,' said George. 'I'm getting sleepy myself. I've been watching him for a day and a night, you know. I'm going to bed. Sheila – it's time to go to bed.'

'Yes, dear.'

'We'll have to keep him here tonight, I suppose,' muttered Parker. 'Has the doctor seen him?'

'We've sent for him, sir.'

'Well, Mrs Fentiman, I think if you'd take your husband into the room the officer will show you, that would be the best way. And we'll send the doctor in to you when he arrives. Perhaps it would be as well that he should see his own medical man too. Whom would you like us to send for?'

'Dr Penberthy has vetted him from time to time, I think,' put in Wimsey suddenly. 'Why not send for him?'

Parker gasped involuntarily.

'He might be able to throw some light on the symptoms,' said Wimsey in a rigid voice.

254

Parker nodded.

'A good idea,' he agreed. He moved to the telephone. George smiled as his wife put her arm about his shoulder.

'Tired,' he said, 'very tired. Off to bed, old girl.'

A police constable opened the door to them, and they started through it together; George leaned heavily on Sheila; his feet dragged.

'Let's have a look at his statement,' said Parker.

It was written in a staggering handwriting, much blotted and erased, with words left out and repeated here and there:

'I am making this statement quickly while he is asleep, because if I wait he may wake up and stop me. You will say I was moved and seduced by instigation of but what they will not understand is that he is me and I am him. I killed my grandfather by giving him digitalin. I did not remember it till I saw the name on the bottle, but they have been looking for me ever since, so I know that he must have done it. That is why they began following me about, but he is very clever and misleads them. When he is awake. We were dancing all last night and that is why he is tired. He told me to smash the bottle so that you shouldn't find out, but they know I was the last person to see him. He is very cunning, but if you creep on him quickly now that he is asleep you will be able to bind him in chains and cast him into the pit and then I shall be able to sleep.

'GEORGE FENTIMAN.'

'Off his head, poor devil,' said Parker. 'We can't pay much attention to this. What did he say to you, Superintendent?'

'He just came in, sir, and said, "I'm George Fentiman

and I've come to tell you about how I killed my grandfather." So I questioned him, and he rambled a good bit and then he asked for a pen and paper to make his statement. I thought he ought to be detained, and I rang up the Yard, sir.'

'Quite right,' said Parker.

The door opened and Sheila came out.

'He's fallen asleep,' she said. 'It's the old trouble come back again. He thinks he's the devil, you know. He's been like that twice before,' she added simply. 'I'll go back to him till the doctors come.'

The police surgeon arrived first and went in; then, after a wait of a quarter of an hour, Penberthy came. He looked worried, and greeted Wimsey abruptly. Then he too went into the inner room. The others stood vaguely about, and were presently joined by Robert Fentiman, whom an urgent summons had traced to a friend's house.

Presently the two doctors came out again.

'Nervous shock with well-marked delusions,' said the police surgeon briefly. 'Probably be all right tomorrow. Sleeping it off now. Been this way before, I understand. Just so. A hundred years ago they'd have called it diabolic possession, but *we* know better.'

'Yes,' said Parker; 'but do you think he is under a delusion in saying he murdered his grandfather? Or did he actually murder him under the influence of this diabolical delusion? That's the point.'

'Can't say just at present. Might be the one – might be the other. Much better wait till the attack passes off. You'll be able to find out better then.'

'You don't think he's permanently – insane, then?' demanded Robert, with brusque anxiety.

'No – I don't. I think it's what you'd call a nerve-storm.

That is your opinion too, I believe?' he added, turning to Penberthy.

'Yes; that is my opinion.'

'And what do you think about this delusion, Dr Penberthy?' went on Parker. 'Did he do this insane act?'

'He certainly thinks he did it,' said Penberthy. 'I couldn't possibly say for certain whether he has any foundation for the belief. From time to time he undoubtedly gets these fits of thinking that the devil has taken hold of him, and of course it's hard to say what a man might or might not do under the influence of such a delusion.'

He avoided Robert's distressed eyes, and addressed himself exclusively to Parker.

'It seems to me,' said Wimsey, 'if you'll excuse my pushin' my opinion forward and all that – it seems to me that's a question of fact that can be settled without reference to Fentiman and his delusions. There's only the one occasion on which the pill could have been administered – would it have produced the effect that was produced at that particular time, or wouldn't it? If it couldn't take effect at eight o'clock, then it couldn't, and there's an end of it.'

He kept his eyes fixed on Penberthy, and saw him pass his tongue over his dry lips before speaking.

'I can't answer that off-hand,' he said.

'The pill might have been introduced into General Fentiman's stock of pills at some other time,' suggested Parker.

'So it might,' agreed Penberthy.

'Had it the same shape and appearance as his ordinary pills?' demanded Wimsey, again fixing his eyes on Penberthy.

'Not having seen the pill in question, I can't say,' said the latter.

'In any case,' said Wimsey, 'the pill in question, which was one of Mrs Fentiman's, I understand, had strychnine in it as well as digitalin. The analysis of the stomach would no doubt have revealed strychnine if present. That can be looked into.'

'Of course,' said the police surgeon. 'Well, gentlemen, I don't think we can do much more tonight. I have written out a prescription for the patient, with Dr Penberthy's entire agreement.' He bowed; Penberthy bowed. 'I will have it made up, and you will no doubt see that it is given to him. I shall be here in the morning.'

He looked interrogatively at Parker, who nodded.

'Thank you, doctor; we will ask you for a further report tomorrow morning. You'll see that Mrs Fentiman is properly looked after, Superintendent. If you wish to stay here and look after your brother and Mrs Fentiman, Major, of course you may, and the Superintendent will make you as comfortable as he can.'

Wimsey took Penberthy by the arm.

'Come round to the Club with me for a moment, Penberthy,' he said. 'I want to have a word with you.'

22

THE CARDS ON THE TABLE

THERE was nobody in the library at the Bellona Club; there never is. Wimsey led Penberthy into the farthest bay and sent a waiter for two double whiskies.

'Here's luck!' he said.

'Good luck,' replied Penberthy. 'What is it?'

'Look here,' said Wimsey. 'You've been a soldier. I think you're a decent fellow. You've seen George Fentiman. It's a pity, isn't it?'

'What about it?'

'If George Fentiman hadn't turned up with that delusion of his,' said Wimsey, 'you would have been arrested for the murder this evening. Now the point is this. When you are arrested, nothing, as things are, can prevent Miss Dorland's being arrested on the same charge. She's quite a decent girl, and you haven't treated her any too well, have you? Don't you think you might make things right for her by telling the truth straight away?'

Penberthy sat with a white face and said nothing.

'You see,' went on Wimsey, 'if once they get her into the dock, she'll always be a suspected person. Even if the jury believe her story – and they may not, because juries are often rather stupid – people will always think there was "something in it". They'll say she was a very lucky woman to get off. That's damning for a girl, isn't it? They might even bring her in guilty. You and I know she isn't – but – you don't want the girl hanged, Penberthy, do you?'

Penberthy drummed on the table.

'What do you want me to do?' he said at last.

'Write a clear account of what actually happened,' said Wimsey. 'Make a clean job of it for these other people. Make it clear that Miss Dorland had nothing to do with it.'

'And then?'

'Then do as you like. In your place I know what I should do.'

Penberthy propped his chin on his hands and sat for some minutes staring at the works of Dickens in the leather-and-gold binding.

'Very well,' he said at last. 'You're quite right. I ought to have done it before. But – damn it! – if ever a man had rotten luck . . .

'If only Robert Fentiman hadn't been a rogue. It's funny, isn't it? That's your wonderful poetic justice, isn't it? If Robert Fentiman had been an honest man, I should have got my half-million, and Ann Dorland would have got a perfectly good husband, and the world would have gained a fine clinic, incidentally. But as Robert was a rogue – here we are . . .

'I didn't intend to be such a sweep to the Dorland girl. I'd have been decent to her if I'd married her. Mind you, she did sicken me a bit. Always wanting to be sentimental. It's true what I said – she's a bit cracked about sex. Lots of 'em are. Naomi Rushworth, for instance. That's why I asked her to marry me. I had to be engaged to somebody, and I knew she'd take anyone who asked her . . .

'It was so hideously easy, you see . . . that was the devil of it. The old man came along and put himself into my hands. Told me with one breath that I hadn't a dog's chance of the money, and in the next, asked me for a dose. I just had to put the stuff into a couple of capsules and tell him to take them at 7 o'clock. He put them in his spectacle-case, to make sure he wouldn't forget them. Not even a bit of paper to give me away. And the next day I'd only to get a fresh supply of the stuff and fill up the bottle. I'll give you the address of the chemist who sold it. Easy? – it was laughable . . . people put such power in our hands . . .

'I never meant to get led into all this rotten way of doing things – it was just self-defence. I still don't care a damn about having killed the old man. I could have made better use of the money than Robert Fentiman. He hasn't got two ideas in his head, and he's perfectly happy where he is. Though I suppose he'll be leaving the Army now . . . As for Ann, she ought to be grateful to me in a way. I've secured her the money, anyhow.'

'Not unless you make it clear that she had no part in the crime,' Wimsey reminded him.

'That's true. All right. I'll put it all on paper for you. Give me half an hour, will you?'

'Right you are,' said Wimsey.

He left the library and wandered into the smoking-room. Colonel Marchbanks was there, and greeted him with a friendly smile.

'Glad you're here, Colonel. Mind if I come and chat to you for a moment?'

'By all means, my dear boy. I'm in no hurry to get home. My wife's away. What can I do for you?'

Wimsey told him, in a lowered voice. The Colonel was distressed.

'Ah, well,' he said, 'you've done the best thing, to my mind. I look at these matters from a soldier's point of view, of course. Much better to make a clean job of it all. Dear, dear! Sometimes, Lord Peter, I think that the War has had a bad effect on some of our young men. But then, of course, all are not soldiers by training, and that makes a great difference. I certainly notice a less fine sense of honour in these days than we had when I was a boy. There were not so many excuses made then for people; there were things that were done and things that were not done. Nowadays men – and, I am sorry to say, women too – let themselves go in a way that is to me quite incomprehensible. I can understand a man's committing murder in hot blood – but poisoning – and then putting a good, lady-like girl into such an equivocal position – no! I fail to understand it. Still, as you say, the right course is being taken at last.'

'Yes,' said Wimsey.

'Excuse me for a moment,' said the Colonel, and went out.

When he returned, he went with Wimsey into the library. Penberthy had finished writing and was reading his statement through.

'Will that do?' he asked.

Wimsey read it, Colonel Marchbanks looking over the pages with him.

'That is quite all right,' he said. 'Colonel Marchbanks will witness it with me.'

This was done. Wimsey gathered the sheets together and put them in his breast pocket. Then he turned silently to the Colonel, as though passing the word to him.

'Dr Penberthy,' said the old man, 'now that that paper is in Lord Peter Wimsey's hands, you understand that he can only take the course of communicating with the police. But as that would cause a great deal of unpleas- antness to yourself and to other people, you may wish to take another way out of the situation. As a doctor, you will perhaps prefer to make your own arrangements. If not—'

He drew out from his jacket pocket the thing which he had fetched.

'If not, I happen to have brought this with me from my private locker. I am placing it here, in the table drawer, preparatory to taking it down into the country tomorrow. It is loaded.'

'Thank you,' said Penberthy.

The Colonel closed the drawer slowly, stepped back a couple of paces, and bowed gravely. Wimsey put his hand on Penberthy's shoulder for a moment, then took the Colonel's arm. Their shadows moved, lengthened, shortened, doubled and crossed as they passed the seven lights in the seven bays of the Library. The door shut after them.

'How about a drink, Colonel?' said Wimsey.

They went into the bar, which was just preparing to close for the night. Several other men were there, talking over their plans for Christmas.

'I'm getting away south,' said Tin-Tummy Challoner. 'I'm fed up with this climate and this country.'

'I wish you'd look us up, Wimsey,' said another man. 'We could give you some very decent shooting. We're having a sort of house party; my wife, you know – must have all these young people round – awful crowd of women. But I'm getting one or two men who can play bridge and handle a gun, and it would be a positive charity to see me through. Deadly season, Christmas. Can't think why they invented it.'

'It's all right if you've got kids,' interrupted a large, red-faced man with a bald head. 'The little beggars enjoy it. You ought to start a family, Anstruther.'

'All very well,' said Anstruther, 'you're cut out by

nature to dress up as Father Christmas. I tell you, what with one thing and another, entertaining and going about, and the servants we have to keep in a place like ours, it's a job to keep things going. If you know of a good thing, I wish you'd put me on to it. It's not as though—'

'Hallo,' said Challoner. 'What was that?'

'Motor-bike, probably,' said Anstruther. 'As I was saying, it's not as though—'

'Something's happened,' broke in the red-faced man, setting down his glass.

There were voices, and the running to and fro of feet. The door was flung open. Startled faces turned towards it. Wetheridge burst in, pale and angry.

'I say, you fellows,' he cried, 'here's another unpleasantness. Penberthy's shot himself in the library. People ought to have more consideration for the members. Where's Culyer?'

Wimsey pushed his way out into the entrance-hall. There, as he had expected, he found the plainclothes detective who had been told off to shadow Penberthy.

'Send for Inspector Parker,' he said. 'I have a paper to give him. Your job's over; it's the end of the case.'

'AND George is all right again now?'

'Thank heaven, yes – getting on splendidly. The doctor says he worked himself into it, just out of worry lest he should be suspected. It never occurred to me – but then George is very quick at putting two and two together.'

'Of course he knew he was one of the last people to see his grandfather.'

'Yes, and seeing the name on the bottle – and the police coming—'

'That did it. And you're sure he's all right?'

'Oh, rather. The minute he knew that it was all cleared up, he seemed to come out from under a blanket. He sent you all sorts of messages, by the way.'

'Well, as soon as he's fit you must come and dine with me . . .'

'. . . A simple case, of course, as soon as you had disentangled the Robert part of it.'

'A damned unsatisfactory case, Charles. Not the kind I like. No real proof.'

'Nothing in it for us, of course. Just as well it never came to trial, though. With juries you never know.'

'No; they might have let Penberthy off; or convicted them both.'

'Exactly. If you ask me, I think Ann Dorland is a very lucky young woman.'

'Oh, God! – you *would* say that . . .'

*   *   *

'. . . Yes, of course, I'm sorry for Naomi Rushworth. But she needn't be so spiteful. She goes about hinting that of course dear Walter was got over by that Dorland girl and sacrificed himself to save her.'

'Well, that's natural, I suppose. You thought Miss Dorland had done it yourself at one time, you know, Marjorie.'

'I didn't know then about her being engaged to Penberthy. And I think he deserved all he got . . . Well, I know he's dead, but it was a rotten way to treat a girl, and Ann's far too good for that kind of thing. People have a perfect right to want love affairs. You men always think—'

'Not me, Marjorie, I don't think.'

'Oh, you! You're almost human. I'd almost take you on myself if you asked me. You don't feel inclined that way, I suppose?'

'My dear – if a great liking and friendship were enough, I would – like a shot. But that wouldn't satisfy you, would it?'

'It wouldn't satisfy you, Peter. I'm sorry. Forget it.'

'I won't forget it. It's the biggest compliment I've ever had paid me. Great Scott! I only wish—'

'There, that's all right, you needn't make a speech. And you won't go away tactfully for ever, will you?'

'Not if you don't want me to.'

'And you won't be embarrassed?'

'No, I won't be embarrassed. Portrait of a young man poking the fire to bits to indicate complete freedom from embarrassment. Let's go and feed somewhere, shall we? . . .'

'. . . Well, and how did you get on with the heiress and the lawyers and all that lot?'

'Oh! there was a long argument. Miss Dorland insisted on dividing the money, and I said no, I couldn't think of it. She said it was only hers as the result of a crime, and Pritchard and Murbles said she wasn't responsible for other people's crimes, and I said it would look like my profiting by my own attempt at fraud, and she said, not at all, and we went on and on, don't you know. That's a damned decent girl, Wimsey.'

'Yes, I know. The moment I found she preferred burgundy to champagne I had the highest opinion of her.'

'No, really – there's something very fine and straight-forward about her.'

'Oh, yes – not a bad girl at all; though I shouldn't have said she was quite your sort.'

'Why not?'

'Well – arty and all that. And her looks aren't her strong point.'

'You needn't be offensive, Wimsey. Surely I may be allowed to appreciate a woman of intelligence and character. I may not be highbrow, but I have *some* ideas beyond the front row of the chorus. And what that girl went through with that blighter Penberthy makes my blood boil.'

'Oh, you've heard all about that?'

'I have. She told me, and I respected her for it. I thought it most courageous of her. It's about time some-body brought a little brightness into that poor girl's life. You don't realise how desperately lonely she has been. She had to take up that art business to give her an interest, poor child, but she's really cut out for an ordinary, sensible, feminine life. You may not under-stand that, with your ideas, but she has really a very sweet nature.'

'Sorry, Fentiman.'

'She made me ashamed, the way she took the whole thing. When I think of the trouble I got her into, owing to my damned dishonest tinkering about with – you know—'

'My dear man, you were perfectly providential. If you hadn't tinkered about, as you say, she'd be married to Penberthy by now.'

'That's true – and that makes it so amazing of her to forgive me. She *loved* that blighter, Wimsey. You don't know. It's absolutely pathetic.'

'Well, you'll have to do your best to make her forget it.'

'I look on that as a duty, Wimsey.'

'Just so. Doing anything tonight? Care to come and look at a show?'

'Sorry – I'm booked. Taking Miss Dorland to the new thing at the Palladium, in fact. Thought it'd do her good – buck her up and so on.'

'Oh? good work! Here's luck to it . . .'

'. . . and the cooking is getting perfectly disgraceful. I spoke to Culyer about it only yesterday. But he won't do anything. I don't know what's the good of the committee. This Club isn't half what it used to be. In fact, Wimsey, I'm thinking of resigning.'

'Oh, don't do that, Wetheridge. It wouldn't be the same place without you.'

'Look at all the disturbance there has been lately. Police and reporters – and then Penberthy blowing his brains out in the library. And the coal's all slate. Only yesterday something exploded like a shell – I assure you, exactly like a shell – in the card-room; and as nearly as possible got me in the eye. I said to Culyer, "This must *not* occur again." You may laugh, but I knew a man who was blinded by a thing popping out suddenly like that. These things never happened before the War, and – great heavens! great heavens, William! Look at this wine! Smell it! *Taste* it! Corked? Yes, I should think it *was* corked. My God! I don't know what's come to this Club.'

This re-issue of THE UNPLEASANTNESS AT THE BELLONA
CLUB *(which has received* some corrections and amend-
ments *from Miss Sayers) has for postscript a short
biography of Lord Peter Wimsey, brought up to date
(May 1935) and communicated by his uncle* Paul Austin
Delagardie.

I AM asked by Miss Sayers to fill up certain lacunae and
correct a few trifling errors of fact in her account of my
nephew Peter's career. I shall do so with pleasure. To
appear publicly in print is every man's ambition, and by
acting as a kind of running footman to my nephew's
triumph I shall only be showing a modesty suitable to my
advanced age.

The Wimsey family is an ancient one – too ancient, if
you ask me. The only sensible thing Peter's father ever
did was to ally his exhausted stock with the vigorous
French-English strain of the Delagardies. Even so, my
nephew Gerald (the present Duke of Denver) is nothing
but a beef-witted English squire, and my niece Mary was
flighty and foolish enough till she married a policeman
and settled down. Peter, I am glad to say, takes after his
mother and me. True, he is all nerves and nose – but that
is better than being all brawn and no brains like his
father and brother, or a mere bundle of emotions, like
Gerald's boy, Saint-George. He has at least inherited the
Delagardie brains, by way of safeguard to the unfortunate Wimsey temperament.

Peter was born in 1890. His mother was being very
much worried at the time by her husband's behaviour
(Denver was always tiresome, though the big scandal did
not break out till the Jubilee year), and her anxieties may
have affected the boy. He was a colourless shrimp of a

child, very restless and mischievous, and always much too sharp for his age. He had nothing of Gerald's robust physical beauty, but he developed what I can best call a kind of bodily cleverness, more skill than strength. He had a quick eye for a ball and beautiful hands for a horse. He had the devil's own pluck, too: the intelligent sort of pluck that sees the risk before he takes it. He suffered badly from nightmares as a child. To his father's consternation he grew up with a passion for books and music.

His early school-days were not happy. He was a fastidious child, and I suppose it was natural that his school-fellows should call him 'Flimsy' and treat him as a kind of comic turn. And he might, in sheer self-protection, have accepted the position and degenerated into a mere licensed buffoon, if some games-master at Eton had not discovered that he was a brilliant natural cricketer. After that, of course, all his eccentricities were accepted as wit, and Gerald underwent the salutary shock of seeing his despised younger brother become a bigger personality than himself. By the time he reached the Sixth Form, Peter had contrived to become the fashion – athlete, scholar, *arbiter elegantiarum – nec pluribus impar*. Cricket had a great deal to do with it – plenty of Eton men will remember the 'Great Flim' and his performance against Harrow – but I take credit to myself for introducing him to a good tailor, showing him the way about Town, and teaching him to distinguish good wine from bad. Denver bothered little about him – he had too many entanglements of his own and in addition was taken up with Gerald, who by this time was making a prize fool of himself at Oxford. As a matter of fact Peter never got on with his father, he was a ruthless young critic of the paternal misdemeanours, and his sympathy for his mother had a destructive effect upon his sense of humour.

Denver, needless to say, was the last person to tolerate his own failings in his offspring. It cost him a good deal of money to extricate Gerald from the Oxford affair, and he was willing enough to turn his other son over to me. Indeed, at the age of seventeen, Peter came to me of his own accord. He was old for his age and exceedingly reasonable, and I treated him as a man of the world. I established him in trustworthy hands in Paris, instructing him to keep his affairs upon a sound business footing and to see that they terminated with goodwill on both sides and generosity on his. He fully justified my confidence. I believe that no woman has ever found cause to complain of Peter's treatment; and two at least of them have since married royalty (rather obscure royalties, I admit, but royalty of a sort). Here again, I insist upon my due share of the credit; however good the material one has to work upon it is ridiculous to leave any young man's social education to chance.

The Peter of this period was really charming, very frank, modest and well-mannered, with a pretty, lively wit. In 1909 he went up with a scholarship to read History at Balliol, and here, I must confess, he became rather intolerable. The world was at his feet, and he began to give himself airs. He acquired affectations, an exaggerated Oxford manner and a monocle, and aired his opinions a good deal, both in and out of the Union, though I will do him the justice to say that he never attempted to patronise his mother or me. He was in his second year when Denver broke his neck out hunting and Gerald succeeded to the title. Gerald showed more sense of responsibility than I had expected in dealing with the estate; his worst mistake was to marry his cousin Helen, a scrawny, over-bred prude, all county from head to heel. She and Peter loathed each other cordially; but he could always take refuge with his mother at the Dower House.

And then, in his last year at Oxford, Peter fell in love with a child of seventeen and instantly forgot everything he had ever been taught. He treated that girl as if she was made of gossamer, and me as a hardened old monster of depravity who had made him unfit to touch her delicate purity. I won't deny that they made an exquisite pair – all white and gold – a prince and princess of moonlight, people said. Moonshine would have been nearer the mark. What Peter was to do in twenty years' time with a wife who had neither brains nor character nobody but his mother and myself ever troubled to ask, and he, of course, was completely besotted. Happily, Barbara's parents decided that she was too young to marry; so Peter went in for his final Schools in the temper of a Sir Eglamore achieving his first dragon; laid his First-Class Honours at his lady's feet like the dragon's head, and settled down to a period of virtuous probation.

Then came the War. Of course the young idiot was mad to get married before he went. But his own honourable scruples made him mere wax in other people's hand. It was pointed out to him that if he came back mutilated it would be very unfair to the girl. He hadn't thought of that, and rushed off in a frenzy of self-abnegation to release her from the engagement. I had no hand in that; I was glad enough of the result, but I couldn't stomach the means.

He did very well in France; he made a good officer and the men liked him. And then, if you please, he came back on leave with his captaincy in '16, to find the girl married – to a hardbitten rake of a Major Somebody, whom she had nursed in the V.A.D. hospital, and whose motto with women was catch 'em quick and treat 'em rough. It was pretty brutal; for the girl hadn't had the nerve to tell Peter beforehand. They got married in a hurry when they heard he was coming home, and all he got on landing was a letter, announcing the *fait accompli* and reminding him that he had set her free himself.

I will say for Peter that he came straight to me and admitted that he had been a fool. 'All right,' said I, 'you've had your lesson. Don't go and make a fool of yourself in the other direction.' So he went back to his job with (I am sure) the fixed intention of getting killed; but all he got was his majority and his D.S.O. for some recklessly good intelligence work behind the German front. In 1918 he was blown up and buried in a shell-hole near Caudry, and that left him with a bad nervous breakdown, lasting, on and off, for two years. After that, he set himself up in a flat in Piccadilly, with the man Bunter (who had been his sergeant and was, and is, devoted to him), and started out to put himself together again.

I don't mind saying that I was prepared for almost anything. He had lost all his beautiful frankness, he shut everybody out of his confidence, including his mother and me, adopted an impenetrable frivolity of manner and a dilettante pose, and became, in fact, the complete comedian. He was wealthy and could do as he chose, and it gave me a certain amount of sardonic entertainment to watch the efforts of post-war feminine London to capture him. 'It can't,' said one solicitous matron, 'be good for poor Peter to live like a hermit.' 'Madam,' said I, 'if he did, it wouldn't be.' No; from that point of view he gave me no anxiety. But I could not but think it dangerous that a man of his ability should have no job to occupy his mind, and I told him so.

In 1921 came the business of the Attenbury Emeralds. That affair has never been written up, but it made a good deal of noise, even at that noisiest of periods. The trial of the thief was a series of red-hot sensations, and the biggest sensation of the bunch was when Lord Peter Wimsey walked into the witness-box as chief witness for the prosecution.

That was notoriety with a vengeance. Actually, to an experienced intelligence officer, I don't suppose the investigation had offered any great difficulties; but a 'noble sleuth' was something new in thrills. Denver was furious; personally, I didn't mind what Peter did, provided he did something. I thought he seemed happier for the work, and I liked the Scotland Yard man he had picked up during the run of the case. Charles Parker is a quiet, sensible, well-bred fellow, and has been a good friend and brother-in-law to Peter. He has the valuable quality of being fond of people without wanting to turn them inside out.

The only trouble about Peter's new hobby was that it had to be more than a hobby, if it was to be any hobby for a gentleman. You cannot get murderers hanged for your private entertainment. Peter's intellect pulled him one way and his nerves another, till I began to be afraid they would pull him to pieces. At the end of every case we had the old nightmares and shell-shock over again. And then Denver, of all people – Denver, the crashing great booby, in the middle of his fulminations against Peter's degrading and notorious police activities, must needs get himself indicted on a murder charge and stand his trial in the House of Lords, amid a blaze of publicity which made all Peter's efforts in that direction look like damp squibs.

Peter pulled his brother out of that mess, and, to my

relief, was human enough to get drunk on the strength of it. He now admits that his 'hobby' is his legitimate work for society, and has developed sufficient interest in public affairs to undertake small diplomatic jobs from time to time under the Foreign Office. Of late he has become a little more ready to show his feelings, and a little less terrified of having any to show.

His latest eccentricity has been to fall in love with that girl whom he cleared of the charge of poisoning her lover. She refused to marry him, as any woman of character would. Gratitude and a humiliating inferiority complex are no foundation for matrimony; the position was false from the start. Peter had the sense, this time, to take my advice. 'My boy,' said I, 'what was wrong for you twenty years back is right now. It's not the innocent young things that need gently handling – it's the ones that have been frightened and hurt. Begin again from the beginning – but I warn you that you will need all the self-discipline you have ever learnt.'

Well, he has tried. I don't think I have ever seen such patience. The girl has brains and character and honesty; but he has got to teach her how to take which is far more difficult than learning to give. I think they will find one another, if they can keep their passions from running ahead of their wills. He does realise, I know, that in this case there can be no consent but free consent.

Peter is forty-five now, it is really time he was settled. As you will see, I have been one of the important formative influences in his career, and, on the whole, I feel he does me credit. He is a Delagardie, with little of the Wimseys about him except (I must be fair) that underlying sense of social responsibility which prevents the English landed gentry from being a total loss, spiritually speaking. Detective or no detective, he is a scholar and a gentleman; it will amuse me to see what sort of shot he makes at being a husband and father. I am getting an old man, and have no son of my own (that I know of); I should be glad to see Peter happy. But as his mother says, 'Peter has always had everything except the things he really wanted,' and I suppose he is luckier than most.

PAUL AUSTIN DELAGARDIE.

WIMSEY, Peter Death Bredon, D.S.O.; *born* 1890,
2nd son of Mortimer Gerald Bredon Wimsey, 15th Duke
of Denver, and of Honoria Lucasta, *daughter of* Francis
Delagardie of Bellingham Manor, Hants.

Educated: Eton College and Balliol College, Oxford
(1st class honours, Sch. of Mod. Hist 1912); served with
H.M. Forces 1914/18 (Major, Rifle Brigade). *Author of:*
'Notes on the Collecting of Incunabula', 'The Murderer's
Vade-Mecum', etc. *Recreations:* Criminology; biblio-
phily; music; cricket.

Clubs: Marlborough; Egotists'. *Residences:* 110A Piccadilly, W.; Bredon Hall, Duke's Denver, Norfolk.

Arms: Sable, 3 mice courant, argent; crest, a domestic
cat couched as to spring, proper; motto: As my Whimsy
takes me.

DOROTHY L. SAYERS

CLOUDS OF WITNESS

The Duke of Denver, accused of murder, stands trial for his life in the House of Lords.

Naturally, his brother Lord Peter Wimsey is investigating the crime – this is a family affair. The murder took place at the duke's shooting lodge and Lord Peter's sister was engaged to marry the dead man.

But why does the duke refuse to co-operate with the investigation? Can he really be guilty, or is he covering up for someone?

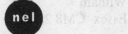

NEW ENGLISH LIBRARY
Hodder & Stoughton

I HOLD BY MY WHIMSY

If you have enjoyed this book, you might like to
find out about the Dorothy L Sayers Society.

Founded in 1976, with members throughout the
world, the Society:

- holds regular meetings throughout the year
  and a Convention every summer
- produces wide-ranging research and writings
  on Sayers and her varied literary output
- has published her Poetry, Letters and *The
  Lord Peter Wimsey Companion* – the ultimate
  enquire-within about the man and his times.

To find out more and how to join, visit our
website: www.sayers.org.uk

Or write to The Dorothy L Sayers Society at:

> The Dorothy L Sayers Centre
> Witham Library
> Newland Street
> Witham
> Essex CM8 2AQ

*The Wimsey Arms are reproduced by kind permission of
Giles Scott-Giles on behalf of the late C W Scott-Giles.*